Kaiki:
Uncanny Tales from Japan

Volume 2 – Country Delights

Kaiki:
Uncanny Tales from Japan

Volume 2 – Country Delights

Foreword by Robert Weinberg
Introduction by Higashi Masao

Kaiki: Uncanny Tales from Japan
Volume 2 - Country Delights

Second printing

Book design by j-views, Kamakura, Japan: info@j-views.biz
FG-JP0008-L22
ISBN: 978-4-902075-09-0

KURODAHAN PRESS
Kurodahan Press is a division of Intercom Ltd.
#403 Tenjin 3-9-10, Chuo-ku, Fukuoka 810-0001 Japan

Contents

The Subtle Ambiance of Japanese Horror

Robert Weinberg

THE SUBTLE AMBIANCE OF JAPANESE HORROR

WRITING ABOUT THE first book in this series, *Kaiki: Uncanny Tales from Japan—Tales of Old Edo,* I called the collection "must reading for anyone interested in the history or development of horror and fantastic literature." With this second volume, *Country Delights,* my recommendation remains as enthusiastic as before. If anything, as a historian of modern supernatural fantasy and horror writing, my appreciation for the dark side of Japanese fiction continues to grow. Considering the rising popularity of Japanese horror films in the United States, one has to ask if an invasion of Japanese horror novels and short stories can be far behind? If so, no doubt this three-volume series will serve as a perfect guide for the uninitiated. And readers of these anthologies will be able to pick and choose among the various offerings from other publishers, recognizing the quality authors from these collections.

Country Delights is quite different from *Tales of Old Edo.* The stories in this volume are all from the modern and contemporary periods of Japanese literature, stretching from 1868 to the present day, while the fiction in *Tales of Old Edo* was from the Edo period (1603-1868). The world changed nearly overnight for Japan with the arrival of Commodore Matthew Perry's Black Ships in 1853. The opening of Japan to trade with the nations of the West swept through the country like a tidal wave. In a short time, religion, social structure, culture, architecture, and technology changed, and the symbols of the samurai - topknots and swords - were banned from everyday life. The ways of the West were everywhere.

Extremely important to the modern period was the formation of the Meiji government, whose main purpose was to modernize Japan and catch up with the powers of the West. This abrupt and forced modernization of the island civilization was accompanied by radical growth and the rejection of traditional culture. It was also a period in which some of the finest Japanese horror stories were written. The very best of these make up the contents of *Country Delights.*

During the Meiji period Japanese scholars investigated old beliefs and folklore, looking to explain and demystify religion. Of course, they never succeeded in wiping out religious beliefs and merely added another layer of believability to the legends and nightmares of ordinary people. Ghost stories were extremely popular, and a number of fine writers participated in writing them. Among the best were Yanagita Kunio, Natsume Sōseki, Izumi Kyōka, and Hirai Teiichi.

Strangely enough, Japanese ghost story writers followed much the same path as their American brethren in creating horror. As demonstrated by this volume, the ghost story specialists in Japan started out writing "subtle" stories of horror, then switched to writing "quiet horror," and then finally experimented with extremely violent, graphic horror. This progression was much the same in America.

In the 1950s, a group of young American horror writers experimented with a new style of fantasy fiction that could be labeled "subtle horror." The stories featured little blood and gore, were extremely well written, and concluded with a surprise ending that hit the reader right between the eyes. Chief among these writers were Richard Matheson and Charles Beaumont. Not surprisingly, a few years later Rod Serling recruited both men to write for his new television show, "The Twilight Zone." Serling's show specialized in subtle horror and fantasy, and stories written in that style became known as "twilight zone fiction."

Following the lead of these two horror masters, other weird fiction writers developed a second new style of horror writing which became known as "quiet horror." In these stories, the dense plot was hard to follow, motivations were often murky, and the horror was rarely seen and often difficult to comprehend. The leading writer of quiet horror was Charles Grant.

Much of Japanese horror fiction can be said to fall within the categories of subtle horror or quiet horror. While there is no shirking from blood and gore when blood and gore are necessary, writers do not use gallons of blood to paint the landscape grisly red. Monstrous doings usually take place off screen and are hinted at more than described in gruesome detail. The horrors in the stories are often understated or left for the reader to imagine. Ghost stories are no longer mere catalogues of terrible happenings, described in detail for the entertainment of the audience. Instead, the stories require some level of emotional involvement to make their point.

Subtle horror and quiet horror depended on the participation of the reader on many levels. Such stories conclude with horrifying shocks which are slowly but carefully developed throughout the tale. A good subtle horror story will often stay with the reader for weeks, a vivid memory undiminished by the passage of time.

The contents of this book equal those of the best horror and supernatural collections being published today in the United States, and with good reason, since the editor had nearly 150 years of Japanese fiction to choose from. Since Japanese horror fiction is virtually unknown in English-speaking countries, putting together an outstanding collection of ghost stories is not difficult. However, reading the introduction to this volume by series editor, Higashi Masao, makes it clear that he didn't settle for merely *good* stories but instead selected some of the very *best* fiction published during the modern and contemporary eras of Japanese writing. Without question, this book contains an all-star lineup of ghost and supernatural stories by some of the finest practitioners of such writing in the Far East.

The introduction to this volume by Higashi Masao is a wonderful description of the growing popularity of weird fiction in Japan. It is also an excellent survey of some of the best books by top writers in the genre. I highly recommend the introduction with one warning: It is best read *after* reading the rest of this book. As is often the case, the editor has a bad habit of revealing some of the major plot twists and turns in his selected stories. Too often, a wrong word or two regarding a piece of horror fiction is enough to negate the wonderful surprise constructed through pages and pages of a masterfully written story. That's definitely the case for the introduction with regard to several tales in this book. The editor is his own worst enemy. Read the introduction, but read it last.

While all of the stories in *Country Delights* are worth reading, I was particularly impressed by the novella "Midnight Encounters" by Hirai Teiichi and the short story "Reunion" by Takahashi Katsuhiko. Both deserve a much wider audience. One is a near-perfect example of the subtle horror story, while the other is an equally fine example of quiet horror. I'll leave it to the reader to determine which is which.

Robert Weinberg
Oak Forest, Illinois
September, 2010

The Rise of Japanese Weird Fiction

Higashi Masao

東雅夫

Translated and with footnotes by Miri Nakamura

THE RISE OF JAPANESE WEIRD FICTION

THE FIRST VOLUME of this series, *Tales of Old Edo,* was an anthology of famous short strange tales (*kaidan*) set in the Edo period (1603–1867). Those period pieces (*jidaimono*) covered a span of two hundred and sixty years, from the establishment of the Tokugawa shogunate capital in Edo to the birth of the Meiji government and the restoration of imperial power.

In contrast, this volume and the third and final volume, *Tales of the Metropolis,* present *gendaimono* (works set in the modern era)—stories written by modern and contemporary authors set in Japan in the Meiji (1868–1912), Taishō (1912–1926), Shōwa (1926–1989), and Heisei (1989–) periods. I have taken the liberty of including a few stories set in other lands, or other times, as well.

The Meiji government was established in 1868, and at its center stood the leaders of the Satsuma and Chōshū clans—the two clans who led the overthrow of the Tokugawa shogunate in the name of the emperor.

After the Meiji Restoration, Japan sought to form a modern nation-state by centralizing its power under the Meiji Emperor. The primary agenda of the new government was to catch up to the powers of the Western nations and surpass them.

One of the main causes of the collapse of the shogunate was the arrival of the "Black Ships" in 1853.[1] With Commodore Matthew Perry's arrival and the subsequent opening of the borders, the West's progressive culture and philosophy of civilization entered Japan. The new Meiji government of course pushed to introduce the social structures, culture, and industrial technology of the advanced Western nations, marking the beginning of the era of "civilization and enlightenment" (*bunmei kaika*). Western archi-

1. Commodore Perry demanded a treaty opening Japanese ports to American ships, demonstrating overwhelming military force and threatening to use it if refused. The shogunate signed the Convention of Kanagawa the following year, leaving Perry under the impression the treaty had been signed by Imperial representatives.

tecture appeared in metropolitan centers like Tokyo and Yokohama, and a host of new public facilities were built. The national infrastructure was upgraded with electric power and rail networks. The symbols of the samurai—topknots and swords—were banned, and Western clothing and food became fads. The new "Western style" permeated every phase of life in Japan.

This abrupt and forced modernization and Westernization, though, brought significant stress and distortions to Japan's spiritual landscape and culture.

This distortion became evident particularly in the sphere of traditional religion and its customs, which were commonly ridiculed and cast off in the new clime. The most famous event was the anti-Buddhist movement at the beginning of the Meiji era called *haibutsu kishaku* (abolish Buddhism and destroy Śākyamuni). In March 1868 the Meiji government ordered the separation of the newly proclaimed "national religion" Shintōism from Buddhism, which had been introduced into Japan from continental Asia. Numerous temples and small shrines were abolished or combined, and many Buddhist objects and sutras were destroyed. It was a time rife with denial of traditional culture, and rampant destruction.

The Buddhist religion, well-established and with a powerful organization, eventually resisted and finally overturned the *haibutsu kishaku* movement, but by then many tiny shrines at village crossroads and in the mountains, and shrines for minor deities, had been lost. Decried as embodying "evil heresies" (*inshi jakyō*), they had been tossed aside as remnants of outdated and ignorant superstition. It signaled the crisis of Japanese perception of the "other world" (*ikaikan*)—the envisioning of major and minor deities that resided in mountains, rivers, grasslands, and forests (the "myriad deities" of Shintō) and folk beliefs such as sensing one's ancestral spirits in the life and land.

This trend greatly influenced Japanese *kaidan* literature and art, which had developed so greatly from the late Edo period. Ghosts and folkloric monsters (*yōkai*), the stars of *kaidan* culture, were forced to retreat and disappear—at least from the main stage—as remnants from an older, outdated time and as representations of shameful superstition. This phenomenon recalls depictions from the famous scroll "Night Procession of One Hundred Demons" (百鬼夜行絵巻, 1766), where various monsters are seen running towards the borders and edges of the scroll in a pathetic, ridiculous manner, fleeing from the light of the rising sun.

> "The *kaidan* is nearly extinct these days. There aren't many artists who perform them anymore, because there aren't any more ghosts. These days ghosts are symptoms of nervous disorders, and Messieurs Enlightenment find *kaidan* to be distasteful."

These are the sarcastic words of the ingenious *rakugo* performer Sanyūtei Enchō, famed from the end of the Edo era to the final decade of the 19th century. Enchō spoke these words at the beginning of one of his best epic *kaidan* works, *Reckoning at Kasane Swamp* (真景累ケ淵, 1888).

Of course, authors like Enchō and kabuki playwright Kawatake Mokuami (河竹默阿彌, 1816–1893), who produced numerous *kaidan* towards the end of the Edo era, most notably *The Murder of Bunya at Utsunoya Pass* (蔦紅葉宇都谷峠, first performed 1856), only pretended to go along with the currents of "civilization and enlightenment." They in fact managed to produce new types of weird tales that fused traditional supernatural elements with the sensibilities of the new era, probing the dark depths of the human spirit under the guise of *shinkei* (nerves, psyche). They were successful in expressing the fear and anxiety of the common people, whose lives were rocked by the tumult of the transition era.

The young Okamoto Kidō ("Here Lies a Flute," in *Kaiki* Volume 1) once said that he got goose bumps when he discovered *kaidan* while attending Enchō's performance of *Peony Lantern Ghost Story* (怪談牡丹燈籠, 1861, published 1884). He was just one of the numerous popular fiction geniuses who went against the tide of rationalism and Enlightenment to produce strange tales. Their efforts eventually brought about the golden age of *kaidan* and weird tales from the late Meiji to Taishō eras.

In April 1890—around the same time that Enchō was lamenting the decline of *kaidan* on stage—a certain man arrived in Japan aboard a ship: Lafcadio Hearn, author of "The Value of the Supernatural in Fiction" (1898) and "In a Cup of Tea" (1902), both in *Kaiki* Volume 1. Upon arriving in Yokohama harbor, Hearn quickly disembarked and headed off to do some sightseeing on a rickshaw. The following are his impressions, from his essay "My First Day in the Orient":

> The traveller who enters suddenly into a period of social change—especially change from a feudal past to a democratic present is likely to regret the decay of things beautiful and the ugliness of things new. What of both I may yet discover in Japan I know not; but to-day, in these exotic streets, the old and the new mingle so well that one seems to set off the other. The line of tiny white telegraph poles carrying the world's news to papers printed in a mixture of Chinese and Japanese characters; an electric bell in some tea-house with an Oriental riddle of text pasted beside the ivory button; a shop of American sewing-machines next to the shop of a maker of Buddhist images; the establishment of a photographer beside the establishment of a manufacturer of straw sandals; all these present no striking incongruities, for each sample of Occidental innovation is set into an Oriental frame that seems adaptable to any picture. But on the first day, at least, the Old alone is new for the stranger, and suffices to absorb his attention. It then appears to him that everything Japanese is delicate, exquisite, admirable, —even a

> pair of common wooden chopsticks in a paper bag with a little drawing upon it; even a package of toothpicks of cherrywood, bound with a paper wrapper wonderfully lettered in three different colours; even the little sky blue towel, with designs of flying sparrows upon it, which the jinrikisha man uses to wipe his face. The bank bills, the commonest copper coins, are things of beauty. Even the piece of plaited coloured string used by the shopkeeper in tying up your last purchase is a pretty curiosity. Curiosities and dainty objects bewilder you by their very multitude: on either side of you, wherever you turn your eyes, are countless wonderful things as yet incomprehensible.

What attracted Hearn in transition-era Japan, where new and old customs co-existed, was "the Old" (*furuki mono*), things that the Japanese were discarding in the face of Enlightenment. Hearn, who wrote "the old and the new mingle so well that one seems to set off the other," learned soon after how Meiji Japan was attempting to erase its older, well-accepted traditions. He came to feel a sense of crisis that the customs and artifacts of the foreign land that had seduced him were facing extinction. It was this recognition that led the foreign author and journalist to study Japan's traditional culture on his own.

One of the results of Hearn's study was the superlative literature he produced, such as "In a Cup of Tea" from *Kwaidan* (1904), and other collections like *Kotto* (1902). These works were eventually translated into Japanese by authors and students of English literature, many of whom were once taught by Hearn at various high schools and universities. They were also rewritten for children and produced as picture books, or eventually as anime. His stories came to be enjoyed throughout the Meiji, Taishō, and Shōwa periods, becoming standard *kaidan* tales. Even today, a Japanese hearing the word *kaidan* is likely to think first of the folkloric tales that Hearn sought out from Edo period books and set down, such as "The Story of Mimi-nashi Hōichi," "Yuki-onna," and "Mujina."

The period around 1900, when Hearn wrote his *kaidan* masterpieces, marked Japan's victories over China in the Sino-Japanese War (1894–1895) and Imperial Russia in the Russo-Japanese War (1904–1905). With these victories, Japan accomplished its goal of achieving parity with leading Western nations. It marked a moment of success for Japan, in terms of living up to its slogan "rich country, strong army"—that is, economic and military strength.

On the other hand, however, many of the younger generation (those born after the Meiji Restoration) perceived contradictions and a sense of *strangeness* in the almost overpowering adoption of scientific rationalism and Western thought. Like Hearn, many of them traveled the provinces of Japan, studying and recording folklore, beliefs and traditions. Others, influenced by studies of psychic phenomena in the West, sought to explore spiritual worlds and other worlds considered by modern thought to be impossible to see or comprehend.

One such man was Yanagita Kunio, honored today as the founder of Japanese folklore studies.

Yanagita began as a lyric poet, enjoying close friendships with Japanese Naturalists like Tayama Katai (1872–1930) and Shimazaki Tōson (1872–1943). He served as a high-ranking official at the Ministry of Agriculture and Commerce, becoming interested in folkloric rituals, customs, and legends as he traveled around the country for his job. In 1909 he published Japan's first folkloric study, *Notes on Traditional Hunting* (後狩詞記), the first of his many works. He also edited and published scholarly journals like *Folklore* (民間伝承), through them meeting numerous researchers in a variety of areas, helping create an organization for work in the field, and laying the foundation of future folklore studies.

The Legends of Tōno[2] (遠野物語, 1910), excerpted in this volume, is a collection of strange tales from *Michinoku* (a term

2. Translated by Ronald A. Morse, Lanham: Lexington Books, 1975.

indicating the distant provinces), the Tōhoku region of Japan centered on Tōno in Iwate prefecture. The original comprises one hundred nineteen short chapters, covering a diverse range of content including strange occurrences caused by spirits or the spiritual powers of deities; monster tales of *tengu, kappa, zashiki warashi,* and snow women (*yuki onna*);[3] weird tales of birds and animals; and records of fairy tales and folksongs. Of these essays, I have chosen three stories dealing with "Mountain Men" (*yamabito*—aborigines of strange appearance and abilities, who live in the mountains), a research topic of great importance to Yanagita, and *kamikakushi* (women or children being "spirited away"), along with the "Preface to the First Edition" (the numbers in the heading of the tales are the numbers used in the original).

I chose to begin this volume with the preface to *Legends of Tōno* because of its eloquent opening words, which serve as a kind of manifesto for the "*Kaidan* Renaissance" in modern Japan:

> I heard all of these stories from Sasaki Kyōseki who lives in Tōno. From around February of 1909 he often came for evening visits and told these stories that I have written down. Kyōseki was not a great raconteur, but he was an honest man. I recorded the stories just as I heard them without adding one letter or phrase myself. There must be several hundred of these types of stories in the district of Tōno. I hope to hear more of them. In the mountain villages of Japan there are countless other legends of mountain gods and mountain dwellers in places even more isolated than Tōno. I would like to tell these stories and cause the flatlanders to tremble.

3. As explained in Volume 1, *tengu* are literally "heavenly dogs," humanoid monsters with wings and long noses. *Kappa* are creatures who live in rivers, said to drag horses or little children down into the current as they try to cross the river and eat them. *Zashiki warashi* appear as little boys and haunt tatami-mat rooms (*zashiki*). They are said to bring financial fortune to the house they haunt. *Yuki onna* often appear holding a child, begging a passerby to hold the child for them. The unlucky person freezes to death.

This famous opening is structured exactly like the Edo-period ghost story anthologies (*hyaku monogatari kaidan bon*) mentioned in the introduction to *Kaiki* Volume 1. A character versed in the ghost stories of the region "visits on a nightly basis," and the narrator (here, Yanagita) jots down what he hears for the reader. This, at least at the formalistic level, is exactly the explanation offered by early modern authors in the introductions or framing devices for their ghost story anthologies. To make the connection even more obvious, Yanagita also writes the following towards the end of his introduction:

> The modern pastime of telling ghost stories in the dark lacks sincerity, and no one can say if those stories are true. In my heart I find it shameful to compare these Tōno tales to such ghost stories. In short, what I write here are stories of fact, and that in itself is sufficient justification for telling them.

During this period Yanagita immersed himself in early modern strange tales. He listened attentively to true weird tales told by his friends, acquaintances, and the elderly he met on his travels, as evidenced by his essays "Discourses on the Hidden World" (幽冥談, 1905) and "Studies on Ghost Stories" (怪談の研究, 1910) and also from the fact that he was involved in editing modern Japan's very first anthology of provincial weird tales, *Complete Collection of Early Modern Strange Tales* (近世奇談全集) published by Teikoku Bunko. It was in this *Complete Collection* that Edo texts like *Teatime Tales of an Old Woman* (老媼茶話, 1742), *Strange Tales of Three Provinces* (三州奇談, 1764), and *New Collection of Things Written and Heard* (新著聞集, 1749) were first compiled and republished, and these texts greatly inspired Meiji writers such as Izumi Kyōka, providing them with original materials with which to work. (Hearn's "In a Cup of Tea" is also based on a story in *New Collection.*) *Complete Collection* opens as follows:

> I hear that even today in the twentieth century, dominated by Western thought and modern mysticism, there are those who

> refuse to listen to the "unvoiced voice," the "tuneless song." I may be just one lone wolf of the Far East, raised in a desolate land, inspired by the sublimity of the spirits and sensing the profundity of fate. My hope is to follow their lead and to turn my heart into a pond that reflects their light like a mirror. *Complete Collection of Early Modern Strange Tales, Volume One* is the embodiment of this hope. Not all tales give access to the mysterious depths, but I do believe that they capture our land's early modern thought on other worlds in an exhaustive manner.

Yanagita refers to "modern mysticism," the rise of spirit studies and occultism in the West. His hope that Japan would produce its own studies is evident in his interest in delving into "our land's early modern thought on other worlds."

At about the same time, in 1900, another author went abroad to study in London to witness first-hand the rise of occultism there. This was the canonical Natsume Sōseki, known for such classics as *Botchan* (坊っちゃん, 1906) and *I Am a Cat* (吾輩は猫である, 1905–1906).

Among Sōseki's works one will find numerous short stories that are strongly influenced by occult studies, such as "Hearing Things" (琴のそら音, 1905) and "The Heredity of Taste" (趣味の遺伝, 1906). The most representative fantastic work, however, is of course *Ten Nights' Dreams* (夢十夜, 1908), a collection of ten tales that all begin with the phrase "I had a dream...." The stories unfold like dreams and are haunted by the dark imagery the author saw as an integral part of his life. In this volume, I have chosen a particularly unsettling tale, "The Third Night." In Japan there is a class of folkloric tales that begin "On a night like this...," often called "blind man murder" tales, and "The Third Night" is very similar. A man carries his blind child on his back, walking on a dark road through rice paddies and under the shadows of herons, heading towards a forest. It should be noted that the dream-like landscape functions like a photographic negative, capturing the landscape of rural Japan from the "good old days."

What is interesting is that Hearn published a similar weird tale in his travel essay "By the Japanese Sea."[4] In fact, there was a strange connection between Hearn and Sōseki: Sōseki replaced Hearn at Tokyo Imperial University's Department of Literature when Hearn left. When Hearn was teaching at the university, he never stopped praising Western fantastic fiction, but even the works of the so-called "Sōseki Mountain Range" (a term referring to Sōseki's classmates and students, later famous in the world of literature), such as Uchida Hyakken (1889–1971, see below), Naka Kansuke (1885–1965), and Akutagawa Ryūnosuke (1892–1927, *Kaiki* Volume 3), all carried on the lineage of *Ten Nights' Dreams*.

> I read an interesting story recently: Yanagita Kunio's *Legends of Tōno*. I read it three times without tiring of it. It is a hearsay work where the author recorded the strange tales and legends from the inhabitants of the mountainous, secluded region called Tōno in the Kamihei district of Rikuchū.[5] He wrote of them in a very realistic manner, as if his pen gave life to these creatures. The stories are literally bursting with folkloric monsters and ghosts.... The mountain man of Tsukumoushi, the river *kappa* of the Hei River's deep pools—they emerge from the pages to the sounds of terrifying panting and or webbed feet, appearing in front of your eyes. Surely one of the most enjoyable treats I've had in some time!

Izumi Kyōka thus writes of *Legends of Tōno* in his critical essay "Anecdotes from Tōno" (遠野の奇聞, 1910). He praises Yanagita, but not undeservedly. Kyōka had already begun to write his own weird fantastic tales about water spirits and mountain goblins as early as the 1890s, following up with his masterpiece "The Holy

4. This essay can be found in *Glimpses of Unfamiliar Japan*.

5. 陸中国上閉伊郡の遠野郷; current Iwate prefecture.

Man of Mount Kōya"[6] (高野聖, 1900). If Yanagita was someone who helped to popularize weird tales through "true stories," Kyōka contributed significantly to their development from the fiction side.

Of the more than three hundred works produced by Kyōka, about two hundred deal with supernatural themes. In other words, approximately two-thirds of his fifty-year career, spanning the Meiji and Shōwa periods, belongs to the weird or fantastic fiction genre. Kyōka was a self-proclaimed "ghost lover." He once quipped in his essay "Why I like Ghosts and My Debut Work" (おばけずきのいわれ少々と処女作, 1907), "I truly believe that there are two supernatural powers in the world. If I had to summarize them, one would be called Kannon-esque force (*kannon-riki*) and the other demonic force (*kijin-riki*). Humans are completely powerless against these forces."[7] Kyōka entered the literary world in the late Meiji period, as part of the literary club Friends of the Inkstone (Kenyūsha), led by the much-admired Ozaki Kōyō. He was a truly gifted writer, producing a steady stream of exquisite prose and plays dominated by the strange and the mysterious. Mishima Yukio describes Kyōka thus: "Cultivating the utmost extravagance and possibility with the Japanese language, while utilizing the parlance of the common people's storytelling and human-interest narrative, [Kyōka] created monumental texts with vocabulary rich as the ocean, and pushed his way through, practically bare-handed, into the dense forest of symbolism and the highest mysticism."[8]Izumi Kyōka's tale "Sea Dæmons" takes place in a dilapidated fishing

---

6. Included in *Japanese Gothic Tales*, translated by Charles Shirō Inouye, Honolulu: University of Hawaii Press, 1996.

7. Kannon or Guanyin (in Chinese) is a famous bodhisattva.

8. *Dangerous Women, Deadly Words: Phallic Fantasy and Modernity in Three Japanese Writers*, by Nina Cornyetz,, p. 72. Stanford: Stanford University Press, 1999.

village on the Bōsō Peninsula (Chiba prefecture), introducing the sea monster referred to as a "sea-monk" (*umi bōzu*) in an uncanny manner, with vivid descriptions of other strange happenings that take place on the boats offshore. This story is apparently based on a story Kyōka heard from one of his students, and the original version is recorded in *Ghost Storytelling Circle* (怪談会, 1909).

Ghost Storytelling Circle is a collection of true strange stories told by Kyōka and twenty-two other literati and scholars. It is thought that they held an actual ghost storytelling session (*hyaku monogatari*). As I explained in Volume 1, this tradition of ghost storytelling, where like-minded people gather at night to tell one hundred strange tales to each other, became popular during the *kaidan* boom of the late Edo period. From the late 1890s, literary circles began to conduct various *hyaku monogatari* sessions, as interest in weird tales grew. Kyōka was one of the central organizers of these events, with regular participants including friends such as actor Kitamura Rokurō (1871–1961), author/journalist Hirayama Rokō (1882–1953), author Hasegawa Shigure (1879–1941), Western occultism authority Mizuno Yōshū (1883–1947) and koto composer Suzuki Koson (1875–1931). Yanagita Kunio also joined them on occasion; Mizuno was the person who introduced Sasaki Kyōseki to him, and in that sense, *Legends of Tōno* can be said to be a product of this ghost story boom among the literary circles.

This ghost story boom that began in the late Meiji period further intensified in the Taishō period, leading to the Golden Age of ghost tales and strange fiction in the early Shōwa period. I will cover this more fully in the introduction to Volume 3.

LET ME NOW move onto the introductions of the authors and works included in this volume.

I have already described the first three authors, Yanagita Kunio, Natsume Sōseki, and Izumi Kyōka. It would be no exaggeration to say that these three, each in his own way, helped lay the foundation for the birth of modern Japanese weird tales. The works of all three are often derived from Edo-period tales spanning Japan, and ghost storytelling collections, redolent of the uncanniness that could only come from popular local oral legend. The grandeur of these three was not limited to the field of weird fiction; they exercised an enormous influence on all modern and contemporary Japanese culture in many ways.

In the Edo period, under feudal rule, each village had a headman called either *shōya* or *nanushi*, who was in charge of each land's administration. The large mansions they lived in functioned as both the administrative and social center of the village, but they were also the scene of dark, mysterious secrets of the lineage, and diverse hauntings and possessions. It was the perfect setting for Japanese gothic tales.

"Midnight Encounters" (真夜中の檻, 1960), by Hirai Teiichi (1902–1976) is a masterpiece of gothic horror, set in one of these "old family homes" in a mountainous region famous for myths and legends. It tells of the romance between a seductive "La Belle Dame Sans Merci" and the scholar who becomes her target. It is a multi-layered tale of a strange and doomed love.

Hirai is better known for his work as a translator of English literature than as a novelist. Immediately after World War II he became known for his translations of canonical Western fantastic fiction, including complete anthologies of Lafcadio Hearn and Arthur Machen, Horace Walpole's *Castle of Otranto* (1764), Bram Stoker's *Dracula* (1897), and Joseph Sheridan Le Fanu's *In a Glass Darkly* (1872). One can sense the methods of these works in "Midnight Encounters." My hope is to make the reader realize that even within Japanese weird tales, there are works like Hirai's that incorporate the world of English fantastic fiction into the world of Japanese folklore and customs. I am eager to discover how such a work based on this kind of reversed literary influence will be received by English-speaking readers and aficionados of strange fiction.

The collection also contains an erotic masterpiece surrounding "the old family home." "Reunion" (大好きな姉, 1993), by Takahashi Katsuhiko (1947–), also takes place at an old family home, deep in the Matsue Mountains of Shimane prefecture. As an aside, Matsue is where Lafcadio Hearn decided to reside as a teacher after arriving in Japan, and where he met his wife Koizumi Setsuko. Matsue's mysterious local landscape is passionately captured in Hearn's *Glimpses of Unfamiliar Japan* (1894).

In this volume, traditional Japanese architecture, in particular the Japanese-style toilet, plays a key role. Sewerage systems were not constructed outside major cities until after the war, and until around the 1950s many homes still used squat toilets with porcelain fixtures mounted over pits. The dark hole beneath and between one's legs resembled a passage into another world, and in Japan numerous ghost stories surrounding toilets have been passed down. In many of these tales, a young girl is using a pit-style toilet when a monster's arm stretches up from beneath to pet her private parts. This type of toilet ghost story did not disappear even with the introduction of flush toilets, and a famous toilet ghost named "Toilet Hanako" is still frightening Japanese children today.[9]

Takahashi Katsuhiko was the first author to win the prestigious Naoki Prize in Literature with weird fiction; his 1991 short story

9. "Toilet Hanako" supposedly haunts school bathrooms.

collection called *Scarlet Memories* (緋い記憶) earned him the honor. He has served on the selection committee of the Japan Horror Story Grand Prize since its establishment, and is recognized as a leading author of contemporary weird fiction. Besides the work included here, he has published works like *Tower of Stars* (星の塔, 1988), a collection of weird tales drawing on the folklore of Iwate prefecture, just like *Legends of Tōno*.

Note that the name of the heroine in his tale, Saki, comes from the folkloric monster "Osaki fox." Osaki foxes resemble other foxes but with split tails. They are said to possess humans and do evil deeds through them. In parts of western Japan there was a belief in "possessed" families who conned money out of others using Osaki foxes. Most of these families were older, wealthy families, as the wealthier you are, the more envious your neighbors. Understanding this kind of cultural background may convey the terror expressed in the work in a more immediate manner.

In Japan and China, from ancient times foxes in general, not just Osaki foxes, were thought to have mysterious powers that allowed them to turn themselves into people or to possess them. The term "fox possession" (*kitsune-tsuki*) was used to describe someone who suddenly became hysterical or insane, or started acting like a different person. As messengers of the Inari deity, foxes are also religious symbols in Shintō. One still finds numerous fox idols of various sizes at Inari shrines. Hearn again captured the otherworldliness of these creatures in *Glimpses*, in a section called "Kitsune," as quoted below. "Izumo" here refers to the eastern part of Shimane prefecture, including Matsue.

> Goblin foxes are peculiarly dreaded in Izumo for three evil habits attributed to them. The first is that of deceiving people by enchantment, either for revenge or pure mischief. The second is that of quartering themselves as retainers upon some family, and thereby making that family a terror to its neighbours. The third and worst is that of entering into people and taking dia-

> bolical possession of them and tormenting them into madness. This affliction is called 'kitsune-tsuki.'
> The favourite shape assumed by the goblin fox for the purpose of deluding mankind is that of a beautiful woman; much less frequently the form of a young man is taken in order to deceive some one of the other sex. Innumerable are the stories told or written about the wiles of fox-women. And a dangerous woman of that class whose art is to enslave men, and strip them of all they possess, is popularly named by a word of deadly insult—*kitsune*.

Uchida Hyakken's "A Short Night" (短夜, 1921) is a story about an encounter with a fox trickster and the terrifying results. It is written in a style that reminds one of *haiga* (Japanese-style ink paintings with connections to the world of haiku). Hyakken had admired Natsume Sōseki since his school days, and he entered the literary world with a short story collection called *Realm of the Dead*[10] (冥途, 1922), which further explored master Sōseki's *Ten Nights' Dreams*[11] in its rich, realistic depictions of dreamscapes. The work won praise from Akutagawa Ryūnosuke and author/critic Satō Haruo. Akutagawa stated, "There is a kind of non-Western, refreshing pathos that flows through the work," and Satō added "It is a fascinating work. The book itself is a modern version of *hyaku monogatari*." *Realm of the Dead* creates a world that blurs the borders between dream and reality, this world and the world beyond. It is a reflection of the magical landscape of the Sanyō region where the author grew up. Hyakken continued to write this kind of literature through his later masterpieces "Tokyo Diary" (東京日記, 1938) and "Disk of Sarasate" (サラサーテの

10. English translation by Rachel DiNitto, Normal: Dalkey Archive Press, 2006.

11. Several English translations exist, including by Takumi Kashima and Loretta R. Lorenz, Bloomington: Trafford Publishing, 2000; and by Akito Ito and Graeme Wilson, North Clarendon: Tuttle Publishing, 2004.

盤, 1948), while also producing numerous satirical essays full of his witty sense of humor.

In the Chūgoku region of Japan, which includes the Sanin and Sanyō areas, there is a legend concerning a creature called the "kudan." It resembles the Greek minotaur, but it has a human face and the body of an ox. It understands human speech, and as soon as it is born, it gives a prophecy of great misfortune, like the coming of war or an epidemic. Hearn wrote of seeing a stuffed *kudan* at a traveling circus in "From Hōki to Oki" (in *Glimpses*), and Hyakken's *Realm of the Dead* contains a fantastic short tale simply titled "Kudan" (件) told from the perspective of a newly born *kudan*.

Komatsu Sakyō's "The *Kudan*'s Mother" (くだんのはは, 1968) is set in the Hanshin region, which suffered numerous air raids towards the end of World War II. A weird tale about war that revives the legends surrounding *kudan* and its prophecies through the eyes of a lonely, frightened boy, it is a masterful work that compares to Arthur Machen's "The Bowmen" (1914). Sakyō is a famous science fiction writer, known for his bestseller *Japan Sinks* (日本沈没, 1973) and *At the End of the Endless Stream* (果しなき流れの果に, 1966), which explore the *raison d'être* of the human species and culture on a grand scale. With a solid scientific background and global perspective, he has also written powerful works in the fantastic and weird fiction genres. He has published several collections of "sci-fi horror fiction"—traditional ghost and monster tales, including about *kudan*, told with a science fiction-esque imagination and an innovative style—such as *The Country of Vengeful Ghosts* (怨霊の国, 1972) and *Fare Thee Well, Ghosts* (さらば幽霊, 1972).

Following foxes and cows, I turn to another animal very familiar to the Japanese. "The Clock Tower of Yon" (猫の泉, 1961) by Hikage Jōkichi (1908–1981) deals with cats and prophecies.

The story, however, does not take place in Japan but rather in the mountains of southern France. In today's Japan, where modernization and land development have pretty much obliterated any "secret worlds" (*hikyō*), exotic foreign venues provide fitting locales for provincial weird tales. The plot of "The Clock Tower of Yon," involving a traveler who wanders into another world to experience strange occurrences, though, resembles Edo-period ghost stories from the provinces.

Hikage's first work "Sorcerer's Song" (かむなぎうた, 1949) won much praise from Orikuchi Shinobu (ethnologist and folklorist, a student of Yanagita) and writer Edogawa Rampo, whose work will be included in Volume 3. He penned a wide variety of works, including nostalgic mysteries about childhood idolizations and horror, exotic mysteries set in colonial-era Taiwan, and of course masterpieces of weird fantasy such as the one included in this volume. His unique style reveals his vast knowledge of Japan, China, and the West. The short story here was originally published in a collection entitled *Terrible Natural History* (恐怖博物誌, 1961), which includes numerous weird tales about small, familiar animals like cats, crabs, crows, foxes, and rats.

Aficionados of British and American weird fiction may recall a particular story after reading Hikage's work: Algernon Blackwood's "Ancient Sorceries" (1908). This, also, is a dream-like tale in which strange cats reside on an unnamed mountain. Perhaps this plot appeals to readers in both East and West.

The final story in *Country Delights* transcends time and space, traveling to the underworld of ancient Egypt during an invasion by the Persian armies. Although it is set in a distant time and land, the style of narration and plot bring to mind the traditional worlds of *Legends of Tōno* or *Ten Nights' Dreams*.

This is "The Mummy" (木乃伊, 1942) by Nakajima Atsushi (1909–1942), which will surely leave the reader dizzy. Nakajima also wrote tales like "Tiger Poet"[12] (山月記, 1942), about the torment of a man in ancient China who transforms into a tiger. "The Catastrophe of Writing," (文字禍, 1942) set in ancient Assyria, describes the retribution dealt an old scholar who reveals the secret of the Spirit of Writing. Nakajima left numerous sophisticated pieces that revealed his profound knowledge of diverse cultures. While he showed promise of becoming one of the finest masters of the provincial weird tale, he passed away at age of thirty-three.

Akiyama Ayuko (1964–) shot to prominence with the publication of her first manga "Only Child" (一人娘, 1992) in the legendary avant-garde manga magazine *Garo*. The story tells of an aging father sitting alone at a wake for his dead daughter, and a heart-warming miracle that takes place right before his eyes. Akiyama's work offers a uniquely Japanese view of other worlds and the "shadows under the leaves" (草葉の陰) where the spirits of the dead roam. Dressed in her wedding gown, the dead daughter is led by small insects. She tiptoes across a strand of hair to her father's palm and, after bidding him farewell, turns into a butterfly and flies off to the netherworld.

Akiyama, known as a manga artist who loves insects, was asked about her motivation for drawing the tale. She explained, "I could say that it is simply because I like drawing insects, but I have to admit it's because I truly believe insects carry away the souls of the dead." Her words reveal that a tradition based on fantastic animism is carried on even today by contemporary artists.

---

12. Translated by Paul McCarthy and Nobuko Ochner, Chicago: Autumn Hill Books, 2010.

It is my hope that her animistic fantasy collection *Honorable Insect* (虫けら様, 2002), full of the trees, grasses, insects and fish of her imagination and including the manga selected for publication here, will someday be well received abroad as well.

Tokyo
Summer, 2010

Selections from "Legends of Tōno"

『遠野物語』より

「序」「第三話」「第七話」「第八話」

(Tōno monogatari)

Yanagita Kunio (1910)

柳田國男

English translation by Pamela Ikegami

PREFACE TO THE FIRST EDITION OF *TŌNO MONOGATARI* (LEGENDS OF TŌNO)

I HEARD ALL of these stories from Sasaki Kyōseki who lives in Tōno[1]. From around February of 1909 he often came for evening visits and told these stories that I have written down. Kyōseki was not a great raconteur, but he was an honest man. I recorded the stories just as I heard them without adding one letter or phrase myself. There must be several hundred of these types of stories in the district of Tōno. I hope to hear more of them. In the mountain villages of Japan there are countless other legends of mountain gods and mountain dwellers in places even more isolated than Tōno. I would like to tell these stories and cause the flatlanders to tremble. Stories like these here are just the tip of the iceberg.

Last year at the end of August I was in the Tōno district for leisure. There are three towns on the road more than ten *ri*[2] from Hanamaki. Aside from that, there are only green mountains and fields. It is even more austere than the Ishikari Plain of Hokkaido, where signs of human habitation are scarce. Perhaps that is because the road is new and few have come to reside there. The castle town of Tōno is a town of fireworks. I borrowed a horse from the innkeeper and rode around to the surrounding villages alone. The horse was wearing a thick black tasseled harness like seaweed because of the many horseflies swarming about. The Sarugaishi Gorge was lush and open. There were more stone stupas by the roadside than I had seen in other places.

Looking out from a high point I could see that the early-planted rice was just ripening and the later crops were in full bloom; all the water had been drained down to the river. The color of the rice varied by type. Three, four or five paddies of the same shade

---

1. Tōno is a district located in a valley in Iwate prefecture in northeastern Japan.

2. *Ri* is an ancient measure of distance used in Japan. One *ri* equals 2.44 miles or 3.93 kilometers.

in a row meant the fields belonged to one family and had the same place name. The name of such an area, smaller than a parcel of land, was known only by its owner. It was something you see in old sales-transfer deeds.

Crossing into Tsukumo-ushi Valley, Mt. Hayachine was lightly hazy and the shape of the mountain was like a reed hat. It also looked like the katakana character へ. The rice ripens later in this valley, and as far as the eye could see it was all a uniform green. As I went down a narrow road in the paddies, a bird whose name I do not know skittered across with chicks in tow. The chicks were black with wings mixed with white. At first I thought they were small chickens, but when I saw them hiding in the grasses of a ditch I realized they were wild birds.

At Mt. Tenjin there was a festival and a costumed dance. It was dusty there and flashes of red could be seen against the green of the village. What they called a lion dance was really a deer dance. Men wearing masks with deer horns danced among five or six children brandishing swords. The flute had a high tone and the song was low, so it was difficult to hear even when standing nearby. The sun sank and the wind blew. Drunken voices called out lonesomely, women laughed and children ran about, but they did nothing to dispel the melancholy of travel. Homes in which there had recently been a death raised red and white flags for the Feast of Lanterns, and a wind beckoned to the spirits of the departed. On horseback through the mountain pass, I saw these flags in about a dozen places east and west.

Dusk came slowly and enveloped those spirits who were about to depart from their eternal home in the village, travelers passing through and the calm, mystic mountain. There are eight shrines in Tōno devoted to Kannon, the goddess of mercy, and the statue in each shrine seemed to be carved from a single tree. On this day there were many people offering prayers of thanks. Lanterns could be seen up on the hills, and the sound of small metal gongs could be heard. In the bushes at a crossroad there were straw figures from the Wind and Rain Festival lying on their backs, as though they were exhausted. These are the impressions from Tōno that have stayed with me.

Books of this type are few and not in fashion these days. No matter how simple a matter it may be to print it, there will be people who say that publishing a book of these kinds of stories and pushing my own narrow tastes on others is boorish. My response to that would be that after hearing such stories and seeing such places, how could I not want to talk about it to others? At least among my friends there is no one who would keep silent and be so modest.

Would I say I am like my predecessor of nine hundred years ago who wrote the *Konjaku Monogatari*[3] ? Well, those stories were already old tales at that time. The stories in this collection are about events that happened before the storytellers' eyes. These stories can't be said to equal to those of the *Konjaku Monogatari* in piousness or sincerity. They have been heard by few people and have been rarely told or written down, and for that Dainagon[4] himself, with his candid nature and innocence, would find it worthwhile to come and hear them.

The modern pastime of telling ghost stories in the dark lacks sincerity, and no one can say if those stories are true. In my heart I find it shameful to compare these Tōno tales to such ghost stories. In short, what I write here are stories of fact, and that in itself is sufficient justification for telling them.

However, Kyōseki is only twenty four or twenty five, and I myself am only ten years older. Why should anyone claim that even though I was born in these industrious times, I have lost the abil-

---

3. *Konjaku Monogatari* (Tales from the Past) is a twelfth-century Japanese collection of tales from India, China and Japan.

4. Minamoto-no-Takakuni (1004–1077), thought to be the compiler of *Konjaku Monogatari*, was often referred to as "Uji Dainagon."

ity to distinguish between matters that are important and those that are trivial? It would be like castigating the horned owl of Mt. Myojin for having ears peaked too sharply or eyes far too round.

Well, who can say for sure what is truth? This responsibility falls to me alone. The owl in the far-off woods may be laughing at an old flightless bird like me.

Yanagita Kunio[5]

5. Yanagita Kunio (1875–1962) founded the field of folklore studies in Japan. He recorded accounts of folk legends at their source during a period of rapid modernization in Japanese history. These accounts would have been lost forever without his efforts to preserve and publish them.

3. *Yamabito* (MOUNTAIN men) live deep in the mountains. A man named Sasaki Kahei, who is over 70 years old, lives in Wano in the village of Tochinai. When he was young he went hunting deep into the mountains. On a far-off rock he saw a beautiful woman with an exceedingly fair complexion combing her long, black hair. Being a reckless man, he immediately pointed his rifle in her direction and fired. The woman was struck by the bullet and fell. He ran over to check and saw she was a tall woman and her combed hair was even longer than she was tall. Thinking he might want some evidence to show others later, he cut off a small lock of her hair, coiled it up, put it into his breast pocket and set off on his way home.

A ways down the road he was overcome by an overwhelming urge to sleep and stopped to take a nap in a shady, sheltered spot. Just when he was on the border between sleep and wakefulness, a tall man came up and put his hand into the youth's pocket. He took back the coiled lock of hair. As he watched the tall man leave, suddenly the young man felt wide awake. He said the man who had come up to him was a *yamabito*.

(Note: Ōaza Tochinai, Tsuchibuchi village)

7. **THE DAUGHTER** of a farmer in Kamigō went into the mountains to gather chestnuts and never came back. Her family thought she had probably died, so they held a funeral using her pillow as a substitute for her body.

Two or three years later someone from the village was out hunting in the foothills of Mt. Goezan and unexpectedly met this woman under a rock overhang. They were both surprised to see the other, and the man asked how she had come to be there in the mountains. The woman said when she went to the mountains to gather chestnuts she was taken away by a terrible man and brought to his place. She had been wanting to escape and go back home, but she hadn't had even the slightest chance to do so.

The villager asked, "What kind of person is he?" She said that to her he seemed like a normal person except he was extremely tall and his eyes had a peculiar color. She had borne several of his children, but he said they did not look like him so they were not his. He ate them or killed them, or took them away somewhere.

The man asked if the man was really a human just like them. She said his clothes and such were normal, just the color of his eyes was slightly odd. Once or twice between market days[6], four or five of the same kind of people would gather together. They talked about things and then they went off. Since he brought back food and other things from the outside world he must be visiting a town, she explained. Realizing the man might reappear at any moment, the hunter was terrified and hurried home. This happened about twenty years ago.

---

6. The market in Tōno was held six times a month, so the period between market days was about five days.

8. HERE, AS happens in other places, women and children who go outside at twilight are often spirited away. At a home in Samuto in Matsuzaki village a young girl went missing, her *zōri* sandals left behind under a pear tree. More than thirty years had passed when one day relatives and friends were gathered at that home and the woman returned, old and emaciated. They asked what had happened, and she said she wanted to see them again. Then she left again without leaving a trace. The wind blew strongly that day. And that is why even today when a strong wind blows the people of Tōno say it looks like the old lady of Samuto will come back that day.

The Third Night
from "Ten Nights' Dreams"
『夢十夜』より (Yume jūya)

Natsume Sōseki (1908)

夏目漱石

English translation by Kathleen Taji

I HAD A dream...

I am carrying a six-year-old child on my back. It's my child. Yet strangely, he is a blind *aobōzu*[1], a child monk.

I ask him, "When did you go blind?" Why, he's always been blind, he says. Although the voice is that of a child, he speaks just like an adult, moreover as one adult equal to another.

To my left and to my right, the rice paddies are lush and green. The path is narrow. The occasional shadow of a heron falls across the gloom.

"We've come to the rice paddies," he says.

"How can you tell?" I ask as I turn my face to him.

"Why, the heron will cry," he replies.

And sure enough the heron cries twice.

I begin to feel fearful of this child of mine. If I continue to carry this little burden, who knows what will happen further on. As I look ahead for a place to put him down, I see a large forest in the shadows. No sooner do I think it would do, than the voice on my back chuckles.

"What is so amusing?"

The child does not answer but asks, "Father, am I heavy?"

"No," I reply.

"I'm going to get heavier," he says.

Wordlessly, I walk on with the forest as my landmark. The path through the paddies winds crookedly and my feet carry me unsteadily. After a while, it forks. I stop there at the start of the divide and take a short rest.

"There should be a standing stone here," says the boy.

And indeed, there is one, high enough to sit on, about eight inches square. *Higakubo* is carved on its right side and *Hot-*

---

1. *Aobōzu*: One of the many Japanese ghosts, goblins, phantoms that may take the form of a child monk; there are many different descriptions and tales according to each prefecture.

tahara on its left. Despite the darkness, the red lettering can be clearly seen, the crimson hue like the red belly of a newt.

"The left is better," bids the boy.

As I look to the left, the forest casts a dark shadow over my head from high above. I waver.

"There's no need to hesitate," says the boy.

I reluctantly begin to walk toward the forest. I ask myself, how is it that he, blind, knows everything so well. As the straight path brings me closer to the forest, he says, "Being blind is such a curse."

"That's why I carry you on my back to make it less so."

"Sorry to say, though you carry me on your back, people somehow think me a fool. Even my father thinks me a fool."

I begin to weary of this. I'll hurry to the forest and rid myself of him; so I make haste.

"You'll see when you go a little further.... It was a night just like this," he murmurs.

"What was?" I ask fearfully.

"*What was?* You're asking when you know already," he sneers.

Suddenly, I feel as if I do know. But, it's not very clear. I seem to remember it was a night like this. And I feel I will know more, as I go further. But, because the knowing will be dreadful, I must quickly rid myself of him to gain peace of mind. My feet hasten all the more quickly.

It continues to rain. The path slowly becomes darker still. I am frantic. The small boy clings fast to my back and sheds light on my entire past, present, and future, shining like a mirror that misses not a sliver of truth. Moreover, he is my child. And he is blind. I can bear it no longer.

"Here. Here. Right at the root of that cedar tree."

I hear his voice clearly in the rain. I stop unwittingly and find myself in the forest. Slightly ahead, I see a dark object, a cedar tree just as the child says.

"Father, it was at the root of this cedar tree, was it not?"

"Yes," I answer in spite of myself.

"It was in 1808, the year of the dragon, wasn't it?"

To be sure, it was in 1808.

"You killed me exactly one hundred years ago, did you not?"

As soon as I hear this, the knowledge comes to me that I killed someone blind at the root of this cedar tree on a dark night such as this, one hundred years ago in 1808, the year of the dragon. I realize now this was murder, and the child on my back suddenly grows heavy like the stone statue of the Jizō[2], the guardian deity of children.

---

2. Jizō, a small stone statue of the Buddhist Guardian Deity of Travelers and Children, often wearing a red bib.

Sea Dæmons

海異記 (Kaiiki)

Izumi Kyōka (1906)

泉鏡花

English translation by Ginny Tapley Takemori

SQUEEZING THROUGH SAND dunes crouched facing each other like two fearsome beasts, a path runs alongside the cliff from the raging sea to a lone fisherman's cottage. The steadfast bluff wages eternal battle against the onslaught of waves, an iron shield against the enemy lines of tides advancing over boundless leagues. Here and there in the dunes, sedges and grasses sprout, scatter and wither, while evergreen pines cling to the great rocks, their color unchanging even in the frost.

Our brave skipper Matsugorō[1] daily entrusts his beloved Onami and their adorable daughter to the cliff's protection and makes his way through the gate and down the narrow path, pausing briefly between the two ferocious beasts before quickly crossing the ocean of sand dunes to the beach. Without delay he rows off through the stormy sea, soaring higher than the gulls as he vanishes into the unbounded clouds.

In his absence, Onami ties back the sleeves of her kimono, which is permeated with the smell of seaweed carried on the breeze from the rocky shore, the scent of the beach lilies, and the smoky fire. She is at her loveliest as she cradles her babe in arms and nuzzles her cheek, sings lullabies, sews and starches cloth, and roasts dried fish over pine needles, accustomed to the loneliness of her days.

Habituated as she is to the sound of the waves, on occasion she is startled by the clucking of chickens breaking into her dreams as she lies sleeping with her child. Wrenching open the gate, she stands beneath a clear moon amidst the chirring of insects, her nightclothes damp in the dew, filled with longing for her husband in the dead of night. With the tiny hands like miniature autumn maple leaves at her breast, she has no eyes for the budding flowers of spring, and with her ears attuned to the sound of oars carried on the balmy breeze, she is surprised by the summer

---

1. Matsugorō's name echoes the pines (*matsu*), establishing an image of him as steadfast, and strong like the trees. Onami's name links her to the sea.

call of a lesser cuckoo. With her terror of migrating winter whales and the roiling surge, amidst a raging storm she rocks her wailing baby, crushing her pillow frozen with tears, for as the mother cradles their daughter, the father is on his boat out at sea in the dark night, plying his trade in a flurry of rain and waves, wind and oars, clouds and fish.

To earn his living this same fisherman travels far and wide, from the warm south to the cold north, his course unwavering day and night. Hōjō Tateyama in the southwest of the Southern Bōsō peninsula is very different from the exposed eastern seaboard, especially the open sea along the haunted coast from Chikura to Emi and Wada, known for its sea spirits. Here on this notoriously rough coastline, there is nothing other than the white sails heading into the wind to block the air currents blowing over the Pacific.

Their house on the water's edge at Emi is neither walled castle nor stone fortress, but a cottage made of saplings from the shore and thatch that is still green, like the straw that adorned Onami's bridal coiffure for, although she has a child, she is just twenty-two or three and not long married.

This time last year in early autumn she gave birth to her first child, named Ohama after the sandy shore. In the pale light of the mosquito net over the crib in the sunlit room, Ohama is like a daytime firefly peacefully sleeping, her waking charm apparent in the playthings and toys scattered all around the tatami and the veranda.

A papier-mâché dog lies beside the child and a tumbler doll sits at rest, while on the veranda the mother works at her starching board, a kerchief around her head and her clothes still in disarray from nursing. Despite the harsh sun, her kimono sleeves are tied back to reveal her arms, their city-bred white skin contrasting with the red silk cloth as she lightly pats it to the melody of the waves, her fingers flexed as if plucking the strings of the koto. Her gentleness permeates the household.

At around three o'clock on this balmy autumn afternoon, a figure appears on the levee beyond where red dragonflies cavort in the millet and calls loudly, "Extra! Extra! Read all about it!"

"WHAT'S UP, SAN-CHAN?" the woman asked without looking up from her work, her voice bored. It was the boy she saw most days at the fishing grounds.

Digging his hand into the breast of his kimono, he brought out a large bag of candies, selected a sugared rice stick and bit off a piece with his front teeth. Still chewing, his large head wrapped in a bandanna darted straight up before the veranda. Wound once round his threadbare dark blue kimono was a pale yellow girdle, probably a hand-me-down from one of the village women, torn and twisted with string, and sagging down raffishly behind.

The boy's old man was a devotee of Amida who never let go of his prayer beads even as he repaired torn nets. From the small window amidst the tangle of weeds, now and then out of the corner of his sharp eyes he would spy a crow beyond the persimmon tree and the roof next door. A musket handed down through three generations lay ever ready on his knees as he squatted bare-chested. Gripping the butt firmly he would leap nimbly to his feet and, ignoring the dust that made his eyes water, hit his mark, dropping the bird in a flurry of flapping pitch-black wings. "Fetch it," he would say to the boy and, muttering *Namu Amida butsu*, return to the work at hand without further ado.

The bird would be stewed and eaten for dinner, like thousands more before it. The old man maintained that his own karma would befall Sannosuke, hence the nickname "Little Crow" for the strapping lad of thirteen.

The boy raised his droopy eyebrows, his large mouth stretched into a broad grin.

"I brought you the latest news. This morning's was that I had a stomachache, and the Inaba-maru set sail without me. But I got better right away."

"Oh, I'm sorry to hear it. Are you completely better now?" she said, all ears as she stretched the red silk cloth.

"Yup. The latest news is that I'm fine now."

"But if you carry on doing that, you'll get a stomachache again!"

"Doing what? What are you talking about?"

"Eating candies, that's what. Crunching away like that, you're bound to make yourself sick."

"Oh, that." He squinted up at her and licked his lower lip, then jiggled his body to rustle the bag of candies. "What's this? What could it be? A gift for my future bride? I bought them at the old lady's shop. They looked so tasty I just had to try one. Just one, though. The rest are for her." Suddenly he turned to face the starching board and, leaning with his hands on the veranda, peered towards the bedroom. "Is she sleeping?

"I put her down for her nap just a moment ago."

"How heartless. Just when I brought some tasty snacks. Hey, Ohama, wake up! Hey!" Sannosuke drooped his head. "Not a peep. Just flies buzzing around."

"The flies are really terrible, aren't they? I have to use the mosquito net even during the day when there aren't any mosquitoes around. The poor child gets covered in flies otherwise. It must be the starch. They're so noisy! I don't suppose it's like that at your place, is it? There's a bit of distance between you and the shore, so there can't be quite so many."

"Of course there are. Not just lots but hordes of them. They're so easy to swat that you could add them to miso soup instead of shellfish," he said with a straight face.

EVEN AT HIS age, living in the humble cottages in the haze of steam rising up from the salt makers, the boy was so home-loving! The woman smiled. "You're such a family man, San-chan. I'm impressed."

The boy laughed self-consciously. "Me? No way! Ever since Ohama was born, I don't spend anything on myself. I'm careful about every penny—it all goes on toys or candy and stuff for her."

The woman dropped her gaze to the cloth in her hands, and said in a subdued voice, "San-chan, how come you're like that? Most kids your age see what other kids have and want it for themselves, even if they have to snatch it away, but you use all the pocket money you get to buy things for our baby. I'm truly happy that you do, but really, we have enough to eat, there's no need to feel sorry for us."

The boy looked down, embarrassed. "It's not that. I don't feel sorry for you at all! It's just that it seems tastier if you eat it than if I eat it myself."

"Do you mean that?" the woman glanced up, smiling. "You're so warmhearted!"

Conscious of her gaze, he nodded to himself, "All men are like that. The skipper said so. Even when he's out on the boat and gets drenched in a storm, he doesn't need a roof over his head. As long as he knows that you and Ohama have shelter, he doesn't feel the cold at all."

"Men are all liars!" He was just a child, yet she found herself blushing.

"No, we're not! But in return, you work for him at home, don't you? When I get married, I want to know that my wife will be starching cloth while I'm out fishing, too."

"Oh, so let's make something for you! How about it, San-chan? What shall I make?"

"Oh, but I didn't mean... well, all I have is what I'm wearing now." Flustered, he took the bag of candy about to slip from the breast of his kimono and hastily put it on the veranda. As he did so, some spent bullets clattered to the ground.

"Extra! Extra! Read all about it!" he yelled, hurriedly dropping to his knees and lightly sweeping them up in the flat of his palm before jumping up again. Then spotting another one, he whirled around in relief with an exuberant "Hah!"

"These candies look tasty. Thank you very much."

Sannosuke gulped and in confusion stuttered "Um.... Extra!"

All of a sudden, the woman stood up holding out her wet hands. "San-chan."

"What?"

"That cloth about your waist, it's a splendid color but isn't it getting a bit worn? How about if I tie this scrap on for you instead?"

"What's that?" he asked, stepping back.

"It's an old satin sash."

Singing a tongue twister to a melody he had heard somewhere, the boy spun round and round, perhaps too fast for he said "Whoa!" and stamped hard to slow himself. "Wow!"

A dog with a speckled coat that had lumbered into the sunshine took fright and fled, tumbling in the sand in its haste.

"WHAT A WIMP! It's only me, Sannosuke, the Little Crow!" He strutted around laughing uproariously.

"Oh, you startled me, yelling out of the blue like that! My heart's still pounding." The woman had sat down on the veranda from the shock and leaned back on one hand, the heel of her sandal caught in her flowing skirt, and a touch of fatigue showed in her downcast eyes as she patted her chest.

"You're a bit spineless, too, aren't you? Trailing your skirts around the residence of that big spender from Tokyo—that's no good. You've got no pride."

The woman picked up the towel and dabbed at the corner of her eyes and then her flushed ears, stroking back some wisps of hair. "What a brat you are, going on about skirts and whatnot. Saying that sort of thing sounds disreputable."

"You're like one of those colored woodblock prints—you know the ones? They all had trailing skirts."

"Those are ladies of days gone by. I'm just a handmaid for that rich man Mr. Inaba. There's nothing immoral about that."

"I don't like this satin sash. I don't know about ladies or handmaids, but you're the skipper's wife. You should have more backbone. To think of Ohama being brought up like that!" Such arrogance did not suit him, jarring like the sound of a mechanical toy.

The woman turned and looked at him. "Ho, ho. I've heard it said that you're awfully strong, but gutless. Now what's that all about?"

"What?" He rolled his eyes.

"Ever since about last May, Genji, Senta and Old Man Riemon stopped calling you the stylish Little Crow and now it's Crybaby Sannosuke, isn't it? Crybaby San-chan! He might sound highfaluting, but put him on watch out at sea where it's scary and tough and he cries, he does." She looked him directly in the face, amused.

The boy mumbled something and pulled his headband down over his eyes, then abruptly looked down and forced a chuckle.

"So, what did you see, Crybaby?" She tapped his hand lightly.

"B-b-but... what do you mean?" he stammered, looking mortified. "There aren't many boys my age who can row a tuna fishing boat.

"The sniveling kids around here can't even swim off these rocky shores. The most they can manage is catching killifish in the weir. Or they make do with splashing around in the lower reaches of the Furukawa for roach.

"The shore is all very well, but try riding the swell, rising slowly up to the heavens, then looking down from its lofty heights. It's no Mount Fuji, it's true, but from its peak you descend into the trough. You can't see the shore or land, but just the starry firmament or the great pallid sun. That's what it's like on a calm day. If you're out at sea when a storm comes along, in the terrible pitch black the waves become torrents. Gulping down a mix of fresh and salt water, cleaning salt from the nets, humming a tune—who'd have time to cry at sea?" The boy squared his shoulders and swung his arms, swaggering like the local policeman.

"So, what's that then? You really are a crybaby?"

"Yup," the boy frowned, his bravado completely gone. Fiddling with his headband, he resumed his call, "Extra! Extra! Read all about it!"

"HEY, JUST A moment! There's something I want you to do." The woman called out to stop him.

The boy had taken to his heels, but stopped suddenly as if pulled back. "I'm busy. Um.... Extra!"

"Listen, it won't take long. What's with you? Didn't I just say to wait?"

She jumped up to go after him, but the boy sprang back from his headlong rush and quickly crouched down before her, his round chin and forehead upturned as he looked at her and said, "What's up?"

She had been fully prepared to charge after him, and now staggered to stop herself falling forward. "What are you doing? You startled me again!"

"Ha, ha, ha! So who's the weakling now?"

"Oh, okay. You're strong. So tell me, was it because you're so strong that you blubbered?" She winked irritably, and said again, "It's because you're strong that you were such a crybaby, was it?"

"What are you talking about? Whoever cried because they were strong?"

"So, you're a weakling then?"

"You'd have cried too if you'd seen that ghost fire. It clung to the boat all night long! Old Riemu and the others might call me 'Crybaby,' but when they saw it they all prayed to Amida." He opened his eyes wide with bluster.

Unsure how true this was, the woman kept her anxiety in check and changed tack, probing him, "So the boat is haunted by a ghost fire?"

"Oops," Sannosuke snapped his mouth shut and turned away, muttering "I should hold my tongue." He appeared quite disconcerted, but suppressed a smile.

Feigning a lack of interest, she said grumpily, "Alright, no need to go to such lengths to hide it from me. After all, you're not family are you, San-chan? It's not as if you're betrothed to Ohama." Squaring her shoulders, she leaned back and fiddled angrily with her sleeve before turning away.

The boy smacked himself on the head, as if to knock some sense into himself. "I've gone and done it now! It's not that I'm hiding anything from you. The skipper, too, and Riemu and the others on board—they were all saying I shouldn't tell you 'cause you'd be scared."

"So they're all hiding it from me. But you'll tell me, won't you, San-chan?"

"Hmm, well, okay. But you mustn't tell the others I told you!"

"Who said I would?"

"Don't tell Ohama either." He craned his neck and peered from the veranda to the mosquito net over the baby's bed.

"What would a baby know?"

"Even so, you might have nightmares and cry out."

"Really? Is it that scary?" the woman clasped a pillar on the veranda.

"Yes, well, enough to make me cry and Old Riemu pray to Amida. It happened in May when we were out at sea for three days and two nights fishing for tuna. It was in the middle of the night. It was a foggy night at sea, the kind when you can't tell whether there's a mountain or a plain up ahead, and we had just finished a late dinner. It had been drizzling since midday and everyone had crawled below decks, leaving Senta to work the oar.

"Suddenly, he came flying down from the stern. *It's freezing out there, and a wind's blown up. You lazy lot! Won't anyone take over?* The boat was rolling wildly, and there was no sign of the waves letting up. Every moment it seemed we would go under, and we had no idea whether we were a hundred leagues or fifty leagues from shore, or in which direction it lay."

The woman hunched her shoulders, desolately clutching her swollen breast.

"*Dinner was too salty. I need a drink, even if it's just rainwater,* said Riemu, as he took over the sculling duty. *Hey, Senta, you're a crafty one. I suppose you're feeling pretty smug now,* he yelled from the stern.

"*Don't be daft! I was frozen stiff,* retorted Senta, snuggling into his padded kimono, looking for all the world like a tumbler doll.

"*Hoy, a-hoy!* called a faint voice in the waves. It was impossible to tell which direction it was coming from, or whether it was from near or far.

"*I shouldn't have come out here. It's really heavy going in this weather, and my back's beginning to act up. Come on, you lot, someone take over. I'm so stiff I can't even bend down!* grumbled Riemu a scant half hour later, trying to shirk his turn.

"*You go. I've got a headache.*

"*You go, you bastard! I've got beriberi.*

"Everyone grumbled, refusing to take over.

"The skipper glanced up from where he was sitting cross-legged with an eye on the compass, and said, *Boy, you go*. Uh-oh! It seemed I was somehow the only one on the boat fit enough, and so it was left to me." The boy made a show of tightening his headband.

"I rushed to the stern just as the boat was bridging the waves, slipping in the rain. Whoa! I thought, bracing my back and pulling hard on the huge oar of heavy zelkova wood. Rain seeped through my headband, and I could hardly tell the difference between the sea and the sky. It was like treading gingerly atop one of those distant mountains we saw during the day, over the roaring seething depths below.

"*Ahoy hoy ahoy*.... that strange voice kept sounding from somewhere within the pitch black sea. If I faced west, it was coming from the west. Facing south, it was coming from the south. Whichever way I turned, I could hear it. It floated up and sank, faded into the distance and came close up, as if borne upon the heaving swell. And in the midst of the pitch black sea, a fire began softly burning. Out to sea, a mile or so from the boat, it swelled as if forming a large bubble, blazing brightly.

"Oh my! I tell you, I was so shocked that I cried out that there was a fire...."

"Ooh," exclaimed the woman, her voice anguished.

"*Shh! Be quiet!* ordered Riemu from beneath the rush matting midships.

"And then Senta, well, he went and said, *It's* that—*a death-fire*[2] *from the shore. They say if you go fifteen years without seeing it, you'll never come across it in your life, but this kid has encountered it at thirteen. He's lucky, he is.*

---

2. *Hitodama*—the spirit of a dead person not buried with the appropriate rites and returning as a small ball of fire to guide the bereaved family to an appropriate site for burial.

"When I heard that, I felt a chill spread all the way up from my hands gripping the oar."

"Well, isn't that just awful? No wonder you cried. Who could blame you? So scary!" Wisps of the woman's hair fluttered in the breeze as she, too, shuddered in fright. The boy's face and the red dragonflies above the spikes of millet glowed in the setting sun.

"But that's not all. You don't suppose that alone was enough to have made Ohama's future husband cry, do you? The flames of that strange fire burned and burned, and seemed to be coming our way, and so I sculled hard to get away from it. But, as I did so, the fire rose up like a huge wave, higher than my head, then sank back to the depths, turning into a cliff rising and falling as it came after the boat, following us like a writhing sea serpent."

"Oh!"

"And then that awful disembodied voice *A-hoy hoy ahoy....* When the fire floated, the voice died down, and when the fire died down the voice rose up—up and down, but always clear, reaching our ears from afar."

"AND THEN, OH! I heard what sounded like someone rowing, just as I was, coming from within those flames. I didn't want the fire to draw alongside us, so I pulled on the oar for all I was worth. But, oh, it was awful. The flames, too, airily sped up.

"It couldn't be! There was nothing for it, so I sculled harder, standing up straight, fearfully keeping an eye on it. But even so, it came up onto the prow, light as a bird, surging up from the water's edge. As it moved around, it started swelling up, bulging, warping, burning yellow and casting a turbid shadow. Half the boat, from the prow to midships, turned yellow. The fire was like a woman leaping, her knees drawn up and skirts spread out. It was enormous! And suddenly the heavy oar rose up light as could be.

"I hastily let go of it. I must have paled, for the others in the shelter told me, *Your face is all yellow, boy! It's a passing ghost flame, that is.*

"*Shut up and row, boy! Nothing can be done about it,* ordered the skipper, so what could I do? I crouched down and quietly watched the flames. Something was moving, swarming, near the base of that golden fire."

"Really? What was it?" pressed the woman from where she sat in the shadow of the eaves.

The boy was caught in the last rays of the setting autumn sun, but soon he too was enveloped in the gathering gloom.

"I have no idea what it was, but it squirmed like the discarded entrails of a red-eyed blowfish. Now ghastly red, now pale blue, it appeared to cling to the deck of the prow. It detached itself and dropped into the sea, going round and round in circles before being carried off on a wave into the distance where it remained glistening like a great fish eye. It was as though a weight had lifted from my shoulders, and the boat again slipped smoothly through the water. The shelter was hushed, with just a barely audible snoring. It was late at night, but the waves were again calm, so I could breathe once more.

"But there it was again! I held my breath. *Ahoy, ahoy.* That whisper in my ear again. I'd been told to shut up and row, and I'm not one to cry easily, but it was as if that voice was coming from the very fiber of my being. It was horrible. I shook my head as if to free myself from it. I could no longer hear it, but, damn it, it must have been haunting the boat for it summoned the fire again.

"Now that the waves had subsided, it was worse. The flames floated, effortlessly spreading as the fire came after us, then billowed up just where I was rowing, right by the oar, and suddenly puffed up to the size of a large room[3]. The surface of the waves

3. Literally "puffed up like a tanuki's balls," a reference to the mischievous shape-shifter of folklore known for its outsized testicles which on rainy nights it

shone yellow all around. Then—oh! A long, thin black island rose up, glistening, from the depths. My old man told me later that sharks are known to turn into monsters after a ghost fire on a night like that.

"But its eyes! Two bright red flames reaching skyward blazed at the tip of its torso for some time. Then the ghost shark seemed to disintegrate, for its large bulk vanished, its place taken by hundreds or thousands, nay, countless myriad fish that flew smoothly over the yellow waves. It was a night of the unknown, of happenings from as far abroad as the China Sea, India or even Holland—but I don't cry over such things," said the boy. The words had been tumbling out of him, but now he broke off and glanced all around.

The sand dunes crouched facing each other like two fearsome beasts black amidst the pampas grass, while over the sea where the waves came to an end the yellow sky faded to deep crimson.

"NOW IT RESEMBLED an ape, and now shrank to the size of a person squatting down, before suddenly darkening. And then the ghostly fire started frothing around the edges, gained speed and surged towards me, its flickering flames winding around the rudder at my feet.

"I covered my eyes, but it was at the tip of my nose. It was about to creep up to the stern! It kept spreading, and was licking at the oar in my hands, so that even my nails were tinged yellow, and I suppose my eyeballs were too. Everything was yellow, from the waves lapping at the gunwales to the boat itself! Maybe it's okay for a boat made of metal to glow gold, but this was because of the ghost.

"At times we couldn't see the boat's outline for the smoke. The waves were forming black ridges, each of which fanned the ap-

sometimes blows up to the size of a room to provide itself with shelter.

parition so that it burned anew. I pulled on the oar with all my might, but the flame entwined itself around the rudder. Oh! It was like the hem of a woman's skirt coiling around it! Now it was an old man crouching down. And now like a great anglerfish that had swallowed a white paper lantern.

"Damn it! Damn it to hell! I stamped my feet. *But if it isn't stuck to the rudder!* exclaimed Riemu.

"Yes, it's wound about it, burning, I replied.

"*It's no good... it's that again*! said the skipper gloomily.

"*Boy*! Ah.... *Look into the middle of that ghost flame. You'll get a glimpse of hell, of the underworld,* Senta told me.

"*He's just a child. Don't say stupid things,* admonished the skipper.

"I couldn't stand it any more and started sniveling loudly. I was so scared, I burst into tears."

The woman listened to his extraordinary tale in silence, her lips pale.

"The rush matting lifted, and the skipper stood there silhouetted in the dull glow against the darkness. *Leave it to me boy. Go and get some sleep. So a troublesome spirit arose, did it*? he said, blowing onto his palms. *Bad weather is on the way, so don't make a fuss.*

"So saying, he took over the oar and pointed it heavenward, and I too raised my head and gazed at the sky, now clouded quite red. The rolling expanse of waves, pitch-black, was like a sleeping army of black-clad monster-monks. I staggered to the shelter. Some eight or nine men already cowered there in a huddle. Out at sea, utterly lost in our lone boat, surrounded by dæmons on all sides and a storm about break, and there was the skipper energetically at work. Just thinking of him there alone made me anxious, but he's the best there is."

The woman sighed deeply. "I suppose."

The boy cocked his head to one side, and cupped his small hands to his ears. "There was a loud roar all around. Imagine the priest at Chōenji wearing the temple bell on his head for half a day. That's what it sounded like. I must have dozed off. I felt myself being hurled as if by a sumo wrestler, and awoke to find the boat full of water. It was dreadful! Everyone was running around yelling to bail out.

"The rush matting and everything else had blown away, and amidst a terrifying din the rain not so much pelted down but poured down as if the heavens had opened, and scores of those black sea-monks were there in front of us, behind us, to the left, and to the right. They were lined up shoulder-to-shoulder, hands linked, standing up straight, and when they raised their arms and opened their mouths, from out of their sleeves and their throats welled up white columns of water that they sent surging down over our boat. And here and there, all around, I could hear that voice calling, *Ahoy hoy*."

"AND THEN THE boat started to move along at a fair clip, but there were also voices calling that were not from our boat. Of course there, still stuck to the rudder, was that ghostly flame, and in its glow the shadowy form of a ship fairly sped along amidst the wisps of gray smoke that came and went.

"*Look, there's an island! Thanks be! Let's go ashore,* cried Senta.

"*Oh my! Have we reached land? Where could it be?* called Riemu. In truth, the shape of a mountain had suddenly appeared, the branches of great trees piercing the darkness, swaying amidst the spray, upright masts swimming above the waves.

"*Are you out of your minds? You too, old man, what are you saying? Islands and mountains appearing at sea, I ask you! You'll not find any pebble beach there. It's a ghost ship calling for a companion, inviting us to run aground. Get a hold of yourselves and stop being such weaklings!* yelled the skipper. Yet even as he spoke we were being blown off course to the far-off Hind. *I don't care even if it's hell. I just want to get ashore and breathe, God help me!* he added softly, the distress clear in his voice. Abruptly he stood bolt upright and, trembling, stripped himself stark naked."

"He did?" gulped the woman.

"Yes, he did. The ghost fire still clung to the rudder, never loosening its hold, bathing his body in golden light as he wound a tuna long line around himself and attached the end to a crossbar on the shelter. *We have to be sure,* he said, *so I'm going to see whether it is of this world or whether it is hell.* Your man isn't called 'The Auk' for nothing. He dived nimbly into the deep sea, and raced through the rolling white breakers toward the mountain.

"The long-line was several hundred fathoms long, and coiled up it reached higher than the gunnels, but it was pulled taut in no time. He swam out thirty or forty fathoms before arching up to get a better view, then bent backwards, stared intently, let out a threatening shout, and swam tossed by the waves right into the middle of the black-clad sea monks who were barring his every way. In the boat, all hands took up the line, and Riemu prayed to Buddha.

"After some time he finally came back. Godlike, he grasped hold of the gunnel and said simply, *It's nothing, just waves from all directions beating on a reef. Steady as you go now.*

"*Skipper, you've saved our lives! How can we thank you?* cried one and all, clasping our hands together in a show of respect. The black-clad sea monks, the island, the shadowy ship—all had disappeared. All that remained were the mountainous waves. But then suddenly the ghost fire was back once more. The entire sky, the boat, the men's faces, the waves, the boundless sea—everything was bathed in that pale yellow glow.

"Oh, what to do? The ghost fire's spreading again! rose the cry of despair. But, no, it was just the heavenly sun rising in the east. And so, the sky and the waves were back in their rightful positions above and below. And just as the ghost shark's back had emerged from the waves the night before, so now the faint, hazy black shape of a mountain rose up in the distance amidst the golden glow."

Looking relieved, the woman said, "Oh, so you were close to shore after all. How fortunate!"

"We hadn't drifted as far as we'd thought. We must have been just thirty leagues out to sea."

"Thirty leagues?" The woman looked shocked.

"But thirty leagues is nothing! And in the faint yellow light of dawn, there in the space between the limpid water and the heavens were bodies sliced in half; one-armed bodies; headless bodies, some like wheezing toads; dogs with flames curling around their backs; cows and horses. All these eerie shadowy figures, just like in a magic lantern, floated uncertainly before abruptly fleeing."

"AFTERWARDS, RIEMU SAID he'd never come across anything like that vengeful ghost in all his life. What the hell was it? As soon as dawn broke, all those sea spirits just slipped away and disappeared. And in the morning light, I saw that all the men's faces were ashen. The oar was now free, but that thing clinging to the rudder hadn't yet gone. Yet thanks to the sun, it gradually paled and little by little it shrank back, as if recoiling from the light. As it reached the water its base swelled right up, growing fat like a sucking leech, and it dropped down into the waves, lighting up the blue-black sea. But under the sun it stiffened and splashed about.

"We all looked at each other and to a man thought, *What a lucky sign!* And so it was. You just got a new kimono, didn't you? And the bonito catch was the biggest this year. As the skipper stood on the prow fishing, the bonito flashed silver all around him."

The boy gazed up at the cobwebs in the darkening eaves, his expression somber. The woman, too, looked skywards, her eyes closed as she turned her gaze within.

"Well, it's early summer and the rainy season, and it always gets rough after nightfall, doesn't it? So you burst into tears, while Riemon recited the *nenbutsu*? And my husband risked his life diving into those terrifying waves. Me, I'm petrified just by the sound of the waves, so when evening comes I lock the gate and sleep inside with Ohama.

"Matsugorō always tells me that however rough the sea, the cliff will never crumble. It's an iron wall. Don't worry about it, he says, and so I take him at his word. Even so, every time a wave pounds it's like a battle between wave and cliff, and I feel that surely the rock must crumble under such an assault, but all I can do is hold my baby close. In the middle of the night, when my milk runs dry, I feel so lonely that I'm consumed with a desire for company, even though I had been sleeping with no thought at all of the cold. Could that be why? In that rough sea, with the terrifying ghost fire and black-clad monks and all the drowned wraiths, and my husband there in their midst clinging to a board of wood like a leaf on a tree."

She hung her head. "He never tells me anything of this...." A single tear dropped onto her collar. "I'm sorry."

Without knowing quite why, the boy tried to console her saying cheerfully, "There's nothing to be sorry about. The skipper works so hard because he doesn't want you to have to ever feel cold or suffer in any way. Me too. I won't ever snivel at that sort of thing again. I'm Ohama's betrothed, and I'd dive into that same sea for her.

"And in return you cook and buy saké for him, don't you? For my part, I don't drink saké, and potatoes are good enough for me. Having piled in the bonito we ride the waves home.... Now that smoke wafting up from the beach, what would that be?" He clapped his hands excitedly. "Let's gather some stones for potatoes and add salt, then boil them in a toy bucket and roast strips of seaweed. So, hey...." The boy abruptly stood erect and, clutching his hands together before his bare chest, declared, "I've really grown up. When will I be able to take Ohama to the beach to play?"

With tears in her eyes, the woman smiled gently. "Why, before you know it she'll be a grown girl," she said teasingly.

The boy gulped.

"LOOK, I DON'T want a new kimono or anything, and the baby doesn't need candies either, so if you really want to marry her then give up the idea of skippering a boat and take up some other trade. I mean it, San-chan. How about it?" She shifted a little on the veranda, sitting up straight as she spoke, her voice full of emotion.

The boy had stayed longer than he intended, and now glanced around restlessly at the sound of a crow cawing. He stood on tiptoe, his eyes darting here and there. "The Inaba-maru went out just for the day today, didn't it?"

"Yes. Matsugorō told me he'd be back by evening. You hear everything!" she said, affecting unconcern.

The boy paid her no heed and continued, "No, it's just that you *don't* hear. Why, those crows have come from the mountaintop shrine, yet they're pretty quiet. They're known for thieving, and when there are fish to be had they soon come. That means the boat has reached the offing, and it's a big catch. A huge catch!" He did a little dance beneath the crows.

"So he'll be home soon. Let's go down to the beach to meet him!" Happy at the thought of her husband's return she stopped, as if suddenly remembering something, and straightened her clothes.

"We won't be able to see the boat just yet, you know. Look over there. Those noisy crows on the branch of that persimmon tree are just sitting and waiting. They can catch wind of the boat coming five or six leagues away, and so they wait there, ready to pounce on the fish as they bring them ashore. When the boat finally heads for the shore, still far off, these crows will be the first to know.

"Ah, look! Another fifteen or sixteen of them have come. They've seen the boat in the offing! Next time I bring home a big catch I'll get you some new clothes!" He clucked his tongue boastfully. "I got some pocket money for going out on the boat, but I spent it on the extra edition, so I can't buy any toys for Ohama."

He hung his head and fiddled with an oyster shell, and kicked stones at scattering red dragonflies and at the shadows dropped by the gathering cloud of crows. "What are those crows cawing about now? Caw, caw! Toys for Ohama!"

The woman had been regarding him in silence, but now spoke again, saying softly, "That's why, I'm telling you, we don't need any toys or clothes, so don't become a fisherman but set your heart on another trade." Her voice was tear-choked.

For the first time the boy looked directly at her, his face utterly serious. "What are you talking about? Not become a fisherman? Whatever next?"

"Look, you never know what you're going to come across at sea! It's scary, isn't it? And when Matsugorō and you both leave us at home and go off to sea, while you're away fishing we're visited by storms and swells. But what if something worse came? What if, say, something from that sea came fishing for us? What then? Even if we shut ourselves up inside this house, like a clam hiding in its shell, if it's stronger than us it will get us, you know! Ohama is just a baby, and I'm not strong myself. Just thinking about it makes me so terribly uneasy."

She spoke earnestly, and the boy listened intently with a look of amazement on his face. "Ridiculous! Ha ha ha! Don't be silly. How on earth is a fish going to come fishing for humans? Stand up on its tail and waddle here clutching a fishing pole in its fins? Come on, really!"

"I'm not saying that a bonito or mackerel or whatever is going to shoulder a pole and come walking up the beach and crouch in wait under the eaves, but all manner of things dwell in the bottomless sea, and who knows what will come riding in on the waves some stormy night? And whoever comes here in the daytime? Today only you came, didn't you?" The woman glanced nervously over her shoulder towards the bedroom.

"OH, IT'S GOTTEN so dark. It's like looking into a hole."

In the melancholy of evening, the still damp red silk cloth appeared black in the darkness, and a breeze blew in off the rocky shore.

The boy looked back down the path alongside which the ears of millet resembled rows of malnourished Jizō[4] figures.

"The skipper is saving up so you can move closer into town and get gas lighting and whatnot at home, you know."

"I'm not saying that I want for anything here. I can bear it, but I do feel sorry for Ohama. Please, take up a different trade. Anything would be better, even a newsboy selling extras. Please, I'm begging you. And I don't want my husband to suffer, so don't mention any of this to him, okay? Do you understand?"

The woman was doing her best to convince him, and even the crows on the branches seemed to nod their approval.

4. Jizō is a compassionate Bodhisattva that strives to alleviate suffering, and is the beloved guardian deity of children and travelers.

"Hmm. So I should go home and tell my old man that from now on I'm going to attach a bell around my waist and rush around selling extras? I'll never make any money that way." The boy wrung his hands, disheartened.

"No, no! I'm not saying you should start right away. You can't just come out with something like that out of the blue. I'm just talking."

She spoke lightly and, pulling herself together, sat up. Softly stroking the starching board, she added, "I overdid it, and now it won't dry."

"Come now, it's because you're weeping."

She seemed unaccountably moved by his remark. "Oh!" She raised her sleeve to her eyes, but then, as if startled, glanced again at the bedroom. "There's a rustling. Perhaps a crow got in there."

Sannosuke laughed again. "Perhaps a fish came from the sea, fishing!"

"How awful! You frightened me."

The mosquito net stirred as Ohama became fretful.

"Look, she's awake. That's what happens when you go about scaring people," the woman chided, half smiling, half scowling. "You see?"

"Well, if she's awake, let me take a peep at her. I've been holding back all this time because I didn't want her to start crying and get in the way of your work," grumbled the boy, wriggling impatiently.

"How about it, Ohama? Ha ha ha! Will you let him say hello?" the woman moved to the baby's mosquito net in the dark room.

The boy leaped onto the veranda, but then exclaimed, "Oops!" He fidgeted. "My feet are dirty."

"That's okay. Come on in."

"But you're so house-proud."

"Really, I don't mind." She snuggled her cheek against the baby in her arms, her profile white in the darkness.

"Why, if those cawing crows aren't laughing!"

The boy hesitated on the veranda, and kept his distance, shaking his head. "Hey, they're being pretty raucous." Suddenly grown-up, he gazed up at the sky. In the midst of the clouds racing through the evening sky from the mountain shrine, a shot suddenly rang out—*bang*!—followed by a few more, sending shockwaves through the air.

"San-chan—"

"Oh, my old man's after the crows again. I really must go—I'll be scolded for staying out!"

"Well, come again soon!"

The woman stood in the doorway cradling her child, the warmth from the infant melting her frosted heart.

"DO STAY! MATSUGORŌ will be home soon. When he comes, I'll give you some of our dinner. That way you won't get scolded. Somehow I'm feeling so lonesome today, I can't help being anxious. So please stay. Right, Ohama? Daddy's coming home soon," she told the baby, nuzzling her cheek as she went out onto the veranda.

The boy's cry of ""Extra! Extra! Read all about it!" rang in her ears, adding to her desolation.

"Oh, he's already gone." Wisps of hair brushed over her face. "Well, he's just a boy," she told herself.

As she peered into the space under the eaves she noticed a dark form standing there. "Really, you shouldn't play tricks on people! Were you here all along, you little rascal?" She stepped quickly forward as if to cuff him, but then pulled back, startled.

The shadowy figure was three times as tall as the boy, with a round head and wide, flat sleeves—a black-clad monk. The woman tensed and clamped her mouth shut.

The monstrous figure swayed almost imperceptibly as it stood there by the starching board, its bulk filling the entrance to the tunnel-like path that led down to the shore guarded by the two fearsome beasts of the sand dunes. Standing slightly to one side, the figure was swathed in the darkness of nightfall, though a streak of daylight remained in the sky over the sea. The Inaba-maru with her husband on board was somewhere below that hazy bank of clouds.

As she watched, a mist came wafting up from somewhere behind the figure and enveloped it. She could not tell whether it was thin or fat, but she could make out its hollow, reddened eyes and haughty, pointed black nose. Its robes were not damp from the brine, yet in its wake it had left wet footprints in a trail that led back over the sand to the sea. She could also see it was quivering, its back heaving as it wheezed.

Timorous though the woman was, it never occurred to her that it might be a sinister sea dæmon come to fish for people. Indeed, she did not at first consider anything beyond what was before her eyes, just shuddering at the sight of it. Then she thought the repugnant, ghastly figure must be a mendicant monk that had drifted into the village, and she immediately rushed inside, dropped down on one knee beside the chest of drawers in the dark corner of the bedroom, and quickly, almost mechanically, took out some small change.

Wanting him to leave as soon as possible, she hurried back out onto the veranda and hesitantly held it out to him. "Here," she said, her voice gentle despite herself.

The black-clad monk took no notice, but seemed familiar with her circumstances and aware that she was holding her baby in one arm as she proffered him alms. Without so much as looking at her outstretched hand, still hanging his head, he slowly, as if it was irksome and required a great effort, shook it twice with evident contempt.

The woman stared at him with limpid eyes, at a loss for what to do as she rocked her baby, who was beginning to wail.

"What is it? What do you want then?" she asked, still believing him to be a beggar.

After a moment, from some invisible sleeve in his drab robes appeared a hand and, raising one finger as if it were a dead weight, the priest pointed to the opening beneath that haughty nose of his. As he pointed, he noisily sucked in air. Why, he was hungry!

"San-chan, wake up! Now!"

If only the boy were here, she thought longingly, quick-wittedly calling his name as she went back inside.

THINKING SHE WAS up against a robber, her heart had started pounding and she had called for the boy, who had long since departed.

Feverishly she knelt on one knee in the kitchen doorway beside the bedroom and pulled the tub of boiled rice toward her. Still cradling her baby in one arm and uncertain of what would happen to them, she apprehensively scooped some water into her hands from the wooden bucket and briskly shaped three rice balls. She placed them on a wooden tray, its lacquer so desiccated by the sea breeze that it resembled a crinkled sheet of dried kelp. Pushing the rice tub away with a clatter, she stood up, rocking back onto her heels, and went straight back out.

"We are a small household and have little, but here, I'll give you my share. Please take it and leave quickly."

This time when she approached the monk and extended her offering beyond the veranda to where he stood still pointing at his mouth, he abruptly brushed aside the hand that been hovering over his soiled, scaly-looking chest and, by design or no, sent the tray and its contents flying. The food lay scattered on the ground like the fragments of a crushed crab.

The monk let out a long breath like a sigh.

The woman stared in stupefaction at the mess. "Why did you do that?" Taking a step back, she said, "You didn't have to be so... so nasty. Did the food look as bad as all that?"

She said this sternly, but fearful of his anger she added, "Perhaps you were saying it was rude of me to give a monk such plain fare? Well, in that case let me prepare a proper meal for you. Would you like that? I would have done that from the start, but I have my hands full with the baby and evening is a busy time for me. The pickled eggplant's about ready by now, so how about if I mix that with some rice and green tea for you?"

In the twilight the woman thought she perceived him nod his agreement and, somewhat relieved, said cheerfully, "Well, that's settled then. You know, we have nothing else."

Seeing her figure retreating into the kitchen, the monk stepped impassively up onto the veranda as night personified, permeating the small room with darkness. Startled, the woman vacillated, yet being alone there was little she could do. Nevertheless, she wanted to send him away as quickly as possible without further ado. Even lighting the lamp seemed to take an age. Vexed at her own feebleness in giving away her husband's dinner, she swaddled her sleeping baby in the breast of her kimono, and finally managed to fix the meal.

"Here, please eat up and be on your way. My husband is headstrong and quick to anger. It wouldn't do for him to get the wrong idea seeing me do this for a stranger," she said, setting down the heaped-up bowl before him.

The monk had been sitting dispassionately cross-legged in the center of the room, his bulk almost filling the space, but now he stretched his legs straight out before him tipping the bowl over soundlessly as he did so.

"Oh!" Shocked, the woman rose to avoid him, quickly straightening her skirt with her hand.

"What is it now?"

The monk opened his huge mouth and again pointed at it. Then he pointed the same finger at her breast sheltered behind her arms.

Give me the child, she thought she heard him say, before she lost her senses.

When she came to and saw her husband there she clung desperately to him, trembling all over. Perhaps she had been hugging her baby too tightly for Ohama had grown quite cold.

This is the fate the sea bestows on the fisherman forced to leave such a fainthearted creature behind at home as he works.

That very night in Emi, with its white sands, indigo cliffs, and brilliant moon, the boy went around the bay calling sadly, "Extra! Extra! Read all about it!" as the deep blue sea raged.

Midnight Encounters

真夜中の檻 (Mayonaka no ori)

Hirai Tei'ichi (1960)

平井呈一

English translation by Brian Watson

(The following document was written by Kazama Naoki, a friend of mine since middle school. After the war, Kazama graduated from university with a history degree, and then worked for a while as a full-time history teacher at a high school in Tokyo. The high school was one of the top five for university admissions. This document was discovered in a closet in the student library there after his death. It was written in his fastidious handwriting, filling a large university notebook, which had been sealed inside a large yellow envelope addressed to me in bold letters. Aside from that, there was nothing—no letter to me or memo even—that could be construed as a will. As a result, it is uncertain what Kazama intended for this document, but as it has been more than ten years since my friend passed away, I have taken the liberty to reprint his work, not to cause any trouble for others, but rather so that the record of his exceedingly rare experiences might be more widely shared. What follows is exactly as Kazama wrote it. I would like it to be noted that I have made no additions to his work, and my only revisions were minor corrections in two or three places.)

—Early summer, 1960

IT WAS A summer in the late 1940s, and I had decided to take advantage of the summer holiday during my first year of working at the high school to travel to Hōgisaku Village in Niigata prefecture to visit the home of the Asō family in the hope of seeing documents that had been in that family for generations.

The Asō line has continued unbroken for the past three hundred years, and is quite prominent in that region. It was begun by a retainer of the Echizen Asai family, who hid away there after the leading branch of the family died out, and then, as family documents indicate, returned to farming. I did my thesis in university on modern rural farming economic history, and it was that, rather than any genealogical connection, that drew my interest. When one of my university professors, Dr. Tsujimura Kiyosuke, wrote me an introduction to Mr. Asō, he offered some kind advice. (Dr. Tsujimura first met Mr. Asō last year when he was asked to give a speech at the opening of a local museum in Niigata prefecture, as one of the prefecture's esteemed residents, an event at which Mr. Asō, a contributor to that museum, was also present.)

The given name of the current head of the Asō family is Ki'ichirō; he is both young for a head of family, and kind. He seems to be very interested in the preservation of local historical documents, although he has a vaguely sickly air about him. It was perhaps for that reason that his wife attended on him; she is an extraordinarily beautiful woman. Niigata is known for its beautiful women, but a woman such as this is akin to something from a famous painting. It might have been that with his pallor, Ki'ichirō simply and naturally paled in comparison to his wife, or that his sickliness only made her shine all the more vibrantly.... He says he has quite a number of documents at home in the storehouse, and he did mention that there had been some effort made to organize them a little, but he guessed that most of them had not been read in many, many years. He did say that he would like to have a young specialist come by to review everything and put it all in order for him, but I didn't have any time for a visit then. From what he tells me, he lives in a rather large old-fashioned Japanese-style home. The locals refer to the house as the Oshaka House. Oshaka *seems to be a dialect variant for* osaka, *the old word for punishment. It was not uncommon for the peasantry to refer to the homes of local officials in that way back in the old days. Regardless, in a part of the country known for heavy snowfalls, they are likely to have unique agricultural systems in use, and if that is your focus, I am certain you will find some fascinating discoveries. Work hard!*

I immediately sent a letter of inquiry to Mr. Asō, including the introduction from Dr. Tsujimura. I included a stamped postcard for his response, should he wish to turn me away. Since I was hoping to visit him later that same month, I wrote that I would come unless he wrote me back in refusal. A week passed without a response. I hoped that meant that there would be nothing wrong with my going and so, just as the mid-summer festival of *O-bon*[1] ended, and the Tokyo heat became unbearable, I boarded the train leaving Ueno Station at 10:56 a.m. on July 21st, for Niigata via Jōetsu.

As I prepared to depart Ueno, I placed a phone call to a friend of mine from middle school, Tozaki Nobuo, who was working for the *Marunouchi News*. Unfortunately, he was away from his desk. Of course, I knew before I called that it would have been highly unlikely for me to reach a busy newspaperman at work during the morning, but for some reason, when I was told that he wasn't available, I was somewhat disappointed. I almost regretted calling him in the first place. We had met at a teahouse in Yurakuchō a few days before, and I had gone into great detail about my plans for this trip, when Tozaki said to me, "I'd love to have a relaxing holiday like that. Of course, it's a shame that the beautiful woman happens to be his wife," he joked. He was happy for me, and there was nothing further I could have said in a phone call, but still, I did want to let him know that I'd be back soon.

I am not ordinarily a very superstitious person. I therefore had to wonder why it was that I began to see Tozaki's coincidental absence as boding ill for my travels, a kind of thinking that had never even occurred to me before. I briefly and seriously thought about putting off my plans for one more day. I am not ordinarily given to such pangs of self-doubt, but in light of all that I know now I might have been experiencing a presentiment. Taking everything together, it would have been at precisely that point that some unseen magic began working its powers. I am now nearly certain of it.

---

1. Most Japanese return home at Obon, as it is a festival to honor family ancestors.

It had only been four years since the war's end, and our rail system remained symbolic of our status as a defeated nation: disordered and utterly confused. Three people crowded in each seat, and the racks above were jammed with rucksacks. Since there was nowhere an idiot like me would be able to sit, I was forced to stand in the aisle, wedged in between other people and their baggage. A group of black marketeers swaggered about disgustingly as if they owned they place. The heat and sweat from all of us jammed together was nearly unbearable. I thought I was dreaming when, at one point, I could look out the train window and see rice fields and then lily ponds with red and white lotuses blooming so refreshingly, but it wasn't until we reached Takasaki that most of the passengers, like a tide ebbing from the shore, left the train, giving those of us remaining on board some room at last. I was very fortunate in that I was able to find a seat by a window, so I removed my jacket and let the cool air blowing in through the window restore me.

I HAD NEVER been beyond Takasaki. I was not someone who enjoyed traveling, so much so that I had never even gone mountaineering as a student, nor had I taken advantage of student discounts on train tickets to explore places I had never been to. Although it's true that my studies in economics would not have allowed such recreations anyway, I also think that my somewhat narrow-minded and solitary nature led me to avoid such youthful activities as a matter of course. Even my trips home each year to my family's mountain village in Gifu prefecture were undertaken solely out of obligation and nothing more. Once my mother passed away, I used my part-time job as an excuse sometimes to avoid going home as well. Even if travel had not been difficult during and after the war, and even if it had not been difficult to find things to eat along the way, I'm just a boor who fails to see the point in, and I exaggerate, I know, spending so much time being shuttled from place to place in this tiny country in cramped conditions in even tinier train cars. Of course, for someone like me, with my complete lack of social skills, to have experienced the kinds of things that I am about to write about, leads me to believe that I was singled out, perhaps. I cannot say whether that makes me fortunate or unfortunate. Regardless, I believe that I met with an inevitable fate. I have often asked myself whether there was any other way to regard what has happened, but I do not think I will ever get an answer.

As the train travels from Gunma prefecture into Niigata prefecture, it traverses a very long tunnel. The scenery beyond the tunnel is quite different, and it was very surprising for me, who had never seen it before. It was as if the tunnel had served as a border between two worlds, even, one of which was the obverse of the other. That was how drastic the change seemed to me. The forests and mountains were bathed in the pale, clear light of northern July sunshine, and it seemed as if the abundant greenery was almost overcome, as if all of nature were somehow holding its breath in stillness. It was an oppressive, gloomy nature that seemed to oppress my spirit. And in spite of the abundance of life all around me, there seemed to also be a ribbon of frozen air seeping forth from some hidden depth. That was the impression I had, and that impression only seemed to grow stronger with each passing station. I was quite strongly aware that I had never seen anything like this in all the years I had been traveling back and forth between Tokyo and Gifu, along which route, perhaps, nature had been brought under a more artificial control.

"In the dead of winter, say, January or February, even the tops of those cedar trees will be buried in snow. The snow is deepest, they say, along these train tracks." Unbidden, an old farmer sitting beside me offered this description. I hadn't the faintest idea, but when I considered it, it made sense that the profound gloom of these mountains and rivers arose from the threat of the long winters that the plants here must endure, and was a voiceless expression of that experience. It was as if a fear of nature's four great powers were buried within, burning like a hidden, secret fire. As this was the first time for me to see the natural wonders of summer in snow country, it moved me greatly. As I continued to look, I was struck by how pitiable it all suddenly appeared, from the roots of the nearby thickets to the thickly thatched farmhouses spread out along the base of the hills further along. I thought to myself, *I'd never be able to understand the history of this place without knowing the weight and volume of the snow. I should come once during a snowstorm.*

WHEN I ARRIVED at O Station, it was a little after three in the afternoon. A glance at the map indicated that Hōgisaku Village was roughly twelve kilometers away. A young railway clerk told me that a bus left the station three times each day for Iwazawa (the village closest to Hōgisaku), and that the afternoon departure had already gone about an hour earlier. Since the last bus wouldn't be leaving until six, I decided to instead ask directions, and to use the map as my guide for walking. The clerk was kind enough to tell me that the road to Iwazawa was rather indirect, but that if I headed directly for Yoshitani first, it would be only eight kilometers to Iwazawa, which should guarantee my arrival before nightfall.

The town in front of the station appeared to have escaped the ravages of the war, although rows of shabby houses, their wooden roofs weighted with river rocks[2], lined the street. I walked the lone street, with barely another person on it, down

2. This style of roofing is unique to northern Japan, which is why the narrator commented on it. Most roofs in rural areas around Tokyo were tile, while in Gifu they were thatched.

a long slope, for a short distance until I came to an iron bridge over a large river. The map had the river as the S River. Across the bridge was the old township of O.

Old-fashioned shops lined both sides of the fairly broad paved street. This might have been the main street, but there were so few people about that I presumed the sleepy air meant people would be shopping at other times of the day. I recalled reading an article once that said that streets in this region were wide because, during the winter months, people spent considerable time weaving crepe cloth, a material this region of Japan was famous for, and that markets for the cloth displayed whole bolts of it across the entire width of the street. Beyond the dark zigzags of the snowbreaks I could see the latticed windows of rows of shops, decorated in the traditional style and proudly indicating their status as manufacturers of famous products.

Further along, within the town itself, there was a modern, narrow, white building whose very existence seemed to mercilessly destroy the elegance of its surroundings. This was the town hall, although right beside it there was an old-fashioned soba noodle shop, complete with an indigo-dyed entry curtain. I looked at my wristwatch before deciding I should do something about my empty stomach and went in. I hadn't been able to buy any lunch when the train stopped in Takasaki, and all I had had for breakfast was a bottle of milk, which the movement of the train had sloshed about in my stomach, it seemed, until now I was famished.

The shop was as old as the curtain seemed to indicate, and once I entered I found it to be dark and not particularly clean, but the noodles were made by hand and were delicious. In fact, I asked for seconds. As there were no other diners there, I ate slowly, and finished by slurping down the noodle broth, whereupon I asked the pale, middle-aged shopkeeper if she knew the way to Hōgisaku. She looked up at the clock on the pillar and said, "Oh dear, I think you've missed the bus long about now. There's only one way, and there's no getting lost. There are just two turnings, and both times, it's to the left, to the left. Who is it in Hōgisaku you'd be after?"

"A family named Asō."

"That'd be Mr. Asō, is it? In the Oshaka House, then?"

"Yes, that'd be him."

"And what would the likes of you have heard of Oshaka House in Hōgisaku? Do you know of it, then, papa?"

The shopkeeper spoke this last to the back of the shop, where the noodle pots were on the boil, and a face appeared from among the clouds of steam. It was an old man, his face so pale as to be nearly blue.

"Welcome. I remember. Oshaka House is the place way up in the mountains." And then, speaking more to his wife, the shopkeeper, than to me, he said, "There's a policeman stationed up thataways. If you head to the right in the mountains, you'll come to a dead-end where the policeman is stationed, you see. Ask that policeman about the Oshaka House, why don't you? He'll know where you're after. But you should know that it was just last year that the master of that place passed on."

"Who is it who died?" I asked.

"The master of Oshaka House."

"Do you mean someone named Ki'ichirō?"

"All of the masters of Oshaka House are named Ki'ichirō...."[3]

The old man then turned to his wife and muttered, "Do you know?"

"And how would I know, then? You shouldn't be going on about things you know nothing about. If this fellow is off to Hōgisaku

---

3. Traditionally, in large Japanese families, it was common for whoever became head of the family to adopt a set name. For the Asō family, that name appears to be Ki'ichirō.

then surely he'll find someone up thataways who'll know more about it than either of us. Wouldn't you think?"

I was hard-pressed to respond to that, and the proprietor seemed to have been put off as well, so he withdrew into the kitchen once more, muttering incoherently to his wife as he did so.

If it was as the proprietor of the soba shop had said and Asō Ki'ichirō was indeed deceased, it would appear that Dr. Tsujimura had never received word of it. For someone off to review the documents locked away in a storehouse, the now explained absence of their master would explain, somewhat shockingly, why there had been no response to my letter. But the fact of the matter remained that the storehouse was undoubtedly still overflowing with a vast number of documents. Had they been donated to some facility after the parting of Mr. Asō, surely one of the bereaved would have thought to respond to my letter, telling me so. I realized, however, that it was pointless for me to conjecture from where I stood and resolved to travel on to Oshaka House anyway. I therefore left the town to follow the route the woman running the soba shop had shared with me.

My route veered to the left in front of the gate of a large elementary school, and then, after climbing a small hill that curved as it rose, I came to a fairly run-down area, with a long strip of small houses, all in a row. Here and there I could hear the sounds of mechanical looms, but they all seemed to be coming from within the houses and were therefore small businesses, but otherwise things were so quiet that you wouldn't know these were shops. There was a small sawmill surrounded by a plank fence beyond a large field of paulownia trees. I attributed it to this being snow country, but whenever I met someone on the road, be it a man, woman or child, they were all exceedingly pale and appeared to be very subdued as well. At long last there appeared a large building, painted white, that I took to be a hospital on my left, surrounded by more houses, and the road dipped from there into a broad expanse of rice fields.

The sun was still high in the sky, but the wind off the fields was cool. I took off my jacket, dangled my overnight bag from one hand, and took deep breaths, feeling thoroughly refreshed for the first time in a long while. It was as if a wild yet gentle wind had been conjured forth from the mountains and rivers to blow away all the confusion, all the roiling avarice known to man, all that was ugly and filthy about life in the city that had accumulated about my person from all the jostling and pushing up against the countless others. Looking on in silent appreciation were the nodding green heads of the rice plants. The truth of this experience would come in what followed, and as I look back I see that greenness as a moment of true beauty.

The sky had an autumnal feel to it, although that might have been because of the northern latitude. Amid the fields stretched out below that sky, I saw men and women, weeding here and there, and a cuckoo cried out in its lonely way from a nearby mountain. The village layouts here were quite different from those I was used to back in Gifu, no doubt because the deeply falling snow encouraged people to surround their homes with thickets, and I was struck by the strangeness of it all. Everything was done in the traditional manner for handling large amounts of snow, from the steeply pitched and thickly thatched roofs, and the deeply set eaves, to the absurdly massive exposed columns and beams that comprised the white windbreaks set around the houses. I don't know much about the specifics of architecture, but people who lived under roofs as thick as a lion's mane must spend the long white winters not knowing day from night, engaged in a pitched battle against the pitiless snow. Although I had always been vaguely aware that people from this part of Japan were renowned for their perseverance, it was only now, with my feet on this soil, that I began to realize, if only faintly at first, how true that must be.

The road diverged at the tiny nearly forgotten village of Yoshitani. Alongside a sweet statue of a roadside deity, stone markers indicated that Hōgisaku was to the left and the village of Nigoro was to the right. Thick growths of trees appeared on both sides of the road, which now began to rise and fall in a narrow ribbon among the mountains. As I walked, tiger beetles rose up from the moist earth beneath my feet, as beautiful as red lacquer, and nightingales flew above my head, their voices lovely to hear. With all the twists and turns, I think it was four or five kilometers from the fork in the road at Yoshitani to Hōgisaku. I encountered an old farmer and his daughter who appeared to have gathered a summer crop of silkworm cocoons and had loaded them in a large hemp bag across their horse.When the sun began to slip behind the shadow of the mountains and a thin blue haze began its descent I finally saw what I took to be the light from a watch fire burning where the police officer that the proprietor of the soba shop had mentioned would be living. An old woman was sitting on a great cedar tree that had fallen by the side of the road, a bundle of faggots at her back, so I approached her and asked, "Do you know how far it might be to the home of the Asō family?"

The old woman pulled on the plank—or so we would call it back in Gifu, where they are made of wood, although here it seemed to be woven from rice straw—of the pack on her back as she said, "There are many families here by that name, you see. I myself am an Asō, you know. Which Asō is it that you're after?"

"The owners of the Oshaka House. I was told to turn before the police box, but...."

"Indeed, that would be the main family, though I belong to a branch family[4]. It is, in truth, just ahead. I'm on my way back

---

4. Since under old Japanese law the majority of property was only passed down to one person to preserve the main family, those not inheriting formed

home now. Shall we go there together, then? Are you after a visit to the main family?"

"I am.... I heard, back in town, that Master Ki'ichirō has passed away."

"He has." Her answer was brief. She then rose, lifting the burden at her back as she did so. "It was last year, before the old celebration of *O-bon* when it happened. Sometimes these things are simply meant to happen, you know."

"Actually, I came in the hope of being able to have a look at the old records that the main family has kept. I had no idea that Master Ki'ichirō had passed away."

"I see. Well, what do you know? I might not know a thing about it, but it seems to me that there are lots of old written things in the storehouse. I wonder what would have become of it all?"

She walked slowly on as she spoke, and then I noticed at the left a great ginkgo tree, whose branches spread out over the road itself. Just beyond it was a widely fronted old store, the old-fashioned type that sold just about anything. On its porch was arrayed a sparse selection of cigarettes and some sundries. Between the store and the ginkgo tree there was a small building that appeared to be nothing more than a rough hut, the paint peeling from it. This was, apparently, the police box. Behind a glass door darkened with dirt, there was no sign of any officer, though. Beside the store, there was an old iron grate for a watch fire, the kind that had been used during the war, although this one was halfway rusted through. But the only light came instead from a single bulb, shining atop the watchtower across the street made from a simple ladder that appeared to have been raised to replace the grate. A glance at the notice board there led me to believe that this was the center of the village. Even so, there was no one around. No children were out playing. There were no dogs,

branch families. Usually the eldest son inherited, but the father was free to designate whomever he wished to inherit.

even, to accompany the old woman and me as we made our way through the falling dusk.

"This is the road. If you walk on for another five or six hundred meters, say, you'll come upon a great gate. I think you'll recognize it."

I gave her my thanks and then made my way up the overgrown narrow path she pointed out to me, beside the police officer's residence. After a while, I looked back and saw that the old woman was still standing there, watching me.

THE THICKLY THATCHED roofs and the large gate stood out more blackly on slightly higher ground, surrounded on three sides by mountains. Since night had nearly enveloped me, I couldn't say for certain, but I would guess that the impressively wide gate was roughly thirty meters across. This was the entrance, then, to Oshaka House, the home of the Asō family. Its immensity gave me pause at first, but when I saw how large the house itself was, I was even more surprised. Calling it a "house" would be misleading. Perhaps "temple hall" or "monastery" would be more appropriate. Behind it rose the dark shadow of a mountain covered in cedar trees, and wings of the building extended to both the right and left, forming a large U. Again, I am guessing, but I think the overall width of the structure was four times that of the gate itself. I couldn't fathom why such a building had been built on such an elaborate scale, but surely something this large was at least partially designed to evoke fear in anyone who looked upon it. In all honesty, when I came upon that place, in the gathering darkness, my first thoughts were of the ancient ghost stories, for in them it was said that ghosts surely inhabited buildings such as that.

To my right were four glass doors, in which were reflected the remnants of the sky's light. That appeared to be the entrance, but it was dark inside. In fact, as far as I could tell, not a single light burned within at all. All the windows facing me were shuttered. Like the quiet crashing of waves, the sound of the wind in the trees sometimes came from the mountains that surrounded the house on three sides, but other than that, all was silence. One by one, the stars began to shine in the night sky.

I was struck with a feeling of loneliness, when suddenly a cold shiver ran down my spine.

I put my jacket back on and approached the entrance. I opened one of the doors and called out, softly, "Is anyone home?" two or three times, but there was no answer. The house was utterly still. I slid the door open further and stepped into the mud room,[5] placing my overnight bag on a shelf along the wall, and stood there waiting for some time, but it appeared that no one was coming.

Although it was too dark for me to make things out clearly, the mud room seemed to be very large, and the shelf at left seemed to continue for quite some ways into the house, with sliding paper doors arrayed above it. At the far end of the mud room, there appeared to be an old cooking hearth,[6] and a faint glimmer of light seemed to be shining on one of its large cauldrons, even though there was no person yet visible. I thought I would be best served by calling out once more when I was suddenly startled and gave a great cry of alarm. A large white cat had sat down at my feet, although how and when it appeared, I know not. I was relieved when I saw that it was a cat. When I first saw it, my eyes had deceived me into thinking I was seeing a white thing the size

5. The entrances to old Japanese homes had two levels. One was floored with dirt, akin to our concept of a mud room, while a proper wooden flooring area would be on a raised level.

6. In traditional Japanese homes, an earthen hearth would be built up from the floor to roughly waist level, completely enclosing the fire below, with large holes into which iron cauldrons for boiling water and cooking rice were inserted. Smoke from these hearths was ventilated from specially designed flues, placed at the rear.

of a seven- or eight-year-old child, which was quite startling. It was then that I heard a crackling, nearly broken and very strange voice from somewhere deep within the house. I was certain that there must have been a parrot or parakeet somewhere. If a cat and a bird were kept as pets there, then there had to be humans as well. The cat remained seated beside me, its two eyes shining as it stared up at me with a phosphoric gaze, utterly silent, so much so that I began to feel ill at ease. I decided against calling out again and left the mud room to return outside once more, walking around to the side of the building. I thought I might see someone there.

The side of the house was enclosed, with an outbuilding that was connected to the main structure—I couldn't tell whether it was a barn or a woodshed—forming a rather large area, but there was no one there, nor was any light visible. As the stars shone on in the night sky, I heard the drip-drip of water falling, probably from a drain pipe somewhere.

There was a small pond to the right in this area, and beyond it a mound of some kind. There were three or four white lotuses blooming on the pond's surface.

I thought perhaps the people who lived there had gone out weeding in the rice fields, and had yet to come home. I knew that I was in something of a fix as this was the first time I had ever been there, but there was nothing to be done. Had I wanted to inquire of any neighbors, I had only to recall that I had seen no houses between there and the police officer's residence. My only choice was to wait. As there were no birds roosting there, I sat down at the pond's edge and began smoking a cigarette, pondering various possibilities, each less likely than the rest, when suddenly, I was startled as if a bucket of water had been emptied on my head.

"It was so good of you to come." Out of the darkness suddenly appeared, in a boldly patterned flowery summer kimono, a woman—the widow Asō—standing as straight and tall as if she had just walked out of a dream. Looking back, there were many other things I recalled, but I don't know why I felt as if I had been doused with cold water. She was as Dr. Tsujimura had said, and possessed of a buxom beauty. Anyone would be startled if suddenly spoken to by someone so beautiful in the middle of a dark night. You might think me common were I to say I suddenly felt as if I had met a fox capable of turning itself into a woman, the kind that appear in fairy tales.

"Won't you please join me in the house? I am so very sorry to have kept you waiting. I had thought you might be arriving today, and was in fact looking forward to it. It was so good of you to come. Please follow me...."

Perhaps I had been taken aback by the widow's politeness and beauty, but I could barely open my mouth to say hello. It was all I could do to follow her as she led me through the side entrance into the house. Although I can't say when it had happened, the house was lit with lamps here and there. We entered the same mud room that I had entered before, but with the lights on it looked much larger. As I had thought, there was a cooking hearth at the rear of the room, with a curtained doorway beside it, through which led a long hallway, with wooden slats over its earthen floor. The large white cat must have gone somewhere else, for it was no longer to be seen.

We passed through the paper sliding doors from the mud room into a large twelve-mat sitting room. In the center of the room was a black table, and above it hung an old-fashioned chandelier with a wicker cover, leading me to believe that this room was where guests were received. In the room's alcove there was an ornate staggered bookshelf with books of various thicknesses arranged on it, and a large white vase in which golden-rayed lilies were arranged.

Beneath the room's bright light, I was hard-pressed to say how old the widow was, but she looked extremely young. Her sweet black eyes shone with a moist, soft light. What I had thought in the darkness to be a summer kimono was actually made from a luxuriant somber blue crepe material, which she wore quite artlessly and which she belted with an obi that was a rusted vermilion in color. The combination expressed a true eye for elegance. Although no maid appeared to assist her, once our initial greetings were past, she rose to prepare refreshments, and as she did so, she did her utmost to make me feel at ease, asking whether the train had been crowded and whether the bus ride had been long. When I said that I had walked from the train station, she looked at me in surprise, and said, "That is certainly something. My, my. The connections out here are quite horrible; I'm afraid you must be exhausted. There's so very little of interest here in the mountains. Shall I fetch you some dinner right away? Or perhaps you'd rather bathe first. The bath is ready, if you'd like. I'm sure you'll find it refreshing. And we can take dinner after that. Let's do that, shall we?"

"Thank you very much. I shall do as you suggest."

The bathroom lay further along the wooden slatted hallway off the mud room. As it was a country house, I was surprised to find a tiled and spacious bathroom, with rocks decoratively arranged along the wall beside the small, one-person tub. From the open window blew the cedar-scented night air, making me think for a moment I was at some mountain hot spring resort. I rested my head on the side of the tub, and as I relaxed in the hot water I thought back on my first meeting with the widow and began to daydream about spending several days in her company and the pleasures that might bring. There was then a great noise outside the window, and a large white thing rose up to the windowsill. When I looked up, I saw it was the cat I had seen earlier. It startled me, so I stood up in the tub and attempted to shoo it away, whereupon it meowed at me and jumped lightly from the windowsill to the sink. It then began to lap at the water that was still spilling from the faucet, until it decided to jump back to the windowsill, from which it disappeared once more into the night. I'm not particularly fond of cats, but there was something about this cat that made me especially wary. I was certain this cat had lived many lives before.

When I finished with my bath, I returned to the room where the widow and I had parted. Beyond that was another traditional sitting room, set for dinner. Beside a large black pillar, shining with a black veneer, the widow—though it pained me to think of her as such, for she was so young—sat beside a small grill, roasting seaweed, I think.

"The bath temperature was perfect, thank you. I do indeed feel refreshed."

"Please, then, come and be seated. I wish we could offer something better to eat."

As I drew closer to the grill, the widow looked up, and, noticing that I was still in my shirt sleeves and slacks said, "Oh, my, I hope you'll forgive me.... I put out clothes for you to change into. I thought perhaps you'd rather put aside the smell of your travels for the day. It might be better if you changed. After all, it can get rather cold in the mountains at night. It may not be what you're accustomed to, but I think you will find the layers to be warmer. I shall of course launder your things in the morning...."

In a basket by the bathroom I found a freshly starched robe, a sleeved jacket that appeared to be hand-embroidered, an obi for the robe and even a pair of underpants. They must have belonged to Master Ki'ichirō, which reminded me that I had yet to express my condolences. Upon changing, I returned and apologized to the widow.

"I am most sorry I failed to say anything earlier, but I was greatly shocked to hear of your loss."

"Wherever would you have heard of that?" The widow's hand paused in mid-air as she set out the soup bowls. I explained that I had heard it from the proprietors of the soba shop in town as well as from an old woman I had met on the road earlier who had said she was a member of one of the branch families.

"That must have been the old woman from Nakaya then. Did she have anything to say about me?"

"Nothing in particular."

"That's all fine and good, but as you can see, we're out in the country and most people have far too much time for idle chatter." Upon saying this, she turned her face from me as if in thought.

"I heard that next month will be the first anniversary of your husband's passing."

"Has it been a year already? The time has gone so quickly.... Well, enough of that.... Are you hungry? We've not much, but perhaps something will tempt you." And with that her pale hand reached forth and picked up the saké decanter.

WITH THE WIDOW'S encouragement, I found it hard to say no as she continued to pour, and although I normally cannot drink much saké, I ended up emptying two decanters. She drank along with me, about three or four saké glasses' worth, and her eyes were faintly rimmed with red. I couldn't tell you what kind of saké it was, but since this was a rice-producing region of Japan, I would think it was a local brew. It was very smooth, rich on the palate, and it gave a very pleasant sense of intoxication. I had never drunk saké as good as this. When I noted in all honesty how good it was, she said, "Relatives have a brewery, and they make special batches without adding any preservatives, which they sometimes send round here. Ki'ichirō couldn't hold his liquor, and said this was the only saké he could drink. He used it to ward off winter's chill, little by little."

"When they say that saké is the nectar of the gods, surely this is the saké they mean. No matter how much I drink, I can't see myself becoming angry enough to argue or kill. When the famous poets like Yakamochi[7] or Bai Juyi[8] mention saké in the ancient poems, this is what they must have been referring to. I don't know what that swill in saké bottles is nowadays."

"Please have as much as you like. If we run out, I can always send for more."

"I've already had plenty. Thank you, though."

Her family owned a fishery, and dinner included carp and char that had been caught that morning, as well as pickled silver vine flowers and nameko mushrooms, which were particularly delicious. Since silver vine blooms in the spring and mushrooms are only available in the fall, she told me that they were salted down in large casks once they were picked. The food was presented to me in a large bowl, yet I somehow managed to eat every last scrap of it.

As we ate, we talked of various things. She was a talented conversationalist, and so it fell to her to do most of the talking and to me, who was usually less skillful in this regard, to be her listener, and as I was somewhat inebriated, her gentle alto, with its tender lisp and muffled tones, rang softly in my ears. She spoke of Dr. Tsujimura, whom she had met once, and then she spoke of Ki'ichirō, and then of the subject of my studies. In all respects, they were rather serious topics for conversations, and I was struck by the scope and depth of her intelligence. I wondered if she had attended university.

"Forgive me, but as I listen to you speak, I notice that you employ none of the local dialect. Might I ask where you were born? Was it Tokyo?"

---

7. Otomo-no-Yakamochi (大伴家持), c. 718–785. A famous poet and statesman and a contributor to the Manyōshū, a collection of Japanese poems dating back to the ninth and tenth centuries.

8. Bai Juyi (白居易), 772–846. A Tang dynasty Chinese poet also featured in the Manyōshū.

"Me? No, I attended school in Tokyo, but my family is from the coast in Chiba prefecture. I know it's rude to ask, but where is your family from?"

"I am from Gifu prefecture. From the mountains above Minō."

"From Gifu? One of Ki'ichirō's friends from university was from Ōgaki. He came to visit us here once. Are your parents in good health?"

"No, sadly they are both deceased."

"Do you have brothers and sisters?"

"I have but one older sister."

"So it is up to you, then, to carry on the family name."

"Actually, no. My sister's husband took our family name to carry it on, so it is no longer my responsibility. I suppose that makes me something of a vagabond, if a healthy one."

"I would think that would be an enviable position, to be able to do as one pleases, study what one wants. Have you any relatives in Tokyo?"

"No. It's quite nice, actually, to live in an apartment on my own."

"I would think that would have its disadvantages, though. You should quickly find someone you like and make a happy family of your own. Or perhaps there is already someone special?"

"Heavens, no! I've no wherewithal for such things. Had I a wife, I couldn't afford to feed her."

We talked about the dire economic conditions after the war. We talked about how black marketeers had even come this far into the mountains at one point. We talked about the rising fortunes of the new tenant farmers. Even topics that would have bored others were fit for our gossip as we whiled the hours away.

We realized that it had become very late. A large house such as this can be as quiet and as discomfiting as a cavern. I no longer heard even the sound of the wind in the cedars behind the house.

Perhaps it was a sign of how well made the building was, but not even the shutters rattled.

And yet, I wondered whether it was only the two of us in this large house. If there were no maids, surely there was a butler or manservant, but there was no sign of him. Stranger still, there was no sound of any mice or rats. I grew concerned, and when I asked about it, for some reason, the widow hesitated before saying, "Yes, well, there is someone over there, but I'm certain he's already asleep. He always goes to bed immediately after his supper...."

"Surely it must be very lonely for you, all alone in this great house. How hard it must be when the snow falls."

"Yes, but I've grown accustomed to it. People from the village come to shake the snow from the roof, so I've nothing to worry about on that account. That said, this society is still very feudalistic in many ways, so it is difficult to live life alone without inviting comment. There's no need for me to go into all of that now, of course. Let me leave it by saying that my neighbors are far more gossipy than I ever would have imagined."

It sounded as if there were indeed complicated explanations behind her story. It would have of course been rude on our first meeting to have inquired further into the matter, but for her to have left her home to marry someone she loved, and then to lose that someone to death would amount to a kind of solitude that even I could well imagine. It would seem that she and Ki'ichirō had not had any children, and I ventured to guess that was a source of criticism from her neighbors as well. When I realized how difficult it must be for her to endure life all alone in this house, I found that her fortitude of spirit, more than her beauty, stood out.

THAT NIGHT, AFTER I lay down to sleep, I had the most frightful dream. I'm not certain what time it was when I went to bed. Both the clock on the pillar above the grill and the clock set on the chest were, for whatever reason, stopped, and I had left my wristwatch in the pocket of my clothes by the bathroom, as asked by the widow, so I had no sense of the time. I was certain that it was long past midnight. The widow led me to my bedroom, holding an old-fashioned candleholder covered with a paper lantern and metal netting. My room was a ten-mat room, at the end of a dark hall, after three turnings along dark passageways where the only sound was our feet on the flooring. The room was lit with a lamp, which gave the mosquito netting over my bedding a pale glow. The house seemed more and more like a disused inn or dormitory, with very little chance of my finding my room on my own, but the room itself was elegant, with an offset bookshelf, a high ceiling, and expensively crafted tatami mats. After the widow kindly told me how to find the water closet, she bade me good night, and politely waved three fingers from the door to my room before leaving. The odd thing, however, was that her footsteps indicated that she had headed not in the direction from which we had come but in another direction altogether. It is a large house, I reasoned, and her bedroom must have been in that direction.

WHEN I CRAWLED under the mosquito netting and turned off the lamp near my pillow, I fell asleep nearly instantaneously. Given the saké I had drunk and the day's tiring expedition, it was no wonder. Soon after, however, began a frightful dream.

However, in all honesty, I cannot say whether I saw a dream, for I think I lost the ability to discern dreams from reality for a time. In other words, I saw something more frightful than any nightmare could ever be. Perhaps that is the most appropriate description.

I do not know how long I had been asleep, but I remember feeling something heavy upon my chest as I slept. I tried to brush it off but could not, and when I began to have difficulty breathing I awoke. I don't know whether I groaned or not, but I think that something made a noise. When my eyes opened, however, the weight was already gone from my chest. For a while I was convinced that I was still dreaming, and so I remained on the bedding, lying face up, looking out into the darkness. It was then that I sensed the presence of something in my room, beyond the mosquito netting. I could not tell what it was, but its body seemed to be bound and it was unable to move. I held my breath and pricked up my ears. I felt my heart begin to pound faster and felt the blood rush to my head.

After a moment, I heard the sound of something crawling outside the mosquito netting. There was a quiet scraping noise, as if something was slowly crawling over the tatami. Given that it seemed to move and then stop, move and then stop, I thought it might be a snake. In old houses, snakes would often hide up under the eaves to find and catch rats. That would have had to have been what I was hearing. I thought I would frighten it off by making a noise of some kind, so I arose from my bedding, but there was no time for me to grope about for the switch to turn the lamp by my pillow on because at nearly the same moment as I arose, I heard from out of the darkness a scratchy voice crying out. It was the same cry that I had taken for that of a parrot in the mud room when I arrived. I had arisen with enthusiasm, but was taken aback at hearing that sound. It struck me as odd that a parrot would be out of its cage late at night and free to fly into rooms where people lay sleeping. Just as I thought how strange that would be, the mosquito netting suddenly fluttered in front of me as if struck by a gust of air, and a face appeared beyond the netting. As soon as I saw it, my entire body seemed to have frozen, such that I was forced to stare at it, uttering no cry of alarm, and I began to lose consciousness.

As I write this, I can recall in great detail the face that seems to have been burnt onto my retinas. To begin, it seemed to be twice as large as an ordinary person's face. Not only was it larger, but everything about it, including its eyes, nose and mouth, was grossly distorted. Neither eye was in its proper place. The right eye was off in the forehead and the eyeball was clouded over like an oyster, and the left had drifted down into the cheek, with the lid weighing heavily over a black pupil that had narrowed to a slit. The nose seemed to be crushed flat, with its nostrils oddly mismatched. Set between lips that looked like badly stuffed sausages were sharply pointed and glistening teeth. Its skin was stained and leathery, wrinkled as if all the life had been wrung from it. For a moment I thought it might have been the cat, but the hands that gripped the mosquito netting beneath that enormous face were the size of a human child's. Striped pajamas were sloppily closed across its chest, and it vacantly stared through the netting to see what was inside.

When I awoke the next morning, the sliding paper doors beyond the mosquito netting were already brightly lit by sunshine. Someone must have opened the shutters as I slept. Concerned that I had slept in beyond an acceptable hour, I rose from the bedding only to notice that I had ended up sleeping with my feet at the pillow end, at which I recalled with a hair-raising shudder the frightful dream I had had. Even now, in the light of day, when I recall that horrifying face, all of my hair stands on end. I remained seated for a moment on the bedding, frozen in thought, but as I continued to consider it further, some things began to make less sense. I certainly remembered losing consciousness, but had I awakened in the position in which I had fainted? Or had that hideous thing not been a dream after all and had it truly appeared beyond the mosquito netting? And to think that all had been so visible in the middle of such darkness was also very odd. Surely it would have had to have been a dream, but had it not been, what in heaven's name had that awful monster been?

I crawled out from under the mosquito netting and opened one of the sliding paper doors. A veranda ran along outside the sliding paper doors, beyond which was a space of greenery too damp to be called a garden; it was more of an extension of the cedar forests from the mountains behind the house. In the shade, the white flowers of the chameleon plants were blooming in profusion. It appeared that my room was located at the very rear of the house. I could see patches of bright blue sky beyond the eaves and among the branches of the cedar trees. From the sun's position in the sky, I guessed that the morning was already well along.

Once I had put the bedding away, I made my way into the hallway, in the hope of finding the bathroom I had used the night before so I could wash my face. The vast house remained as quiet as ever, with not a soul to be seen; the widow was neither in the dining room nor in the kitchen. When I reached the guest room with the glossy black pillars, I found my overnight bag, as well as my clothes, freshly laundered and folded neatly in a wicker basket, so I removed by toothbrush, facecloth and soap from the bag. I wondered what time it was, but when I removed my wristwatch from my jacket pocket, I found that the hands had stopped at three-twenty. I tried winding the stem, but it was tightly wound. I thought perhaps it needed oiling, so I shook the watch lightly and held it to my ear, but the second hand made not a sound. As I inclined my head at the strangeness of it all, the widow arose from the mud room.

"Oh, dear, I didn't realize you had awoken. I trust you slept well?

"Good morning," I said, somewhat bashfully. "Indeed, I overslept, it appears.... Do you happen to know what time it is? My wristwatch seems to have stopped...."

"Well, I wonder what time it might be. As you might have noticed, there isn't a single working clock in the house. The radio has broken as well, and it has never been fixed.... Things are a bit haphazard, I'm afraid." Upon saying this, she smiled. I wasn't getting anywhere. Things were indeed haphazard if, out here in the mountains, there was no sense of the date or time and no radio as well. I didn't know this until later, but once her husband had passed away, the widow also stopped the newspaper subscription.

I thought about how much I had relied on those things, but then I also stopped to consider how those of us living in the modern world were afflicted by the trappings of civilization, and how we were pursued, night and day, by those three things—clocks, radios and newspapers—made to do their bidding, continually manipulated by them. It can also be said that we are most unhappy and at greatest risk when we no longer consider the various noises of civilization to be loud and bothersome. Has modern man, in his pursuit of progress and civilization, already passed the point of no return? Is he doomed to suffer from the afflictions that will result? In that light, I began to respect the widow for abandoning the three typical expressions of modern civilization. Undoubtedly, there was Ki'ichirō's influence at work, and certainly the environment had much to do with it as well, but it was quite incredible for a woman to have such a philosophical view of things. My respect for her grew ever greater.

Once I had returned from washing my face, I found that she had prepared breakfast for me in the dining room. As she put on a pot of tea, she said, "I've put a few things for you to wear in your bedroom. They belonged to my departed husband, and I can certainly understand should you not wish to wear them, but as no one else will ever wear them again, you may wear whatever you like."

I had seen the crepe men's kimono in a black splashed pattern and the waistband belt set out before the offset bookshelves in the bedroom, but they were so expensive-looking that I hadn't dared to touch them.

"I am grateful, but I should refuse. I would feel terrible should I end up getting those things dirty, although, madam, I was wondering if I might be permitted to enter one of the storehouses today to see some of the old documents."

"I will be happy to show you there later, certainly, but you needn't worry about getting anything dirty. Since the receipt of your letter the other day, the entire house has been cleaned.... Of course, the second floor of the storehouse is quite cool when the windows are open and the air blows through."

As we ate, I made no mention of the dream (if indeed that was what it was) that I had seen the night before.

BEHIND THE HOUSE, space had been cleared to grow eggplant and potatoes. The sound of logs being split could be heard from within the sawmill. That was the first sign of activity I had heard since arriving at the house. Perhaps a manservant worked in the sawmill. Behind the barn there was a tall arbor built from bamboo, upon which ranged moonflower vines, their blue blossoms facing downward toward a patch of red hibiscus, which was riotously in bloom. To the left of a small path that climbed into the cedar forest beyond the potato fields were three storehouses. The two wide-fronted storehouses were for rice, and the one in the middle, with a second story, was where the old documents were kept.

We stepped up onto the stone platform at the storehouse's entrance, and the widow opened the rusty hinged iron doors.

We then ducked through a small but solid screen door and put on woven straw sandals, replacing our outdoor shoes. As we entered the semi-darkness, the overwhelming smell of dust assaulted my nose.

"Please watch your step. Oh, my, there are spider webs everywhere!"

Thin beams of light entered from narrow windows high along the walls, and the space was filled with boxes and antiques, all of which were covered with dust. The antiques spoke to the glorious past of Oshaka House. There was a long locked chest, embossed with the family crest, an old wicker hamper for clothing, a portable safe, and boxes marked with their contents, such as, "serving dish for fifty people" and "painted tea caddy," stacked one upon the next, covered in dust and reaching up to the spider webs hanging down from the ceiling in curtains.

"I suppose there's nothing here but useless old knickknacks. I've heard that some of the things here are worth tens of thousands of yen, but I've never opened any of the boxes. Let's go up to the second floor. It's as dirty up there as it here, so let's keep our straw sandals on."

I followed the widow up a rickety staircase immediately beside the entrance and we came out into a ten-mat room, floored in tatami mats. At the other end of the room was a large window, paned in glass. One of the other walls was covered with bookshelves packed full of books and documents that rose to the ceiling. Opposite that was a large set of shelves made from zelkova wood, with columns of shelves set on rails to maximize storage space. It appeared as if this room had been cleaned every now and then, with everything in the room fairly well organized.

"Well, well. Quite the impressive study. It's bright and quiet...."

"Yes, it is. My husband found it to be a very relaxing place and put in the effort to have it properly restored."

The widow brought a rosewood table that had been leaning in a corner to the center of the room and said, "Perhaps because there are windows at both the north and south ends a nice breeze blows when they're open. And even though there's no fire in the grate anymore during the winter, it stays fairly warm in here, perhaps because the walls are so thick."

As I opened the window and looked out over the cedar trees, I realized how right she was as a cool breeze blew across my face.

A framed photograph above the beam caught my eye. A variety of personages in formal attire were arrayed on what appeared to be a grass lawn before a building I took to be the local museum that Dr. Tsujimura had spoken about, for he stood among them in his frock coat, in what was perhaps a commemorative photograph.

"Was this taken when the museum was opened, madam?"

"Indeed it was. You can see Dr. Tsujimura standing there in the center. There I am in that horrid outfit...."

"Oh, you're wearing a dress. It rather suits you, I would say."

"Oh, listen to you.... I really had no interest in going, but my husband would hear none of it. It was quite the topic of conversation, how I went all the way to Niigata to buy that dress."

"Would that be your husband, the gentleman standing to your left?"

"Yes. He was still healthy when that photo was taken. The museum opened in May of that year, and it was in the autumn when it came on, his falling asleep and waking up at odd hours...."

"Is that when his illness began? What exactly was wrong?"

"He had had a respiratory condition when he was younger, so we thought it was a recurrence of that." She had been wiping the dust from the table with a tissue as she spoke, but her hand paused as she said, "As you might imagine, it is rather unhealthy to spend six months with nothing but snow. I asked him to go somewhere with healthier air, to a hospital or clinic, for surely surgery would help to make him better. I begged him, even, but he would hear nothing of it. He insisted that I would leave him if he left. All he wanted, he said, was to remain here and die with me at his side. And he just grew weaker and weaker. But we did as he asked, and he passed away in the house in which he was born." At this, the widow's gaze fell downward with emotion.

I was unable to prevent myself from feeling sympathy for her plight. From the photograph, Master Ki'ichirō, in his fashionable apparel, was every inch the country gentlemen, the young master of an old local aristocratic family, and I thought it all the more likely that he should have therefore fallen victim to his delicate health, exacerbated by an earlier exposure to some respiratory illness. He had not yet reached forty, and had contracted an incurable illness which would force him to leave his beloved and beautiful wife, so perhaps it was not all that difficult to understand the choices made by Ki'ichirō. And yet it was the position of the young widow left behind that warranted even more sympathy. She had hinted the night before that those around her were given to gossip, but perhaps someone among her relations had found a potential suitor for her to consider remarriage to. I knew it was none of my concern, but to be frank, I thought that it would have been a terrible loss were such a beauty to have had to spend the rest of her life locked away in these mountains, regardless of whatever mitigating circumstances there might be.

It was then that the widow opened the lock on one of the sliding shelves, removing a very thick door to expose an interior stuffed to overflowing with papers. Seeing them, I involuntarily gasped and moved forward, as if to keep any from falling.

"This is truly incredible!"

"This is all of the family records. Anything else of historical interest, for example, the instruments used for punishment, the antique filing cases, the swords and the like, all of that was donated to the museum. As far as we were concerned, we had no need for any of them. I lost count of the number of cartloads that were driven away. And of course, none of us knew what we were looking at then, so we had no idea if any of it was worth anything...."

There was a strong odor of camphor. The interior of the sliding shelf was divided into several small shelves, and documents appeared to be stored in a very organized manner. I was taken aback by the sheer number of books and papers there.

"Wow, this is something else altogether! I am amazed that everything has been maintained all in one place and not scattered about."

As my heart beat wildly with excitement, I was content for a while to merely take it all in, keeping my hands to myself for the moment. It was as if I had found a vast treasure.

The shelves were marked with small labels, such as "rice field production," "taxes" and "court cases," and documents that had been sewn together into bindings were marked with the Imperial eras on their bindings, dating as far back as Kan'ei[9] and Genbun[10]. I had hardly thought that someone like myself, with so little experience, would ever encounter such a rich historical record, and then to suddenly encounter, hidden away here in this shelf, documents representing hundreds of years of one family's lives and history made me feverish with excitement.

"Please take as much time as you like to review them. They were sealed in old hampers for a very long time, so I suspect you will find they are worm-eaten in more than a few places. Still, he said we should do everything possible to maintain them in their original condition, and with the exception of ironing out a few wrinkles, he did very little else to them. He had this shelving custom made for them, and it took him nearly three years to organize all

9. 1624 to 1644

10. 1736 to 1741

the papers. I suppose he was something of a fanatic, once an idea took hold of him."

"Well, this is certainly far from ordinary. Your husband's desire to preserve these papers is indicative of his respect for history, and I, for one, am extremely grateful. Records such as these are less the property of an individual and more something that should belong to the public."

"I see. That's as he always said. 'These are not my things,' he would say. They were entrusted to him on behalf of the Asō family. That was why he considered it his responsibility to save them, to keep them from being damaged or lost, or scattered to different families. He said it so often. His intention was someday, when he had the opportunity, to donate all of these papers to an institution such as a university. I can't imagine how happy he would have been had he been able to meet someone like you before he passed away. I was never much of a fit partner for his conversations on the topic...."

"You mustn't say that. I'm just barely out of school myself, and if there's anything you want to ask me please go right ahead. It's truly a shame that he passed away so young.... Of course, with such a large collection, I'm at a loss as to where I should begin."

I withdrew a few volumes from the section marked *rice field production* and carefully began to peruse them. They appeared to be old records of irrigation schedules, beautifully handwritten on quality handmade paper, similar in appearance to Minō paper and cut in the old-fashioned size, with separate entries for each plot of land.

"If you'd like to study things more thoroughly, perhaps a room in the house would be better? There is a clean, empty one available, and we can bring you everything you would need. It would be quiet."

"Thank you for your kind offer, but there is nothing to impede my work here...."

"That said, it is still much quieter there. I know it seems selfish, but I think you will find it better there...."

"I see. Well then, shall we do that?" I withdrew the remaining volumes from that section and said, "I'll begin by reviewing these, if you wouldn't mind, madam. It might be good to leave the shelves open for a while to allow some air in."

"Yes, please do leave them open, but let's close the windows, then." She rose to shut the windows and, doing so, said, "You needn't ask me every time you wish to enter this room; please feel free to come and go as you wish. I will leave the door downstairs unlocked.... Please, follow me, and watch your steps on the ladder, as it can be quite dangerous."

"Thank you."

I followed the widow down the steep staircase without any handrail, both of us climbing down it as if it were a ladder, facing the stairs, until we reached the lower floor.

JUDGING FROM THE view of the mountains from the veranda surrounding the room, I believed it was at a further remove from the room where I had slept the night before. At the end of a long, curving hallway, we came to a tiled archway, which we needed to duck under. This brought us into a short and narrow space, roughly four mats long, which had the air of a vestibule. We then opened sliding doors to come into a library-like room, eight mats in size, floored in tatami, bright and facing a garden. The garden was rather small in size, with low-growing maples and azaleas on a landscaped hill overlooking a small pond, and with a stone lantern and other decorative touches off to the side. The wind gently stirred the broad lotus leaves that floated on the cloudy green water of the pond as the bright light, nearly as white as washed rice, was filtered and dappled through the leaves of the trees. I moved a large desk made from Burmese rosewood to a position near the veranda, and there I opened a new notebook as well as the irrigation schedule I had brought from the storehouse.

In all honesty, the moment I laid eyes on that treasure trove of historical documents there, it was as if the poor academic longing that had lain dormant within me had been rudely and abruptly awakened. They say that life is a game of chance, and I trembled with excitement and joy to think that I had been offered a great opportunity to roll the dice for once, and I knew that such opportunities do not happen to everyone. I'm not exaggerating when I say that my heart was pounding as if I had just discovered a gold mine. I was on fire with excitement. I also realized the need for extreme care and diligence in going forward. Even if I were not on the brink of a brilliant new discovery, I knew I would need to proceed with the utmost care in my research as I strove to gather information.

Where should I begin my excavations, as it were, in such a massive amount of source documents? I resolved to begin by perusing everything first, taking notes as I went. It was highly unlikely, however, that I would be able to make my way through it all in a mere ten or twenty days' time. A gold mine of good quality, they say, will continue to produce year after year. Theories and genealogies should naturally be based on any information uncovered. There might be something of profound importance hidden within, which would otherwise only be donated to some academic society on behalf of the Asō family. I was unable to repress the emotions beginning to bubble up within my breast. I was suddenly and strongly taken with the sensation of a glittering light, signifying that the world was mine to do with as I pleased.

I firmly believe and have never doubted that the eyes with which we view history are the same with which we should view ourselves. The converse can also naturally be said to be true, and it must be the case that the basis of a historical perspective likely lies in those mutually reflexive actions. History is not merely the past. Little by little I myself am becoming a historical entity, but what we know as time is a profound mystery, with historical facts simply representing data that was, at some point in the past, stopped within the flow of time. History comes alive when we focus on the causal relationships within the flow of time that center on such data. Records are as a matter of course never absolute, but for any given place, there will be things that live there, human beings included, each of which possesses its own predestined factors that comprise its history within the flow of its time, and as such, these factors will have a very real existence, regardless of how inconsequential the records they represent. These factors are further swathed in layer upon layer of conditional causes that are restricted by time. Records present only one view of that.

Upon the desk in front of me I opened the record of irrigation schedules, and I wondered how vast the scope of time, the layers of time, would have to be as I reviewed it. I had already been made a captive of the flow of time within that document. I could even hear the noise that time made as it rushed by.

Yields for Individual Holdings (official Keichō era land survey)

—eight *seki*, two *to*, two *gō*, four *shaku*, five *sai*[11]

Nakanokubo Hikobei

—two *seki*, eight *to*, one *shō*, seven *gō*, six *shaku*

Tanoue Sukesaburō

—six *seki*, seven to, two *shō*, seven *gō*, nine *shaku*

Sodeyama Shirosaku

—three *seki*, seven to, one *shō*, four *gō*

Nishibora Jirō, Saburō

This was the dry array of numbers that filled the pages of these records expressionlessly. Whatever did they mean? What were

11. The units here are old Japanese volume measures. One *seki* is roughly 180 litres. There are 10 *to* in a *seki*, 10 *shō* in a *to*, 10 *gō* in a *shō*,10 *shaku* in a *gō* and 10 *sai* in a *shaku*.

eight *seki*, two *to*, two *gō*, four *shaku*, five *sai*? What did 'yields for individual holdings' refer to? I began to fantasize about what was hidden beneath the numbers, eight *seki*, two *to*, two *gō*, four *shaku*, five *sai*. What kind of a person was Hikobei? Surely he had had a wife and children. What was his day-to-day life like? His work? His financial situation? Did Hikobei from Nakanokubo get along with Sukesaburō from Tanoue? Did they quarrel over water use? These were the kinds of fantasies that captured my imagination and roamed broadly until they collided with a particular limitation—perhaps it would be better termed a framework. But in the broadest sense this refers to the government, environment or simply the times in which we live. History is merely a summation of the illusions within such frameworks.

As I considered such things and read on for a few more pages, my head bent over the desk, I felt as if someone's shadow had gone quickly past, right in front of me. At first I thought it would have had to have been a bird flying by, but it seemed too large to have been a bird. There was no one in the garden. I thought little of it and had returned to reading when, after a brief moment, the same dark shadow passed before my eyes. I raised my eyes, but throughout the whole of the garden and the room I was in there was only silence and no one but myself. I thought it strange, and as I stared blankly at the garden I had the sensation that there was someone behind me. I quickly turned to look, but there was no one there. I was certain that it would happen again, so I got up from the desk, and opened the sliding door that led out into the dark, four-mat vestibule, but of course there was no one there either. I suddenly felt a little ill-at-ease. Surely there had been someone behind me. Thinking that perhaps I had imagined it after all, I sat down once more and reached for my cigarettes when all of the sudden there appeared a dark shadow over the surface of the irrigation schedules records spread out in front of me. In the very instant it startled me, I suddenly felt a very heavy weight press down on both of my shoulders. Without thinking, I dashed out onto the veranda.

I am sure that my face went very pale at that moment. My heart continued to race for quite some time after that. It goes without saying that there was nothing in the room. I had no intention, however, of immediately returning to my place at the desk. As I wondered what the weight I had felt could possibly have been, I was again overcome with fear.... As I looked out once more into the bright garden, I noticed that the large white cat was beside the stone lantern by the pond, although I couldn't say when it had arrived there. The cat seemed to be looking up at me, and I was quite surprised to see it perhaps because I recalled the frightful dream of the night before. At that point, the cat, its eyes locked upon me, slowly rose and then lay on its side and began to roll in the dirt. Its behavior made me think that it was in heat, as it moved in such an enticing way. It curled up its four paws, and wrapped its body around the base of the stone to the left and right, again and again, rolling in the dirt in a way that suggested either agony or sexual pleasure. When I saw two rows of flesh-colored nipples arrayed within the white fur I realized that it was a female. It grew even bolder, raising its haunches to expose its genitals and then began to rub its body more and more against the stone. It was as if the cat found me sexually attractive, a thought I began to find very unsettling. Unable to re-enter the room, I remained standing on the veranda, although I averted my gaze—for perhaps an interval of a few seconds at most—and when I looked back, the cat was no longer there. In the blink of an eye, that nimble creature had snuck away. Just as I marveled at that, the sliding door to the room quietly opened and the widow entered, smiling, carrying a tray with a teapot and cups on it. Her sudden appearance gave me a deep sense of relief.

"I have no idea how it got so hot all of a sudden.... Is there still a breeze in this part of the house?" She placed the tray out on the veranda and then went to the offset shelves in the room to find two leather cushions for us to sit on, whereupon she began to pour the tea. There was also a dish of sugared beans upon the tray.

"I suspected you might be a little hungry as you went about your studies, so I thought I might come and bother you a bit. There were so many beans left over from the delivery.... Please try them."

"Thank you very much. Don't mind if I do."

As we sat on the veranda, sipping the fragrant *bancha*[12] and nibbling the sweet beans, we made small talk for a while. At that time, I dared not speak to her of the frightening experiences I had just had. It was as if I was consciously attempting to forget them even by seeking out other topics of conversation, although, truth be told, I failed in that attempt and was silent more often that not.

"Oh, I know. Would you like to look at Ki'ichirō's and my photos? There are so many of them." The widow cast about for a new topic of conversation.

I seized the opportunity and said, "Yes, I'd like that very much." I had been wondering what Ki'ichirō had looked like when he married, not to mention the widow.

"I'll just go and get them, then. But are you sure it won't disturb your studies?"

"Not at all."

She left the room quite quickly, and then returned, carrying a large, thick, leather-bound and clasped box in both hands.

"I can't imagine where Ki'ichirō's album would have gotten to. I can't find it anywhere.... I must have lent it to someone," she muttered to herself as she sat beside the desk, opening the clasp

12. Japanese green tea, of a coarser grade than *sencha* or *matcha*.

to remove a handsome leather-bound album. She began to open it on her lap, and said, "These are all photographs of me, nearly all of them taken by my husband. I'm sure you'll find some of them quite silly."

"Oh, please, let me see."

She gave me the album, and I began by lifting the thick cover, under which was revealed the black flocking paper. In the left corner, there was an elegant signature in white ink: Asō Tamae. It was only then that I learned the widow's given name.

"It's rude of me to ask, but is this your handwriting?"

"Oh, my. How could you even look at that?"

"It's very well done. Do you also write *tanka*[13] poetry?"

"Heavens, no. My husband wrote haiku[14] poems now and again, and he often told me that I should try it, because how hard could seventeen syllables be? But I have no talent for haiku or anything like that. I'm much happier reading other people's poetry...."

As I began looking at the photographs in the album one by one, I found them to be as I expected—a collection of smiling snapshots that most amateur photographers specialize in. Tamae dressed in kimono, in Western dresses, in bathing suits, in gardening pants.... The settings varied as well: indoors and out, an innocent smile, laughing, affecting an air of nonchalance, a look of candidness or with her eyes shaded against the sun. The naturalness of her expressions was captured skillfully, but it was her youth and beauty that truly shone through in each photo. Furthermore, the sensation of the deep love shared between the

---

13. *Tanka* is a traditional Japanese poem form, comprising 31 syllables, arranged in lines of five, seven, five, seven and seven syllables each. The ability to read and write *tanka* is considered a mark of superior penmanship in Japanese calligraphy.

14. Haiku are shorter than *tanka*, and were a later development, historically. They consist of seventeen syllables, arranged in lines of five, seven and five syllables each.

people on both sides of the camera was so profound that I felt a twinge of jealousy.

In one photo she was wearing a dress, smiling as she lay in the grass atop a hill with a handful of white flowers, a few contentedly lazy cattle in the background with an ocean visible beyond them. It seemed to be spring, with a soft light suited to that season, lending Tamae a fairy-like air.

"Excuse me for asking, madam, but how old were you in this photograph?"

"It isn't written there?" She leaned over the album perched on my lap, and said, "No, it isn't written there. That was the first time I visited Sado with my husband, so I must have been twenty-two...."

"And yet, as I look at this photo, I can discern no changes between the woman in it and the woman before me. If anything, you have only become more beautiful."

"The things you say! All that for just some tea and sweet beans! Whatever shall I do with you?"

"No need to worry. I'm sure that after a fine dinner there'll be plenty more compliments."

"Oh, can I have that for a second?" As if she had suddenly recalled something urgent, she reached out and removed the album from my lap. "There are some quite horrible photos.... Where were they...."

She placed the album in her lap and began flipping through the pages rapidly, shading them from my view with her hands as she did so and giving me a teasing look. "You mustn't look beyond this point!"

I gasped when I caught a glimpse of white skin in one photograph through a gap her hands had inadvertently made. I quickly averted my eyes to look out on the garden, but I knew my face was growing redder by the second.

Tamae set the album down on the veranda, still open to that same location, and then raised her arms so that she could remove a hairpin from the back of her head, which she then used to clip several pages of the album together so that they couldn't be opened.

"I have to ask. These pages are forbidden for general viewing.... It isn't that the photos themselves are of bad things. I'm just embarrassed, that's all. So you mustn't look!" Upon saying that, she smiled at me with a meaningful look and then placed the album beside the desk.

Clearly, it was I and not she who had become flustered. The shock of seeing something obscene had made me very nervous, and I had no idea how best to answer her, nor could I conceive of a suitable place for my eyes to rest upon. I noticed that at some point the ash from my cigarette had fallen onto my knee, and as I hurriedly tried to brush it into the garden, Tamae began cleaning up the tea things.

"I really shouldn't have interrupted you.... Would you like some more tea? The hot water has cooled off a bit but I can leave the pot if you like."

"No, thank you. It was delicious tea, though."

"Well, at least let me leave the dish of beans, then. Feel free to have as many as you like."

Leaving the album on the floor in front of the offset shelves, she placed the teapot and cups on the tray and made to leave the room, saying, "Would you prefer to bathe before dinner? Or perhaps after?"

"It's very kind of you, madam, but there's no need to draw the hot water every day just for me. I've hardly raised a sweat today, and a good washing with cold water would suffice."

"Nonsense. We light the fire for the hot water every day regardless, so there's no need to stand on ceremony. Now that you know that, please feel free to bathe whenever you feel it would be good to end your studies for the day."

ONCE I WAS left on my own, I remained on the veranda smoking for a while to breathe in what remained of Tamae's fragrance, but once the cigarette was extinguished in the ashtray, I opened the album on the desk to remove the hairpin and open those pages. Her *you mustn't look* was surely an invitation to do precisely the opposite. As I gently pulled the hairpin from the album, the dreaded content fell open before me. As expected, nude photographs of Tamae were arrayed in a variety of poses. My pulse suddenly quickened, and my eyesight seemed to grow weaker. My entire body was suddenly seized with a series of shivering convulsions.... There she was, stretched out upon a bed, and then here, posed standing before a backdrop as if she were modeling for a painting by Modigliani. Here she was lying on her back in a field, a small flower in her hand brushing against her lips, and here she was in a forest beside a tree, her hair disheveled, nymph-like. In each, she was completely and utterly nude. As I continued to look, there was a series of photos in which she was lying on a bed, her legs spread apart in a licentious pose, the camera focused between her legs, from various angles.

As my heart raced, my mouth grew dry as I tried to mentally absorb each and every photograph as I viewed it. Although I began with an urge to cover my eyes, thinking I was looking on something that was somewhat cruel in nature, the more I looked, the more a very different feeling came over me. Regardless of the image, regardless of the licentiousness of the pose, in every instance Tamae clearly appeared to be innocent. At the same time, there was also an air of austerity. I had seen instances of pornography on several occasions in the past, and the impression I had from viewing the nude photos of Tamae was markedly different from the obscene filth one would associate with pornography. I wondered, however, what caused such a marked difference. It would have to be all the photos in the beginning of the album that I had looked at earlier, the portraits of Tamae in myriad poses, and how they expressed a deep love and affection between her and the person taking the photo, such that when I began to view these more licentious materials they were actually more refreshing in nature. I could little know what kind of person Ki'ichirō had been. However, had anyone seen these clearly pure nude photographs and then taken him to be abnormal in some way, I would consider that to be grossly mistaken. Tamae herself said that the photos were not of "bad things," and indeed they weren't. When you truly love a woman and her body, then indeed you should commemorate that love. I was even jealous of Ki'ichirō for the doting love he felt for Tamae. The umpteen photos of her beautiful nude body spread out across the pages were a testament to the happiness of their life together as husband and wife.

And yet there is no doubt that the photographs also represented a secret world that existed only for husband and wife. That may be why Tamae would have wished to have hidden them from my view, but it almost seems, given the end result, as if she produced them for me to see in the first place, and, if that was indeed the case, what was the meaning of that? Had she been planning it all along? The more I thought about, the more confused I grew as to her motives and then, thinking about that, I realized that confusion was also part of the confusion I felt about Tamae in general. Or at least that's what I thought.

How, though, could I describe how truly beautiful her body was? The abundant flow of lines, the rounded muscles that appeared to have a plump resilience, the thinly tapering waist, the deep navel, the gentle slope of the hips, the seductively fertile line between two rounded buttocks, curved like commas about to whirl in on themselves.... Ki'ichirō was able to accurately capture the beauty of each with his camera's lens. And the whiteness of her skin was such that in each photo it seemed to produce its own halo-like effect as if backlit, and glowed like pure white porcelain. Her body seemed to produce a matchless natural luster, so much so that when she posed lying in the grass or standing by a tree, it was the grass or the tree that appeared somehow unnatural in comparison. What is more, one of the things I noticed when I first looked at the photographs—and it shocked me—was that she was utterly and naturally without any hair on her body. In each and every photograph, her skin appeared a pure white expanse, without blemish or hair, fresh and youthful, as if it had sprung forth from some fairy tale. And in keeping with Tamae, it only made her all the more beautiful. It was as if my thoughts, even the blood in my veins, had all ceased; I had become entranced and had forgotten everything but the beauty before me.

IN THE EVENING, when I went to the storehouse to return the materials I had borrowed, it was already growing dark, and although the light from sunset remained in the sky, the cedar-covered mountains were already nearly black with night. Beyond the screen door the lower floor of the storehouse, packed to the ceiling with antiques, was already quite dark.

I placed the borrowed materials under my arm and began ascending the rickety staircase, one step at a time, with one hand on the steps above and a careful eye on my footing. Just as my head and shoulders emerged above the level of the second floor, I noticed that there was something else already in the room before me, and with a jolt I froze.

From the pale light that entered the room from the windows at either end there remained some light within the room itself. As the light hovered between dusk and darkness, I saw something black standing ominously before the bookshelf within the room. When I first saw it, I took it to be a man dressed in a very dark kimono. Although I couldn't quite tell which way his face was looking, given how sudden everything was, in that moment of my shock the man suddenly and rapidly grew in size, up to the ceiling, whereupon, the new giant suddenly became a wisp of smoke that vanished out one of the glass windows until, in the very next instant, I could see him no more.

I was frozen where I stood, my hand clamped tight to the stairs. I have no idea how long I remained there in that position. Unable to descend the staircase like that, I somehow continued up to the second floor and managed to replace the materials on the proper shelves. I remember that I descended the staircase without even looking where I was going. I experienced a sense of relief and of being returned to myself only after I had exited the storehouse.

This was no dream. I was certain I had seen it with my own eyes. I might have been hallucinating, but even had that been the case, I know that I saw it. To this day, however, I still do not understand what I saw. There is the possibility that it was Ki'ichirō's ghost, but in the main ghosts are not known to show their faces, so I cannot say one way or the other. Regardless, the sensation of utter fear that I felt at the moment remains with me still, and as I recall it, cold chills run down my spine. After that incident, I went up to the second floor of the storehouse on many an occasion but I saw that frightful black specter only that once.

ONCE THAT OCCURRED, I began to grow convinced that there was something strange about this household. That would have been the third day—I think. I say it was the third day, but by then my sense of the passage of time had, as I look back on it now, had become very vague. Strangely enough, upon arriving at the house, it was as if I had lost the ability to distinguish between the present day and the day before, and began thinking of the previous day in terms of three days ago, or a month ago or even a year ago, which was exceedingly odd. The seeds of this confusion, as I only realized much later, had been planted from the very beginning of my stay there.

Regardless, there was something odd about the Asō family. The first thing that I could point to was that after my arrival no other visitors came to the house. There seemed to be a manservant or butler of some kind, but I had not yet seen him. There was a strange squawking noise, which I would hear now and again throughout the day as if there was a parrot being kept somewhere within the house. That said, I never saw any indication of a birdcage anywhere. What's more, the squawking had a strange broken sound to it which, every time I heard it, brought to mind my first night's stay in the house, a thought that never failed to send chills down my spine, given that horrible dream I had seen then. But even had that dream been just a terrible nightmare, what was it then that had come upon me in the middle of the day out in the room by the garden? And what was it that I had seen on the second floor of the storehouse?

I've never been given to belief in odd phenomena—what some have taken to calling spirits and others to calling ghosts. If it were a hallucination of some sort, then it would have been the first time in my life I ever experienced such a thing, and I would still be wont to consider that something dark and sinister lay within this vast old house to call forth such a hallucination in the first place. For even though I had never been given to such thoughts as these, there was something about the house, about the very air there that would give anyone such ideas. It's a fact. The fact that the house's very nickname referred to punishment would naturally lend an unhealthy bent to anyone's imagination.

There must also be some unknown and unfortunate mystery buried deep within this house and its family's long history.

Perhaps an important key to solving that mystery lay hidden within the innumerable records kept within the storehouse. As I thought about that, I realized that with enough time I might be able to investigate the matter further. This was not simply a matter of my own curiosity. When you come from common stock as I do, something in your heart chafes at the privilege and lust for power that is still on display, even now in Japan, among our so-called betters. Here, within a distant corner of the remoter part of Japan's snow country I had come upon a strange example of just such a family of privilege, and undoubtedly there were many interesting issues bound up within its origins and aspects. This preposterously enormous house was most certainly an outward expression of this family's strangeness, but I suspected that the problems themselves could fill a house as large as the Punishment House itself.

The only person I saw each day was Tamae. She remained as lovely as ever, and was continually and exceedingly kind to me. Perhaps she had grown tired of waiting on me as she did, but I lacked for nothing in my studies, for which I was truly very grateful, although there was something strange about her. It goes without saying that she remained unfailing in her sweet disposition and was the gentlest woman, and I have not the slightest intention of causing her any harm whatsoever. Although perhaps I have simply thought too much about things, I am still forced to say that I had no idea where, within that great cavern of a house, Tamae spent her days. The more I thought about it, the stranger it seemed. Admittedly, I knew very little of the house's vastness, but surely she had a room of her own somewhere within it. Surely that was where she slept each night and arose each morning, but I did not know where it was. During the day the house was utterly silent, with nary a sound to be heard. She might have simply been a quiet person to begin with, but I could detect no sound of a sliding door, no sound of windows opening or closing, no sound of her walking in the hallways, no sound of her working a sewing machine pedal, no sound of her clearing her throat, no sound of a flushing toilet—no sound of anything that might indicate the things she would be doing during the day. There was no sound of any meal being prepared or any sound of dishes being washed afterward either. When, I wondered, were meals being prepared? When was she doing the washing up?

There was something else that was strange as well. Not once, in all the time since I had arrived at this house, had I ever come upon her in a room. Whenever I saw her, it was always when she had come to find me in whatever room I was in. I had never come across Tamae in the kitchen, at the fireplace or in the garden. The kitchen, the sitting room and even the garden were always devoid of people and silent when I came upon them; a few moments after my arrival, however, she would come to find me there. Yet, I never had the faintest idea of what she had been doing before she came to see me. I might have been overly suspicious. After all, she may have needed to be in the same room as I for legitimate reasons. For someone like me, raised in the country and with only a school trip to experience city life for one week, I can imagine that she must simply have been used to life in such a large house and I was not. Our lives were on different planes. Even without the behavior of Tamae, however, the house remained a very strange place. Had it not been for the work of copying the old records and for the presence of the very lovely Tamae, I would have fled days before.

IT WAS THAT day, or perhaps the day after—my memory of it is somewhat vague. It was probably the day after, I think. I had run out of cigarettes and walked to the old store—Nakaya, it was called—to buy some.

It was the first time I had gone out from the gates of the Asō house. I had only been there three or four days, but the moment I stepped foot from beneath the beams of the gate, it was as if I had been released from years of care into a completely different world once more. The shining of the sun, the feel of the wind on my skin even, everything seemed different once I was away from that house.

Although while someone like me was inside a great house like that, I had no real sense of this, from outside I could see how craggy the mountains there are, and although the sky up above is clear and bright, the air is unexpectedly stagnant amid the rocks and trees. The leaves from the rice plants, in paddies arranged on steep terraces along the slopes of the mountains, sparkled in the bright sunlight, and the air was hot and humid. I found out later that the rice grown in these conditions, which reminded me of being inside a sauna bath, was particularly delicious with a fine small grain.

Nakaya was the only other building in the village, next to the hut where the police officer was stationed, and was the local dry goods store, run by an old offshoot from the Asō family. It was also the home of the old woman that I had met along the road when I had first come to this village.

Beneath the red sign advertising cigarettes, there was a round sign indicating that salt was sold[15] here, as well as a sign whose peeling paint indicated that the proprietor was one Asō Gisaburō. Behind a half-closed and dust-covered glass door was a broad black-paneled entry, and on the shelves were arrayed a scant few goods—some scrubbing brushes here, some laundry soap and some bags of cleanser there. It was a store in name only, it seemed, and even though I hailed from a similarly

15. Salt was originally controlled by a government monopoly, so anyone selling it had to clearly indicate that they did so.

small and remote mountain village, we had nothing quite this desolate.

When I stepped into the entry and called out, the bald head of an old man appeared. The skin was drawn tight over his scalp and flashed brightly as he stepped from behind the shadow cast by an old metal sign advertising a children's medication that was hanging on a pillar. I asked for five packs of Peace cigarettes and, without a word, he went to the back to fetch them. Then, before my eyes, he broke the silver foil on one of the packages, carefully withdrew one of the cigarettes, and then, just as carefully, replaced it. Perhaps he didn't sell very many of them, and was making sure they hadn't gone moldy. It was kind of him, but he was so blunt in his kindness. As he stood there, stiff as a rod, to receive the money for the cigarettes, he started to stare at me. In a husky voice, he asked, "Are you the one who's up at the main house?"

When I said that I was, he withdrew for a brief moment leaving me to wonder what he intended, and then said, "Wouldn't you like to come upstairs for a bit?"

This blunt, rough and off-putting old man was Gisaburō. As you might expect from someone who lived where the snow fell deeply, he was a man of few words, and he was forthright in his opinions. If you looked closely, his eyes were deeply set within wrinkles of age; those eyes, however, could flash with a cold steel. His appearance was one of a deep reserve, although he would likely never describe himself that way. I later heard that Gisaburō was a scion of the Matsushiro family of Shinshū[16], and that he had married into the Asō family. The old woman I met on the outskirts of this village with the bundle of faggots on her back was Gisaburō's wife and the mistress of this house.

---

16. Shinshū is an old name for the region of Japan now known as Nagano prefecture.

Thin round cushions were placed beside the open hearth in the dim room above the store, and once I had sat down, I properly greeted Gisaburō. But in response, all the old man could do was nod his head as his hands picked up two pokers to stir, as if by rote, the embers on the hearth. Once a flame had arisen from among the pokers, his voice, as husky as smoke, stirred within his throat.

"I don't know much about learning or schooling, but I suppose you're here after those papers up at the main house, even though the prefecture got most of 'em. It's an old house, so there's all kinds of things all mixed together up there, especially with what happened in this prefecture. Excuse me for asking, but just exactly what is it you're looking into? It's none of my concern, and I wouldn't be saying this to a blood relation, but you need to keep an eye out for your own self, hear? There's something about that house, and I wouldn't get too deeply involved if I was you...."

I wasn't sure what the old man was trying to say. At first I thought he meant that the information in the papers was not for a stranger like me to uncover, but then I realized that was not was he was hinting at. When the kettle hung above the hearth finally began to boil, the old man poured me a very hot cup of tea and, after taking a drink from a large cup he poured for himself, he said something very strange.

"Since Master Ki'ichirō passed on up at the main house, there hasn't been anyone to carry on the line, and I don't know whether it's right or not for us down here to be talking like this on the subject of it or not, but the village is in pretty poor shape after all. There's the inheritance taxes taking their share and all, but with that woman still there, we're like as not to get a thing done."

"When you say 'that woman,' do you mean Tamae?"

At my question, for some reason unknown to me, Gisaburō stopped drinking his tea and placed his cup in his hands. He then fixed me with such a stare that I was forced to lower my gaze without saying a word. This continued for a moment and then he said something else odd.

"I'm not from around these parts originally, so I don't know much about it, to tell you the truth, but if you want to know the root cause of all these goings-on, there have been strange deaths in that family for near on four generations now. It's not like they've exactly been trying to cover things up, mind you. The whole village knows all about it, and I suppose you should as well. Each master, generation after generation, met his death in a strange way. That house up there was built by a Ki'ichirō from three generations ago. He was my wife's grandfather, you know, and he built that ridiculous house with nary a blueprint. But then the year after the whole thing was finished, they say they found him strung up by a noose, out in the study by the garden. They say he had lost his mind, but he was well known throughout the village for his nasty ways, and two men in a nearby village hanged themselves because of him. Was their hatred strong enough to curse him and end his life in a hanging? Some people in the village still say so, but nobody knows. Nobody could think of any other reason. Even my own wife says as much. But one of the beams in that study has been cut. You can go and see it for yourself. It's been cut right through."[17]

The study by the garden could only be the room where I was doing my research. I hadn't noticed that any of the beams had been cut, but as I sat there listening to Gisaburō, I recalled the weight of that black shade upon my shoulder, and I suddenly felt my knees stiffen. That room, it seems, had been an unfortunate place after all.

Gisaburō continued.

---

17. It was customary, when someone used a beam as a support for a noose when hanging oneself, for the beam to be cut through afterward. It was seen as a way of breaking the bad luck that would therefore be associated with the beam.

"The Ki'ichirō from three generations back, the one who built that ridiculous house where he ended up being hanged? Well, his father and his son as well also met with strange deaths. The master from four generations back was found hanged in the barn that stood where the house is now, and one of his other sons was found up in the mountains behind the house, near one of the old shrines to a sacred lingam,[18] shot through the neck with his rabbit-hunting rifle. They say, from the blood loss and the mess he made of it, that he must have been in terrible pain, but everyone says it was suicide. That was my wife's elder brother, and from what they tell me, he went mad with lust in his middle years and chased anything that moved to slake his unnatural thirsts. Once he had what he wanted, he was just as quick to abandon it. I have no idea what kind of turmoil his poor mother (the daughter of a wealthy family from O township) went through trying to clean up after all his wantonness. He got several girls pregnant, and two were so desperate with sadness that they threw themselves down the well to drown. Later that year, his own father, in part because of the growing anger among the villagers, built a paddock and threw his own son inside, with nary a thought for his toilet, so all the world could come and gawk, in the hope it might knock some sense into him. And then, just before he died, they say he somehow managed to come around a little bit, and that he found a way to sneak out of the paddock while his watchers were off duty. How he found the rifle and bullet, I don't know, but then he ran up into the mountains. The next Ki'ichirō was just twelve years old when his father went mad and died like that.

"And, of course, you would not have met him, but there used be a younger son named Jisaku up at that house as well. He was one of the bastard children from that lust-crazed Ki'ichirō, except that his poor mother happened to be an idiot child in the village.

18. Rock formations that naturally appear in the shape of male and female genitalia are often revered in Shintō as expressions of life-giving energy.

Her older sister took pity on the baby and brought him up to the main house. Given all the crazy things that happened there you'd expect him to be an idiot as well, but in spite of everything he managed to reach the age of forty as an old farmer. I heard about the Ki'ichirō who died when I was young, but his son was an intelligent boy. He got good marks at the university.... and then he was taken in by that woman.... both families insisted on firm agreements for their engagement, but all of us in the extended family were dead set against the marriage. But when my sister-in-law passed, he brought her in here without so much as a by-your-leave, holding the wedding, just the two of them, out at one of them Christian churches in Niigata City, with nary a reception. And then when they came back here to set up housekeeping, it was as if they did everything possible to insult everyone all over again, ignoring anyone worth anything. I got so angry that I called the rest of the family together, and we decided that there'd be no more contact with them whatsoever, and we sent them a letter to that effect, and that was our last word on the matter."

As I listened to him speak, the less I understood what it was that Gisaburō really meant to say to me. Surely such stories that were embarrassing even to members of the same family were not meant for my ears. It was almost as if he was making things up, but the emotions were too strong for that to be the case, it seemed. Regardless, he had come to think of Tamae as an enemy of sorts, and therefore had taken to abusing her, which I found repulsive to listen to. So great was my discomfort, in fact, that a sense of righteous indignation began to arise in me. I began to wonder whether Gisaburō's feelings for the main branch of the family, which would now mean Tamae, had developed into hatred. As I had no knowledge of all the facts involved, and could only venture a guess, I could no longer listen to what Gisaburō was saying. I was no longer curious about whatever motives he might have had. For example, I didn't know whether Gisaburō had any children, but all of the relatives he spoke of seemed to be perched like vultures, waiting to reject Tamae outright, instead of coming together to solve the issue of the continuation of the main family line after the death of the last Master Ki'ichirō. This must have been the 'idle chatter' that Tamae had briefly mentioned before, but I had never expected that it would take this form. If that was indeed the case, then she was truly alone and beset on all sides and even more deserving of my sympathy....

I had had quite enough of Gisaburō's rants and was about to take my leave, when through the curtained doorway came an old woman, up from the store below. She was Gisaburō's wife and the same old woman I had met when I first arrived in the village. I sat back down as she entered, greeting her in the process, and she immediately sat beside Gisaburō by the hearth, neatly on bended knee, and politely bowed her head.

"Did Jisaku come back with you?" Gisaburō ignored our exchange and asked her this directly.

She poured herself a cup of tea and answered, "Yes. We parted ways at the bottom of Nenokuchi hill.... He was in high spirits today."

She then sipped some of the astringent tea from her old teacup and continued with a question for me. "And how goes your work, then? Found anything?"

"I've only just begun."

"There's not much to eat up here in the mountains. Jisaku dug up some great big wild potatoes...."

"What do you know about that? He should bring some in. He's been sneaky of late, that one has. Where was he digging?"

"I couldn't tell you, but I think it was beyond the big patch of rushes, up where he has that netting laid out...."

When I looked more closely at her, I could make out a resemblance to Ki'ichirō in aspects of the old woman's features. But I had heard nothing of the main family from her lips. I then got up, took my leave, and thought that would be the last time I would ever visit that little store and the hearth above it.

After a cool rain fell for two days, the sun came out once more, but the sky took on an autumnal hue, and the cries of the birds and insects seemed to reflect that as well. When the rain fell, the damp, gloomy air in that big empty house grew thicker. But there was something about that sensation that seemed to relax me, and it made my work go all that much faster.

And, yes, just as Gisaburō had said, one of the beams in the study where I was working had been cut through. Coincidentally, the location of the cut was precisely over the desk where I had been sitting. *Aha,* I thought to myself, *that was the reason.* The beams lay flush against the ceiling and there wasn't even an inch of space between then. When that unfortunate event happened, I suspect that the heaviness I felt upon my shoulders was some form of spirit of the dead madman, the Ki'ichirō from three generations ago. It was a strange occurrence, and I do not know exactly what it was or even if I am correct in calling it a spirit, but I do know that simply calling it to mind is sufficient to raise all the hairs on my body, for it remains a frightful experience both in fact and in memory. Once I moved the desk from that position to another and began to work from that new position, no further frightening things happened to me. I also took care to avoid stepping underneath that beam, as I considered it unfortunate from that moment on.

GISABURŌ SUGGESTED THAT there might be a deep sense of retribution involved, or a karmic debt being played out, in the strange deaths in the past four generations of the Asō family. But leaving aside thoughts of karma, when I attempted to view things subjectively, historical facts clouded my vision as well. Clearly those who died were insane. Old aristocratic families, of which the Asō family was one, were known for continually refining their recessive traits and impure blood, although incidents of insanity and strange deaths were not recorded. History lies in wait for all of us, and although it might be difficult to decide where to look, there was the Ki'ichirō who, to borrow Gisaburō's word, built that "ridiculous" house, which was clearly not the action of a sane person. People would naturally think that if a bout of madness came upon him, it would be easy to explain away his sudden death by hanging.

And then his son was a pervert. They say he shot himself after a return to sanity, but it's doubtful whether he actually was sane or not when that happened. And then his son, Ki'ichirō, went to university and excelled. It goes without saying that there's a fine line between genius and insanity, and we all know examples of that. If I were to use a karmic vocabulary, it would have to be fate, then, for a brilliant Ki'ichirō to be the son of a perverted father, for fate does not have to mean a bad fate. If we then carefully consider the work of genetic scientists, we might find solid evidence that the strange death from insanity-related causes, generation after generation, with their children being born as idiots, was not as strange as we might have originally thought. Gisaburō had warned me not to get involved with this family because of his strong dislike for it, I suspect, but whether the family was blessed with good fortune or cursed with ill fortune had little bearing on my research.

I should also confess that I too am the child of quite an impressive madman. When I was five years old and my sister eight, my father went mad. Perhaps he was a little bit strange to begin with. They say it was brought on when he suddenly realized exactly how much he was in debt to our relatives. At the end of his years he was thrown into an asylum and died a miserable death. As a result, my sister and I were raised solely by my mother and had very few happy memories of our childhood. From elementary school onwards, we were both treated as the children of the crazy man. When my father passed away, I was eight years old and my sister was eleven.

By the time I turned twelve, the neighborhood children, who called me Kadoya (after the store we lived over), were convinced that I had inherited my father's insanity. And then, the year after the war ended, I graduated from what was known as middle school in the old system and entered what was then known as university in the new system, all in the same prefecture. However, my education during the war was something of a blank, and I ended up feeling very little confidence in my abilities. For someone with intelligence, like my friend Tozaki, with whom I had grown up, it was easy to get by, but I knew a dullard like me would be left behind in an instant. I talked it over with a few friends, and then left school without seeking permission from either my mother or my sister, returning home to study harder than ever before. At the time, my sister had already gotten married and was running the variety store that my grandfather had run before her, but my decision to come home had created a dilemma for my old mother, who had worked nearly her entire life and was now facing a few years of even more work. I was still known as the son of the crazy man in that village, so I sealed myself up in a second-floor room that had once been a silkworm nursery, and when too much studying made me start seeing things, I would pretend I was having fits, throwing things, yelling, pretending to fast, etc. In the dead of winter I would plunge myself in the middle of the night into the frigid river that ran behind our flat until I lost consciousness, nearly drowning in the process, until a neighbor rescued me. Whenever I did such things, it was as if there was another me standing beside me, brandishing a long polished sword above his head from which a beam of light shone forth, and that me was shouting encouragement to me, saying, "Do it! More! Better!" and so on, in truly desperate fashion.

Fortunately, I never went truly insane, and the next year I followed in Tozaki's footsteps and successfully entered a university in Tokyo. Perhaps it was out of relief that my path had finally been decided, but my mother sickened and died at the end of that year, at the age of sixty-eight. Her entire life had been one of struggle and hard work. It seemed she had been born for a life of working and pain. When I thought that I had contributed to the pain that might have brought about her death, I decided to work three times as hard as anyone else while at university. And whenever I would have wanted to spend time with her, I spent time instead with my books, becoming something of a boring scholar. It was my sister who had inherited most of our mother's realist tendencies, whereas my narrow-minded and boorish behavior tended to indicate that I favored my father more than my mother, I feared. When I looked back on my short life thus far, the son of a crazy man seemed to exhibit a few crazy tendencies himself. Fate, it would seem, is about as useful as a chocolate teapot.

But whenever I saw the place where the beam in the study had been cut, I wondered again what the connection was between what Gisaburō said had happened—how the master of this house three generations ago had hung here to his death—and that heaviness I had felt upon my shoulders. I don't believe in the spirits of the dead, but neither can I deny that I was sitting precisely below the cut in the beam. When I consider that I had moved my desk because the thought of working in that spot made me uncomfortable and that, furthermore, nothing frightening had happened since then, it stood to reason that there was something underneath that cut in the beam. Had some unseen frightful power tried to communicate with me in some fashion? What warning could the shudders that convulsed my body have possibly been meant to convey?

And although I knew that both the black shade in the upper story of the storehouse and my fright in the study by the garden were nothing to be trifled with, I had no idea what their true nature was nor what they signified. All that I can recall, with a vivid clarity as if it is still happening now, is the fear that gripped me. Those things seemed to be beyond the realm of human beings, and if I wished to move my desk a little to remain in that realm, then that seemed a reasonable course of action.

I PASSED SEVERAL quiet days. There was little else for me to do but my work. I became accustomed to deciphering the old handwriting in the documents. My goal was to gather as much of the historical fragments in this rare collection in my own hand as possible. I wanted to piece together as many of these myriad items as I could. Breathing life into them once more might take an eternity, but collecting the fragments themselves was not an easy task. As I copied the dry text into my notebooks, I frequently made asides to myself, although they were never very clever, such as *historia longa, vita brevis.*[19]

As I read the old records, I began to understand just how much of an impact the unique climate had on the happiness and sorrow of people living in a land accustomed to heavy accumulations of snow. The Great Famine of 1786–1787 was one of Japan's disasters from recent history, and its effects here were as appalling as they were elsewhere in the country.

...July, there was frost. Cold rain fell over a ten-day period. No sign of the sky for rest of the month. Both rice and mulberry withered and died. Eighth of August, midnight. Two red lines visible in eastern sky. Remained there until sun set the next day. Do not know significance. Noon, tenth of August. Sky covered with black clouds, sudden downpour of black rain. Rain dissolved everything

19. *History is long, life is short.*

into mud. Homes, fields, mountainsides, all washed away in seconds, without time to stopper the dikes. The rain has made us all, young and old alike, black from water and mud, from head to foot, and we look like barbarians from foreign lands. The people fear we have fallen under a curse, and they have taken to praying day and night at the shrine, offering up amulets and prayers without number. First snow fell on first of September. It immediately stuck to the ground. This is unheard of this early. [...] Of course there was no rice harvested, and there is not a single grain of millet nor any beans nor anything to eat under the snow. Several households have already starved to death, and two houses have been crushed under the weight of the snow as there was no one to go up and clear the snow from the roof. Today there were three more, which makes forty all told in the village, and if this is not a curse from heaven then perhaps, as the wandering monk said, we are living in a branch of hell now. We've broken open five containers of rice to distribute to the poor people, but I doubt it will ultimately be of any use....

For the first time I realized how much income was derived, even in normal years, during the winter, from everything from clearing snow from roofs and roads and the forced labor used to prevent avalanches, to the indoor work, including the weaving of ropes and linen. My inability to see how the snow could form people's economies and customs was being remedied the more I read the old records. In order to truly understand them, however, I began to think that I should come here once more during the winter, when the snow lay thick upon the ground and every last cedar branch bore a blanket of snow. Regardless, it would be impossible, I realized, for me to get through all of the records in the storehouse that summer. And to hear Tamae tell it, the snowfall in the few years since the war had been growing less and less.

THE SPATTERDOCK THAT bloomed along the edge of pond had a yellow flower. The leaves of the water lily, which responded to even the slightest breeze, were quite broad. As the sun set above the cedar-covered mountain, the birds that nested there began to grow quiet at once. In the garden there was a stone, and the white cat seemed to appear upon it suddenly when I was not looking. The quiet was such that time appeared to be standing still.

In fact, since I had arrived, I had not read any newspapers, nor listened to a radio nor seen any clocks, so the notion of time had become quite a remote concept altogether, and I had lost track of how many days had passed since my arrival. Was the person sitting at the desk doing my work the person I was the day before, or the person I was that day? The days seemed to run into one another such that I could, strangely enough, no longer tell them apart. It was as if my body was floating in some vague mist, or as if my feelings for Tamae were like the hands of some great clock, and she were all its numbers, such that my heart kept spinning about.

I remembered that I hadn't sent any letters of any kind since my arrival. I had brought stamps and postcards with me, but I hadn't even bothered to let Dr. Tsujimura or my friend, Tozaki, know that I had arrived safely. They knew that I was a poor correspondent, but to forget to write when I was at such a remove was something else altogether. It was a solitary pleasure, one that I did not want to share with anyone. I wondered how far this aspect of my personality would express itself. I knew which aspects of me would relate to the outside world, but I also thought that I'd never again have another opportunity quite like the one I'd been presented with. In some small way, I had become the master of this little realm.

And as the days went by, Tamae became even more beautiful. Each time I looked at her I seemed to discover a new beauty in her, as if I were discovering some secret treasure she had hidden away for only me to find. And each new discovery only served to deepen the beauty of the whole. For example, there was her lovely nose, which I would find very hard to describe to anyone else, especially the way the curves of her nostrils seemed to form such warm, tender shapes that moved with a tender elegance as she breathed. It allowed me to glance inward at more loveliness, surrounded, as it were, by a pale peach color which then turned to a pale tawny color as my gaze moved further inward until, once, for a moment I was able to discern a still hidden beauty that even then was shocking to my eyes. Unbeknown to her I was able to revere such secrets of beauty everywhere upon her person.

Her long, silky eyelashes, curved and rich with moistness, always seemed to have a sparkle to them, as if her eyes were looking out at stars. Her eyes were as deep a black in color as a freshly made pot of ink. Her ears seemed as small as to be unreal; they were less the ears of a real person than small white mushrooms found growing at the roots of an ancient tree deep within a mountain forest somewhere. Her eyebrows were of a form that reminded me of hearing bells ringing in the capital through a spring mist. Her mouth seemed to be designed less for talking and eating and more for smiling. And when she smiled, there was a glimpse of secrets of a love that she dared not speak to anyone, hidden away within the deep recesses of her mouth. Each time I saw that I thought in all honesty how much I would want to hear just one of those secrets. But her loveliest feature was the fact that she was in no way conceited about any of her natural beauty. She was truly without art. I never once saw her apply any cosmetics. Although I didn't know when she bathed, her skin was always as white as powder, and shone as if it had been polished. Hers was indeed a natural beauty.

It was around that time that a growing intensity within my heart, like a bubble of steam rising up within hot water, began to worsen day by day, straining toward confession. I had become a prisoner of my fascination with her beauty.

When I grew tired of my work in copying out the old records, I would secretly start looking through the album of her photographs once more. To me, that album was heaven-sent. The collection of her licentious poses made her into a truly sublime gift from the gods, an angel. The only problem with this angel, however, was that she appeared before me each morning and evening in a kimono. Where precisely should I look when it came to an angel wearing a kimono? It was all, after all, visible to me within the album. And yet there remained a door between the two of us and I knew it was Tamae who held the key. I had no idea how to open the door without it.

One day, a cold rain fell from early in the morning on, and Tamae brought a *haori*[20] for me to wear over the other clothing she had lent me. I put it on and went to work in the study by the garden. When Tamae brought me some tea later in the day, when she saw me she exclaimed, "Oh, my, with that *haori* on, and in that pose, you look exactly like Ki'ichirō. You took me quite by surprise when I came in just now...."

Thinking to use that to my advantage, I said, "I remind you of Ki'ichirō? Why, thank you.... I feel honored that you should say that."

It's curious that women should always see something of the first man they knew in every subsequent man.

After she poured some hot roasted green tea for me, she said, "I noticed the resemblance the first time I saw you, but now, the way you hold your cigarette reminds me very much of how Ki'ichirō held his cigarette in just that way. It's so strange. And

20. A quilted jacket worn over a kimono.

then the way you purse your lips like that.... He did exactly the same thing."

"I don't know what to say. Thank you."

I grew embarrassed and made a point of looking at the cigarette between my bony fingers, but she suddenly seemed so very close to me, and my heart seemed to be pounding within my breast.

IT WAS AS if I were seeing a very odd dream, one that repeated night after night. Once I entered the mosquito netting of my bedding within my room, the dream would begin. In that dream, I would be sleeping with Tamae. And the Tamae of my dream was as she was within the pinned-together pages of the photo album. And when I was in my dream, I behaved as if I were afraid of nothing, but once I awoke, a dread came over me. I hesitate to write the details of the dream on these pages, but suffice it to say that the fantasies that entered my mind when I saw her photos—that smooth white body, which engendered a fire within me—were the likes of which I had never felt before. As it was a dream, the image I saw would fade fairly quickly and then be replaced by the next, but there was a natural continuity and flow over a long period of time. Every night I learned of a new world, previously unimagined. Here within my dream I learned of a burning beauty in such quantity and passion, it could nearly be called voluminous in measure. I, too, within my dream became akin to an angel.

When I awoke each morning, I realized with a sense of disappointment that it had once again been only a dream. I would be ashamed to see Tamae. As I worked during the day, I realized that I was seeing parts of the dream again, and to shake off the illusion, I would put down my brush, get up and walk out to the veranda for a cigarette. As I looked out on the garden, with the sun shining brightly on it, I began to think how happy I would be to live here always, together with Tamae. During meals, or even during times of no particular significance, I would fantasize that Tamae was my wife, and would find myself seized with an urge to suddenly grab her about the shoulders and kiss her. I considered that these illusions might be the products of my nighttime dreams, and although I did my utmost to avoid them during the day, at night, that dream would always return to me, without fail, no matter what I did. Ultimately, the illusion—although the sense deep within me was that this was more than an illusion—ended with the sensation that Tamae had become mine. It might very well be that at the time I was slightly addled in my senses, but there was something that made me feel that way.

Even now, as I write this, as I think back on the dream, the distinction between dream and reality is very vague, and it is hard to tell the one from the other. Of course, at the time I did believe myself to be dreaming, and could think of it as nothing other than a dream, but there were aspects of the experience that were strange, even for a dream. When I sleep, for example, I have to have every source of light extinguished around me. While I stayed at the Asō house, I always turned the lamp off within the mosquito netting before falling asleep. And yet, strangely enough, within the dream, like clockwork, and only for scenes involving the two us in bed together, the lamp within the mosquito netting would be on. The actions of my dream every night were lit by a faint incandescent light. Yet when I awoke every morning, the lamp would be off. Of course, the more I thought about this, the less strange it seemed, as it was certainly possible within the realm of dreams, but I wondered why it happened within the dreams with such predictable consistency. I know next to nothing of the psychology of dreams nor what objects within them might signify, but for the same scene within a dream to repeat itself night after night struck me as odd. And even if that could be explained, there were other issues that left me with even stronger doubts. It is only now that I can say these things, but once I started having the dream for a few nights, in the morning as I went about my ablutions and in the evening as I had my bath, I noticed something in secret that amazed and horrified me. The revelation so startled me that I nearly fainted. My body was doing things I was not conscious of. And yet, I remained somewhat doubtful of that at the same time. Was that part of the dream, or reality? Although my doubts would directly involve Tamae, my complicity in my actions would of course be doubly, if not triply, worse. I thought it had to have been a dream, but then I became frightened of any possible conclusion that it might not be a dream.

In spite of all of my worries and doubts, the dream continued to visit me night after night. And I found myself unable to wake from it.

And then one day something happened. I had grown bored of my work and was drinking tea all alone when a man suddenly appeared in the garden. His appearance was so unexpected and strange that I was taken aback at first, but then I realized that it had to be Jisaku, the idiot.

He was short and stout, and although he appeared to be quite muscular, there was something of a deformed air about him as well. His short jacket and pants were made from threadbare hemp, and everywhere his skin was exposed, including his chest, face, arms and legs, he was deeply tanned. He called to mind a pig being forced to wear a monkey's clothes, so silly was his appearance.

"You there, are you Jisaku? You gave me quite a turn just then.... What do you say to a cup of tea?" I beckoned to him from beside my desk, and Jisaku, without a word in response, smiled as he crawled up onto the veranda and on into the study. He sat cross-legged beside the desk, his eyes like saucers as he took in the room as if it were a marvel. I went on, saying, "It's very hot today. Are you off work, then?"

He made no answer and simply stared at me.

When I poured him some tea, he drank the whole hot cupful in one gulp, and then began staring about the room once more in silence. I began to look more closely at his features, noticing that his head seemed disproportionately large, given his small body. His eyes, nose and mouth were all much larger as well, and his dark lips seemed to be strangely thick, with his eyebrows a thick unbroken line running in parallel above them. His face seemed to be void of any spare fat, and the skin was leathery in appearance.

"Would you care for a cigarette?"

"Ah, yeah." He smiled as he answered, taking the box I held out for him so that he could select his own cigarette, drawing it out clumsily and comparing both ends before placing it in his mouth. When I lit a match for him, his eyes went wide in shock at first, and a great exhale of breath extinguished the match before I could even light the cigarette for him. I lit another match and watched as he clearly enjoyed his cigarette, stretching his legs out in pleasure as he smoked.

"There's a great view from the mountain behind here. It's all my mountain, but the view is great. I can show you if you want next time."

"Yes, I'd like that sometime. You go up from the path behind the storehouse?"

"Ah, yeah.... You can see the Black Princess and all the way to Sado Island, and even Mount Hakkai and Mount Ginzan. There are bears up in those mountains. And snow in summer. It's really high. It's so high, I don't know how high it is. It's a great view, it is."

"Well, please take me with you next time. You must be very busy, though. This is the first time I've seen you in the more than ten days since I arrived here."

"Ah, yeah. I am very busy...."

When his cigarette had dwindled to no more than an ash he casually tossed it out into the garden and then reached for another without asking.

To paint a better picture of his character, as he sat there fidgeting, his dark and fleshy penis began to work its way out from his pants leg. It was disproportionately longer and thicker than his size would have led me to believe it should be, and I sat thinking that, after the death of Ki'ichirō, here was the last remaining scion of the Asō family. If I remembered Gisaburō and our conversation at Nakaya correctly, the extended family spent a great deal of time discussing the issue of family succession. But with all its twists and turns was the history of this old family to end here? Surely the extended family would have known of the existence of Jisaku in their search for an heir; they could have come together to propose a guardianship for Jisaku. I couldn't say how old he was just by looking at him, but by the nature of his monstrous physiognomy and by the very large size of his manhood, the evidence of the long years of suppressed anger and sexuality within the Asō family were clearly on display within poor Jisaku.

"Do you want to go dig up *jinenkos*?"

"What are *jinenkos*?"

"They give you energy, they say."

"Oh, wild potatoes. Yes, they are quite good."

"Old Nakaya says I'm good at it, but the old man says I shouldn't. He won't give me any money for 'em. But next time he'll give me a snake."

"A snake? That could be dangerous! You should watch out."

"Watch out for what? Snakes are delicious. And they give you energy. See?"

Then he suddenly stood and, right in front of my face, exposed himself to me. Not content to simply show me his manhood, he then proceeded to bring about an erection.

"Hey, now, stop that! That's quite enough! Be on your way."

Even though I knew he was only an idiot, I was so shocked by his behavior that I couldn't keep from yelling at him. A smile played on his lips, and a strange gleam came into his eyes. I feared that he might become angry with me, and I moved to put the desk between us. Jisaku, however, smiled yet again, and began to walk lazily about the room. I remained seated at the desk, but he ignored me, looking out at the garden, smoking the cigarette, and when he returned to the other side of the desk, he sat down, cross-legged, once more. When I looked at him again I saw that he had somehow taken the photo album from the shelf and was now opening it upon the desk. The sight of that made me gasp.

"You shouldn't be looking at that. The mistress of the house will be very angry with you!"

I reached out to take it from him, but Jisaku held on to it firmly, with all the strength he could evidently muster in his burly arms. After he looked through it two or three times, all I could do was simply sit by in silence. But then I suddenly became very angry, my whole body shaking with rage. It was as if Tamae were suddenly here before me, being violated by this idiot. Then Jisaku suddenly cried out in a strange voice, "Ah, yeah, ah, yeah." He began to make a deep moaning noise as he rocked backed and forth; his eyes became slit-like as they focused more intently on the pages of the album. Just as I thought that this had become very strange indeed, Jisaku proceeded to rip one of the photos from the album and to ball it up in his fist. It happened so fast that I had no time to prevent him from doing it. Before I could even yell out, "Hey, what are you doing?" he jumped out onto the veranda, the album still within his grasp. "Wait!" I yelled after him, and made to follow him, but I was suddenly thrown backward with a great force. In all of the excitement, I had forgotten to avoid the spot directly beneath the beam, the one place that I had assiduously been avoiding. I was suddenly seized with fear, and watched as Jisaku ran away carrying the album.

I ran into the hall and on past the sitting room without thinking what I was doing, but as always, Tamae was nowhere to be seen. The house was utterly silent in the middle of the day. Thinking I could still find some way to catch up with Jisaku, I searched for a pair of *geta* in the mud room, and then burst out of the house.

"Mistress! Mistress!"

I ran about the front of the house, yelling at the top of my lungs, but the only sound that reached my ears in reply was that of the cicadas. In truth, that was the first time that I felt the house to truly be a house of punishment, a wicked place. In my carelessness I hadn't realized how truly frightful a place the old house could be.

I was concerned about the loss of the album, but I was even more frightened to suddenly realize how alone I was. My first thought was that I should I go to Nakaya and somehow confess the whole sordid tale to Gisaburō. But when I made for the main gate, a situation arose that I had never expected: the gate, which I had always seen open, was now closed for the first time since my arrival. Thinking it very odd, I drew closer, only to see that the gate's bolt had been thrown as well, locking it tight, together with the smaller side door, where a stout iron lock was affixed. No amount of pushing on either portal would afford me any egress whatsoever.

I was thrown into confusion. There was no way for me to get out the gate, but I then recalled my conversation with Jisaku, and his mention of a path up into the mountain behind the house. I realized that if I went up that way, there might be a way for me to gain access to the village. It might be my only way to get to the outside world again. Once I came to that conclusion, I hurried around to the back of the house, past the barn and toward the garden, passing through the vegetable patch where the potatoes and eggplant were still growing, up to the narrow path past the storehouse that Jisaku had taken until he had disappeared from my sight. I was unsure where he had gone, but it was surely somewhere beyond the garden and storehouse.

The path leading up the mountain had a sharper incline than I thought, and tall grass grew thick on both sides, higher than my waist. I had to push it out of my way as I climbed up, but I couldn't find any path that led down to the village. After a while, the path entered the cool shade of a grove of cedar trees. The fragrance of damp earth was cooler here against my skin, and I could hear the cicadas more keenly. The path seemed to level out, and there was an old shrine ahead. I guessed that this was the shrine to the sacred lingam where Ki'ichirō's father was said to have shot himself. Given the somewhat morbid air of the place, I did not linger there, and pressed on, holding my robe more tightly to me as the incline continued more gently, although I had yet to come upon any downhill slope. I felt silly, but my breath had already gone ragged several times. Normally this much exertion would be nothing for me, but given how I had been shut up inside the house for so long, it was no wonder that I had lacked sufficient exercise. I kept wiping the sweat from my brow and stopping to catch my breath, but I guessed I had only climbed about a half a kilometer when suddenly the path emerged from the cedar grove onto the side of a grassy hillock. A great vista suddenly spread out in front of me, and a powerful gust of wind blew up from the valley below, blowing away the clouds which had lain overhead until now. Looking up, I saw that the peak appeared to be quite nearby. That must have been the place from which Jisaku was boasting of the great view he wanted to show me. The path led directly up to the gentle peak itself. From there you could undoubtedly take in even more of the incredible view that I was already seeing. Since I was already nearly there, I cleared the grass from the rest of the path and made my way up to the very top.

Once there, I was glad that I had come all the way up for, indeed, the view was splendid. The peak was broad, with just a few low shrubs scattered about. For all of Jisaku's insistence on how high it was, it was still just a foothill, but it did have views in all four directions. Looking off to the right was a clear white band, almost like a string, running through a flat area, and then a cluster of black houses, which would have been the town that I passed through so many days before. The river sparkled with a dull shine, like pieces of tin plate. Most of the low mountains beyond the river appeared deep purple, but one of them was still white at the peak. I thought it must have been the one that Jisaku had referred to as Mount Ginzan, the Silver Mountain.

Off to the other side, on the left, there was a wall of jagged deep blue mountains rising higher and higher above me, whose peaks were eventually lost in the clouds. I wondered which of them was the mountain that Jisaku had referred to as the Black Princess. Immediately below there was a stream flowing by in a narrowly twisting course.

With such a vista, there was nothing for the eye to settle on, however, and I had a hard time deciding where to look next. The sun was strong, and my head was uncovered and I could feel it beginning to burn. To dry off, I sat down at the edge of the cliff at the peak and stripped to the waist. Although the sun was hot, the breeze was cool enough to dry my sweat.

I thought I would have been able to see the Oshaka House from there, but the cedar grove obscured the house from my view. The foot of the hillock was covered with forests of cedar and cypress, which also hid any path to the village. Thin white clouds floated across the sky, taking their ease. I could hear nothing from the world below. My head was filled with a calm emptiness and stillness.

In the distance I saw something black that seemed to appear and then disappear, moving like an insect, although I could hear no sound as it did so. It was the train bound for Tokyo. While I marveled that a train could be far enough away to appear as an insect, suddenly all the things that I had forgotten came back to me.

I wondered what day it was. I knew it could no longer be July, and that surely it had to be August already, but what day in August? I had no way of knowing for certain. I had completely lost all concept of time. In the interval since my arrival, where had my time flown away to? I know that I had been fairly well governed by time prior to my arrival at the Asō house on the twenty-second of July, but what had happened to me such that I was unbound by the destiny of time thereafter? Although it's a fact that I spent my days working on copying out the old records, all I had to show for it was one notebook. Other than that, the only record of my life at the Asō house was the meals I took with Tamae and then the strange dream I had night after night, but what proof would they provide? Was my existence here simply an illusion? I was suddenly overcome with fear. Could it be that everything—Tamae, the idiot Jisaku, even Oshaka House—was all an illusion? Was it possible that the vista I looked out upon—the fields, the sky and clouds, all of it—was part of that illusion? The more I thought about it, the more I was seized with panic, with a sensation that I could no longer simply sit there and do nothing.

I arose, drew my *yukata* back onto my shoulders, and began walking in circles there on the peak of the hillock, only to sit back down and get back up again once more, when I found a place in the distance to lock my eyes on, as if that would somehow calm me. I breathed deeply, and tried to relax once more, but I only grew more and more anxious. But then something in the near distance caught my eye, a white fluttering movement. I thought at first that perhaps a bird had arisen from the trees, but it wasn't that.

Directly below me was a small barren field tightly enclosed by low shrubs, standing on a lower hillock and surrounded by a cedar grove. I hadn't noticed it before, I suppose, because I had been so taken by the more distant views, but from above it was completely exposed to the sun, giving it a round, bald appearance. The rounded portion was covered with grass, and thereon was an odd sight, one that took my breath away in its strangeness.

Amid the sparse grass, a pale body was entwined with a darker body, and the two bodies were moving against each other with a heated passion. At first glance, the darker body, with its shorter spine and rounded form, was obviously Jisaku. With her head thrown back and her entire body pressed against his, Tamae, whose body I had seen in my dream every night, was clearly the possessor of the other body. As I watched, my eyes grew dim, and something caught in the back of my throat. The two bodies rebounded against one another throughout, and then the darker one, which was on top, appeared to suddenly somersault, and the white body leapt up to mount him from above triumphantly. When the white face looked for an instant in my direction, without thinking I cried out. And yet no sound came forth from my throat. I was frozen where I stood, trembling in fear. I saw, upon Tamae's white forehead, two horns. Her face seemed to shine with intent as it looked up at me, but I might have been mistaken about that. What I most clearly remember is those horns and the fact that the hands and feet with which she held Jisaku tightly to her were not the hands and feet of a human being.

I have no memory of how I clambered down from the peak. I ran without thinking, somehow finding the path in the cool of the cedar grove, when I finally came to my senses somewhat. When I thought back on what had just happened, I realized that no one had seen me. I was suddenly seized with a nearly unbearable sorrow, and my tears came unbidden. The sadness was such that

I could no longer stand any more, and I sat down on the damp, cool earth and cried. I had been polluted by that evil magic. I realized that it had not been a dream that had come to me every night. There was no way for me to take such things back any more. I would bear the mark of my guilt for this for the rest of my life. *Whatever shall I do? Whatever shall I do?* I kept wondering that as I walked, crying as I did so, following the path down the mountain. I had to get away from there. The sooner I got away from that accursed house the better. Strangely enough, the path that I followed did not take me the way that I had come, back to the storehouse, but instead led me out to the gate at the front of the house. Since I had been crying the whole way, I must have made a wrong turn somewhere. This was not the time, however, for me to exercise my curiosity; I entered the main house immediately.

I ran into the sitting room, removed the clothing I was wearing, and dug out my shirt from the basket in the corner of the room. Just as I removed my pants and jacket from the hanger on the wall there was a great thundering boom, like that of a tree falling, from within the vast house that was otherwise always so silent. I thought perhaps one of the beams had fallen. I quietly snuck out of the sitting room and thought to leave, but with fear and surprise my knees were knocking together quite loudly, no matter how quietly I had been hoping to move. I am not certain now exactly how quiet I was, but after that loud boom, the house had reverted to its usual unnatural stillness. For a short time, I remained frozen in the mud room, listening carefully for any movement. Then I decided that that was my chance, and I returned to the sitting room without wiping the dirt from the mud room from my feet. It seemed a shame, however, to leave without all the notes I had so painstakingly transcribed, so I resolved to at least take those with me.

I removed my jacket and softly made my way along the many hallways to the study. When I peered into the frightening study I found it deserted, and all my things were on the desk just as I had left them. I snuck into the room and quickly picked up my notebook and fountain pen from off the desk, as well as my cigarettes and the four or five photographs that had been crumpled into a ball. I looked at the desk to see if I had forgotten anything else and then turned to leave only to experience a great shock. I don't know when she came, but there was Tamae, standing at the entrance to the study. Upon seeing her, my legs locked, and I froze where I stood.

Even now, as I write this, to recall the look in her eyes gives me chills. Her eyes appeared as if they were carved from ice as they stared out at me. The emotion in them was utterly separate from human feelings such as resentment or anger; they were so frightening to look at I could hardly guess what feelings they encompassed. They shone coldly and without expression, without blinking even, and seemed to accuse me of having seen her with Jisaku. Even had I wanted to scream, I knew no voice could arise within my throat, and even had I wanted to run I knew my legs would be unable to carry me. I had become as rigid as a stick, standing there, unable to will myself to do anything beyond look at her. I don't know how long we stood there, looking at one another—she with that frightening gaze in her eyes—but after she had blinked strangely two or three times, it was as if a dark curtain had been drawn across my eyes and everything went black. I remember thinking that I must not lose consciousness, but I have no memory of what happened after that.

WHEN I CAME to, I was in the bedroom, naked, atop the bedding. Tamae was asleep beside me, although I don't know when she joined me. The mosquito netting was gone, but the lamp at the head of the bed was lit, and beside it my shirt was on the floor, which made me think that Tamae must have carried me there from the study. It appeared to be nighttime already, as it was dark beyond the paper screen windows. I clearly remember that there was a lonesome sound as the night wind blew through the cedar trees on the mountain.

I sat for a while and thought things over. It seemed that I had undergone some form of mental collapse, and even though there were many things for me to think about, I could barely pick up any threads to begin with, and I wondered if perhaps I was back within the dream once more. But I well knew by then that there was no dream. It was not a dream when I had engaged in intercourse here in this room with Tamae; it was as she had said. She and I had indeed done such things here every night, and it was never a dream. At long last I was finally awakening from the deception I had been all to willing to believe.

When I first saw her true nature at the top of that hillock, it rightly shocked me to the very core of my being, but now that I had knowledge of both that nature and her physical self, I no longer found it strange that I should be fostering a deep affection for her and lacking in fear. Human beings are indeed strange. Before I take up the changes in my own psychology, I am still profoundly surprised at the mystery that lies at the core of the two genders, that the male can lie within the physical self of a woman. She pressed her sweet white breast to mine and then whispered into my ear, "I won't ever let you go. No matter how much you might run, I won't ever let you go." People will say that I was simply bewitched by her magic. But what isn't magic? Is not beauty itself a simple form of magic that bewitches us? I don't know whether Ki'ichirō ever knew her true nature, but I think that he did realize that it was the source of her beauty. The depth of Ki'ichirō's unique love for her was surely based on that. That his profound love encompassed a witnessing of her true nature was perhaps one of the ironies of our limited lives, but at the same time it was also proof that love is stronger that death. Ki'ichirō's death was a rare death. He must have died happily. Perhaps I am bound to experience the same fate as he did, but would the depth of my love also be the same?

She whispered in my ear. "You should go on ahead to Tokyo." She said she would follow me after she finished things here. She said that we should live somewhere we could enjoy, where no one knew us. Her words were like a divine revelation to me. In all honesty, I would not have wanted to live anywhere she was not. When I said that, she cried tears of happiness. "I am so happy. I am so happy." Her voice was thick with tears as she leaned her head against my shoulder, lightly biting me here and there and hugging me tightly to her, so tightly that I knew that this was what it meant to be alive, and I too began to cry tears of happiness.

That was when I first began to consider Tamae as my lover, and that marked a change in my whole world. It's a strange comparison, but it's almost akin to becoming a convert to a new religion. There was a very fine line separating my old life from the new, but I did not regret crossing that line. Of course, I would have had no regrets had I remained on the other side of the line, either. But she opened my eyes to a world of magic. And now that she had brought about my enlightenment, I belonged fully to her and had therefore lost a part of my humanity. Having seen her true nature, however, I felt no regret at having lost that part of my humanity, even though there was some sadness at the loss, for the reason for my loss could only be described as miraculous. Furthermore, the ability to differentiate between the magic world and the ordinary world of humans was not something that could be found in our existence, nor were humans possessed of the faculty or talent to determine which world was the better of the two. My life was therefore set to begin by pondering this unanswerable question.

IN THE DIM light of the lamp I sat thinking, and before my eyes came repeatedly the faces of my mother and sister, appearing and disappearing in turn. Deep within my mind I could hear the voice of Tozaki, calling out to me over and over again. All of them, however, were too late. My support now was neither my mother nor my sister nor even Tozaki. I was suddenly struck with the sobering thought that if I had to rely on anyone anymore my body would collapse as there would be no one to support me. I was struck with a loneliness that blew through my body like a freezing wind, so much so that I could actually hear it as it blew. Although I first thought such bad feelings were impossible, I corrected myself, thinking that they were more appropriate now, and ground my teeth to ward them off. They were so bad, I felt for a moment as if I had been bound tightly, head and foot.

I wanted to see Tamae once more. She was my sole support in this world. She had at last made my desires come true, and I was about to depart for Tokyo for her. But how could I go without seeing her once more? Surely we could plan things more thoroughly. Surely there was no need now for her to leave me alone like this.

"Mistress? Tamae? Tamae!" I called out in a loud voice as I took my shirt from the floor, and then stumbled out into the dark hallway. I followed the handrail to the room at the front of the house where I normally took my meals and found that it was brightly lit with an electric light, but Tamae was nowhere to be seen.

"Mistress!" I called out, two or three times, but there was no answer. I was not certain what time it was, as the clock was stopped, but I was certain she had withdrawn to her own room by then. I was thirsty, so I went down to the kitchen and drank a ladleful of water from the water barrel. Through the paper screen window above the kitchen stove, I could tell that the moon must have been shining very brightly, as the paper was lit with a pale white glow from outside. When I went to the sitting room, I found my trousers and socks in the basket in the alcove there, and then lit a candle in a metal lantern I found in a corner bracket there. Lantern in hand, I set off to find her room. When I came to the turn in the hallway that led to my bedroom, I decided to go in the opposite direction, following the wall along to the left, as I had never been down the hallway in that direction before. With the light from the lantern burning faintly before me, I moved gingerly forward, my eyes at my feet.

In the middle of the night, the vast house was an expanse of unnatural and almost deathly stillness. As I walked along the hallways, my own footsteps were magnified in their loudness and creaked as I went. Following along the wall, the hallway curved to the right, with rain shutters along one side and the sliding doors for room after room continuing along on the other side until I came to a somewhat wider area. The sliding doors were worn and riddled with holes, but these parts of the house seemed to correspond to its front. From gaps in between the rain shutters, the pale blue-white light of the moon was admitted into the hall in stripes.

I ran into a spider web. As I cleared the dusty web from my face I opened one of the broken sliding doors that led onto the hall. Room after room was lit by the faint glow of the lantern. They all appeared to be similar in size, but the tatami mats had been pulled up from each of them, with the flooring appearing to be no more than piles of dust. Although the lantern's light did not permit me to see very clearly, there didn't appear to be anything resembling supplies or tools in any of the rooms either. It was extremely unsettling in one room to see an alcove with absolutely nothing in it but dust.

I was fairly certain that Tamae's room would not be in this part of the house and so, when there came a turn in the hallway that led deeper into the house, I took that turn. I thought perhaps it would lead me to the back of the house instead.

I had gone no more than ten steps along that hallway when it ended in a small three-step staircase leading down toward the rear of the house and another hall. *Aha,* I thought to myself, *there's another room down here.* But just as I began to descend that staircase, the flame in the lantern began to flicker, even though there was no breeze to be felt, and my face suddenly felt very cold as well. I shielded the lantern with my other hand to keep the flame from going out, and when I reached the bottom of the staircase, I involuntarily screamed, throwing out my lantern hand, and becoming frozen at the wall there.

The face of a man, as pale and as emaciated as that of a corpse, his hair unkempt and disheveled, suddenly appeared before me from a side hallway. It was as if all the blood had suddenly stopped flowing within my body, yet I could not take my eyes off the man. We had been plunged into darkness when my lantern's candle went out, but he appeared to look straight ahead in a frozen stare. He wore a pale blue kimono and his arms were tied behind his back. I couldn't see below his waist, given the darkness, but I remember quite clearly even now how his head drooped onto his shoulder and how the blood pooled below his neck.

I subsequently thought that this might have been a creature condemned to die in the asylum Gisaburō had told me about, but at the time, of course, I hadn't the luxury for such a careful analysis of the situation. It was as if my brain had been bathed in ice water, such was the level of my paralysis. In the next instant, the figure of the man disappeared again into the darkness. For a brief while, I lost all control of my legs and could move neither forward nor backward, but then a sensation of true fear came over me. After slowly regaining some of my senses from that overwhelming fear and shock, I somehow managed to retrace my steps back up the staircase in the dark and back through the hallway, as if I was swimming through very dark water. All of a sudden there was a loud noise immediately behind me. It so startled me that I jumped up, but I tripped and fell. I crawled forward on my hands and knees and then got up once more to look behind me, only to be shocked to see something long, shining with a white light, heading toward me in the darkness. I instantly realized that it was a snake. A snake had fallen from the ceiling. When I saw that it was a snake, I jumped backwards two or three steps without thinking.

Do snakes ordinarily glow in the dark like this? I dislike snakes to begin with, but now I was faced with one that appeared to be more than two meters long and slithering toward me as its entire body emitted a phosphorescent light that lit up the surrounding darkness. All I could do was stare at it as it grew ever closer for every step backward I took. The snake slithered toward me much faster than I could back up, and I realized that I would soon be cornered there in the hallway. I then backed into the very thing I had feared, the end of the hallway, leaving me with no place to go.

I had reached an impasse in the truest sense of the word. The snake was no more than two meters away and getting closer by the second, all the while glowing with that strange white light. I knew I'd never be able to jump over it, either. There was another one meter of space in the hallway behind me and then it ended there. Suddenly from farther down the hallway we had just come from, there came a bright light. I gasped and nearly doubted my own eyes as I saw several dozen long snakes, all in a jostling tangle and emitting their own whitish glow, come twisting and slithering up the hallway at a rapid pace. I began to tremble, and my knees began to knock. At that point I began to frantically look around for any possible means of escape, and considered trying to break through the rain shutters. I was stopped in the middle in the hall, watching the snakes' movement, when I stepped backward some more into what I thought was the end of the hallway. That was when I found my escape path. What I thought was merely a dead end turned out to be another hallway that curved around yet another room along this hall, and was therefore the key to my avoiding disaster. In the darkness, I had not noticed it, surrounded by walls and rain shutters as it was, and it had simply looked like one more window with the moonlight shining on it. With a rush of sudden happiness, I burst into that newly found hallway and ran down it without looking back.

The end of the hallway was similar to the one I had just escaped from in that it also had a three-step staircase leading to the house's interior. I looked back and was relieved to see that none of the snakes had followed me. Worried that the frightful man I had encountered before might reappear, I hesitantly stepped down the staircase and peered around the corner at the bottom to the right, but I could discern nothing whatsoever, terrifying or otherwise, in the darkness.

Again relieved, when I looked to the left, I noticed a sharply pitched ladder staircase at the end of that hallway, at the top of which was a high window. Through the window the moonlight shone so brightly, it almost made me think it was midday. When I looked up at the landing at the top of the ladder I could see sliding doors there and a faint flicker of light.

Who would have thought that this old house had a second floor to it? Is it just a dormer room, perhaps, because the roof was built so high?

The flickering light made me suddenly excited, and I climbed the ladder, taking care to make as little noise as possible. The steps were thick with dust and very slippery as a result. When I reached the top, I found that the landing had a space at the right for the broken sliding-door entrance to one room, as well as for the small glass window at left, through which the moonlight came streaming in. But everything was covered thickly with dust as well and had a strangely disused feel to it. Oddly enough, the flickering light that I had first seen coming from the sliding doors up was gone, and the only light to be seen was that of the moon.

"Tamae! Tamae!" I called out her name in a low voice by the sliding door, but there was no answer. I suddenly had a terrible feeling, and my heart began to race.

"Tamae!" I called out once more to no response and then slid the door wide open. When I did so, I saw that, contrary to my expectations, the room within was empty, with all its tatami mats removed. Along the wall to the left, in the light from the moon, I could make out what appeared to be a sort of cage. Something white seemed to be inside it, and, wondering what it was, I bent down to have a look, whereupon I noticed its two blue eyes shining out at me. It was the cat. The moment I realized that the cat was there, something white seemed to flutter in the dark recesses of the room. As it approached the cage, it made the screeching noises of a night bird, and then suddenly the deformed eyes and nose of a monster child were pressed against the bars of the cage. I cried out and without thinking, backed away, falling headlong down the ladder staircase, at the bottom of which I must have hit my head and blacked out.

I MUST FINISH this journal as quickly as possible. Tamae is already aware that I am writing it. I surely do not have much longer to live. I doubt whether I can finish writing this. I am resolved to write as much as I can, however.

When I returned to Tokyo, I was shocked to discover that it was past the tenth of September. The school at which I worked was already well into the new term.

It must have taken me some time to regain consciousness that evening after falling from the landing where the dormer room with the cage was, but I was able to escape from Oshaka House well before dawn. I somehow managed to walk to the town of O without seeing Tamae or letting anyone know. I waited at the station for an hour for the first train to arrive, at 6:02. After being unable to tell the time for the duration of my stay at Oshaka House, I noticed that my wristwatch was suddenly, and accurately, working once more.

Once I was on the train bound for Tokyo, I determined to move out of my apartment in Nakano. I was terrified of Tamae. It was as if I were haunted by feelings of regret and shame. I resolved to find a way to cleanse myself of the dissolute state I felt I had fallen into.

On the third day after returning to Tokyo, I found a room to rent in the Umegaoka area of Setagaya and quickly moved there. I lied to my old landlady and told her that I was moving into an apartment that a friend of mine had built. I said nothing about the move to the school at which I worked. I did, however, file a change-of-address card with the post office.

After returning to Tokyo, I did not visit Professor Tsujimura nor did I let Tozaki know that I had come back, although I knew that it was wrong of me on both counts. I knew, however, that had I met with them, I would have been forced to talk about topics I would rather not discuss. Furthermore, there was the issue of my notes that I had been forced to leave at the Asō house after working so hard on them all summer long, even though I now had no regrets about my decision to leave them behind. I wanted to completely obliterate all traces of my connection with that house and its magical power over me. That said, I wondered at what traces had been left behind in me physically. I worried about what it would take to forget it all. And yet, as the days went on, I seemed to forget more and more, and a peace and calm began to return to my heart, such that I even called it happiness. Looking back, however, it is clear that it was only a temporary state. A doctor would have called it a remission.

One day, about ten days after I had moved to Umegaoka, I was returning to my room in the evening from school when the landlord's daughter came running out to greet me, saying, "Mr. Kazama, there's someone waiting for you."

I had to wonder at that. I had told no one where I lived, so how could anyone come to visit me? "A guest? Surely you're joking."

"No, I'm not. She's very pretty."

"Pretty, you say? A woman?"

"Hurry up, now. Don't stand there gaping at me."

Hardly knowing what to think, I opened the door to my room, only to be utterly surprised. I don't know how or where she found me, but the Tamae I had tried so hard to forget, the unforgettable Tamae was now all smiles there in my room waiting for me. The moment I saw her, my feelings were a mass of not only surprise and confusion but also, and in direct contrast, of a nostalgic happiness that I wanted to openly embrace with all my heart. I suppose it might be more accurate to say that my confusion arose from the fact that I was suddenly so happy.

"How well you managed to come to Tokyo! And how clever of you to have found me!"

"No matter how hard you might try to hide from me, I will always see through your schemes. Have you forgotten? I said I would not let you go."

When she reminded me that she had said that, I was filled with a deep regret that I had betrayed her. I was utterly ashamed. Just as a strip of litmus paper turns from blue to red, at the time I did not find it strange that my feelings had changed so quickly from fear to affection. I could not see the inherent contradiction. I was simply heeding my own nature.

From that day forward I was once again held prisoner by her strange power.

She had with her a small black purse. When I asked how she had managed to arrange the affairs for the Asō house, she wrapped me in her delicate white arms and whispered in a husky voice, "There's no need for you to concern yourself with that any more. I'm certain that Gisaburō up at Nakaya is, at this very moment, looking after everything."

"Now that we're away from there, I can say this, but I think Gisaburō said some really awful things about you."

"Yes, I'm certain he did. After Ki'ichirō passed away, whenever that old man saw me he would say the most dreadful things. He simply wanted that house for himself. He is nothing but greedy, that old man. Simply awful, human beings are. That's why I hate them so."

"What about Jisaku? Without you there, what will happen to him?"

"He died."

"He died? When?"

"I wonder when it was.... When you think about it, it was rather sad, but there was nothing that could be done, after all."

"That may be so, but, yes, it is rather sad. That reminds me: what was that monster-like child in the cage?"

"I took care of that child as well. In truth, that child was the product of my union with Ki'ichirō. There was too much magic in it, I suppose. It was really unlike me, how human my feelings were, and then all of sudden we had that child together. But you needn't worry about it any longer. I've taken care of it all."

Her words struck me as neither particularly strange nor cruel and as I listened, I suspected nothing.

"You should continue working where you are for the time being. But let us move away from here tomorrow, shall we? I'll go and find us a nice place to live, so put your mind at ease on that account. As for money, Ki'ichirō's inheritance will ensure that we will always have food on the table. Everything will be perfectly fine.... But I have to say I am so happy that I can be together with you again. Are you happy too?"

"Yes."

I could see a small reflection of my own face in her deep black eyes. I was suddenly shocked, however, to see small bumps upon my forehead that appeared to be small horns.

Two days after that, we moved from my room in Umegaoka to a large house at a remove from Mitaka. I had no idea how, in just one day's time, she had been able to find such a house so easily, but I doubted nothing she did and followed her in everything.

The house was a thirty-minute walk from Mitaka Station on the national railway line and was surrounded by a grove of different types of trees. I was somewhat taken aback when I first saw how large it was. Of course, it was nowhere near as large as Oshaka House. The house appeared to have been built before the war, and comprised five rooms of fairly ordinary appearance in the Western style. But it was sited on a plot of land that must have been dozens of acres in size, with its own ponds, hills, valleys, streams, and several groupings of old-growth trees that cast enough shade to block out the sun during the day in places. The only sound we could hear was that of the birds. It was so quiet I thought we were back in the mountains once more, with the house located in the center in a somewhat toy-like fashion, smack-dab in front of a pond. Since Tamae had done all the negotiating, she was the one who knew who had owned the property, who had built it, who had lived there and how much they had charged her, but I knew none of those details. I could hardly imagine there could be such a paradise, completely removed from all earthly cares and utterly quiet and retiring, merely an hour and a half from the center of the city. After we moved there, I began commuting to work every other day with an innocent look upon my face.

We lived the life we wanted to, wild and unfettered, unbothered by anyone, on this plot of land that seemed to recall the last vestiges of old Musashino[21]. In situations involving a husband and wife or a man and his lover, it is invariably the man who is principally concerned with day-to-day activities, but I believe my case may be the first in which this was turned on its head. Tamae was in charge. I was her dependent in all things: I was a drone, attendant on a queen bee. But never did I feel any resentment for my status as a dependent. Rather I happily accepted it. I do not know when it was that human beings insisted on subverting the natural order of things, for it seems to have occurred so far back in our history as to be lost to time, and accepted as normal by one and all. But if we stop and think about it, the concept of male chauvinism is indeed a contravention of natural laws and is, without doubt, one of the greatest of mankind's follies. It is only proper that the male should worship on bended knee before the might of the beautiful female. I did so. I was happy to do so, boundlessly happy to do so.

One day, I received a phone call at school from Tozaki. "Hey, I went by your apartment last night, but they said you had moved away. I haven't seen you in a while so I was wondering how you were. For a man to keep his whereabouts a secret from his friends, I figure there must be a woman involved. Am I right? Well? Are my instincts as good as ever?"

"What? No, that's not it at all. I've been so busy with the start of the new term I just fell out of touch. You've really put me in a tight spot, calling like this.... I'll be by to see you soon. We can talk then."

"I was just joking. I've been busy too, so I know how it gets, but do come over and visit. Oh, and I've got a new office now, so the phone number has changed. It's extension xxx. Just call before you come, okay? I'm telling you, these days we've had to go out

21. Musashino was the old name for the region around Tokyo.

drinking every night around here. I'm a complete wreck.... Okay, okay. I'll be waiting.

When I put the receiver back on the hook, I remember feeling a sudden sense of panic. I had no idea why. I ran off to the school library, where I knew I would be alone, and began to cry. I didn't understand why I was crying, however. There seemed to be a very fine line separating my resolve from this fit of tears. Even though Tozaki had said he was joking, had it been Tozaki's journalistic intuition that had led him to say something about the woman in my life? Or was it because he knew me as a friend? Regardless, neither of those aspects of my relationship with Tozaki was of any use to me any more. The Tozaki on the other end of the line had become distant from me. For him, day and night was an endless cycle of news stories involving murder, embezzling, fraud, political intrigue and corruption, all washed down with alcohol. I don't want there to be any misunderstanding, however. It wasn't that I lacked respect for Tozaki as a reporter. It was just that I was beginning to want to distance myself from the actions of all human beings, myself included. Through Tamae, I found myself moving away from my fellow man, as far as some distant planet. I supposed that would be the last time I would ever hear Tozaki's voice. It did indeed turn out that way, but I also resolved at that same time that I would therefore write this journal and leave it for Tozaki. In writing this, I offer myself a form of more complete separation from myself and can therefore see myself as so separated.

At that time, it was well into autumn, and the fall colors were deepening with each passing day. Tamae seemed to grow more beautiful, together with the glories of nature. I might be biased, but to me she appeared many times more beautiful than when I first saw her at the Asō house. When I asked her about it, she would say that it was because I was here with her, but her appearance seemed to be that of a freshly beautiful young woman, of a flower whose white petals had only just begun to open and release their sweet fragrance. And she burned with the passion of early spring as well.

There were times when she reverted to her wild nature. When that happened, a sunny place among the dry grass, a pile of fallen leaves within a stand of trees or a spot beside the pond late at night when the moon shone as brightly as daylight would become like those she posed in for her photographs in that album. The light sparkling in her eyes as she reveled in the light of the sun, clouds scudding overhead, or drenched in moonlight, revealed a passion far more intense than when she was in bed with me. I had never known until then just how beautiful nature could be. As I embraced her, I wanted to shout out as if my life depended on it, so very mad with happiness I was. My passion and intensity were such that I felt I had become one with the earth below and the heavens above.

When autumn had passed and winter arrived, our lives began to center mainly on sleep, both night and day. I no longer went to the school. During the cold winter, we became like wild beasts, going for days without eating, simply sleeping. Our sleep was deep, like hibernation. I stopped thinking about things. To think about things was something I had forgotten about long ago it seemed.

Tamae and I had both become extremely lazy and very languid in our movements. The clothing that I had worn had become threadbare and torn, but neither of us paid it any particular care. We gathered all the worn-out clothing together under a tree, set fire to it and cooked food over the fire. Asleep or awake, Tamae simply wrapped her beautiful white body in a blanket. Her listless form then struck me as more divinely lovely than Venus draped in furs.

Every day the winds blew through the forests and stands of trees on the property. On clear days and cloudy days, from morning until evening and then from nightfall until dawn the winds continually blew. Whenever I stepped out onto the balcony into the bright sunlight, clouds would be moving quickly overhead, blown by the winds on high. All of the leaves had fallen from the trees, and the pond had frozen over. The rushes by the pond's edge blew in the cold wind. When night came we could hear the cry of an owl from somewhere nearby. Those would be, we knew, the nights when the moon would shine most brightly.

I couldn't remember the last time I had heard Tamae speak. For that matter, I too had come to find human speech extremely annoying. The use of words in our day-to-day lives had become rather bothersome, in fact. We had become as withdrawn as beasts, bringing our bodies closer together and sleeping more and more. When we awoke in the morning, the house would be surrounded with a white covering of frost, and once it even snowed. That night I mistakenly left all the windows in the house wide open, and the snow blew into the house in great drifts. It took me two whole days to sweep out all the snow, and I still couldn't get all of it. Although for the most part Tamae stood and watched me in silence, she suddenly started to giggle. There was so much snow that eventually I had to laugh along with her.

When I grew cold, I would rise from the bed and take some of the wood that we had collected into the bedroom and place it in a small stove near the wall to light a fire. I have become strangely fascinated by fire now. When I hear the branches crackling in the grate and watch them burn, it strikes me as utterly beautiful. When Tamae rises from the bed and joins me by the stove, removing the blanket from her shoulders to sit naked in the chair there, the glow of the flames is reflected beautifully on her white skin, making her appear red all over, like Ganesh. The beauty of the burning logs is reflected in perfect stillness in Tamae's black eyes as she sits there silently watching. It seems almost as if these burning sparks are the last fireworks I am destined to ever see, so perfect, so beautiful and so still.

The burning logs eventually become embers. Then, they in turn, become cold ashes. It is a condition of my humanity that some time in the near future I shall meet the same fate as those burning logs. And when I have become but cold bones, I will have finally arrived at a place of true freedom. And there memories that will last forever await me. It has been a long winter, but spring is not far off. I can hardly wait to be done with this human form! I want to rid myself of all these annoyances!

Editor's postscript—Here ends Kazama Naoki's journal. His death has yet to be confirmed. No body was ever discovered. The journal was sent to me by the school at which Kazama worked some two months after the principal there received his letter of resignation. After reading it, I was so surprised that I immediately contacted the principal and asked to meet him to discuss the situation, although I was able to glean no further insights into the case. I also called upon the landlord of his apartment in Nakano, but could learn nothing regarding the location to which he had moved. The apartment in Umegaoka had been found, I learned herein. As a result of my investigation, I determined it was the Rokufūsō at 1683 Umegaoka, but again, there was nothing further to be learned once I found it, and when I contacted the police department in Mitaka, they indicated that there were no homes matching the description in Kazama's journal within their precinct. I wrote to Kazama's sister, Ikuno, at their home in K Township, Kamo-gun, Gifu prefecture, and it was the first she had heard of her brother's death. She and her husband rushed to Tokyo to meet with me at my place of employment. There was, unfortunately, little else I could tell them regarding the case, and I sent them home with what little was left at the Umegaoka apartment: several dozen of Kazama's books, some clothing and a few other personal possessions. At the time I had been working for several weeks on a story about unprecedented postwar political changes and living rough with no free time whatsoever, so I was forced to leave an investigation of the Asō family to an acquaintance of mine, Mr. S, who worked at the city desk in N. I had the following report from him:

According to the records in O City Hall, Asō Ki'ichirō died on 9 August 19xx, but there are no records of his ever marrying anyone named Tamae.... According to reports from the O Police Department, Uchiyama Jisaku (Uchiyama was his mother's family name) was found dead within a valley known as Hell's Rim approximately two miles distant from Hōgisaku Village in what appeared to be a fall from a cliff above the valley. His body was found by loggers working in the area. An autopsy was performed because the body was found in an area the deceased was not known to have frequented and because deep wounds near the base of the skull seemed to indicate that his neck had been at least partially eaten by something. As the victim was mentally disturbed, however, it was felt there was little point in continuing the investigation....

At the time, the incident only deepened my feelings of friendship for Kazama Naoki, and I resolved to bury my journalistic instincts and not to bring this story to light. I felt that my personal feelings were more important than the potential for headlines. I am willing to accept that this may indicate that I am less of a reporter for having done so. But is it really true that Kazama Naoki has died, as his journal would seem to indicate? I have been plagued with doubts for the past ten years, doubts which have gone unresolved in spite of the fact that I have kept this case hidden the entire time. It goes without saying that I have nothing to substantiate my theory. But for someone like me, who is unable to believe in the strange and mysterious, I cannot believe my friend's journal as written either. By making the journal public, I am not simply attempting to satisfy the curiosity of those who seek out the strange in this world. If you can forgive someone like me, who believes nothing of the strange and mysterious, then it is possible that my friend who wrote this lives on somehow, having faked his death, tempted by a woman who somehow laid her hands on a massive inheritance and is now living somewhere in secret. Of course, that is merely conjecture, and in no way casts blame or aspersions on the deceased. I wonder wherein the truth really lies. Kazama Naoki might have left this world as surely as Asō Ki'ichirō and Uchiyama Jisaku before him, but am I alone in thinking that Tamae is still alive and living somewhere among us?

Reunion

大好きな姉 (Daisuki na Ane)

Takahashi Katsuhiko (1993)

高橋克彦

English translation by Andrew Cunningham

– 1 –

ON A RAINY, chilly day near the end of September, I received word that my father had finally succumbed to his illness. Given my reasons for moving to the city, I had been firmly convinced I would never return to my parents' home, but the news of my father's death disturbed me. After thinking it over for a full day, I told my mother I would at least show up at the funeral. But my family lived in the mountains, and the bus ride from Matsue was an hour and a half, followed by a forty-minute walk along narrow roads. And Matsue was a considerable distance from Izumo Airport, should I decide to fly. Including transfers, I was looking at a good eight hours. I finally made up my mind in the evening—too late to fly. Instead, I took the sleeper train to Matsue.

Between thoughts of my father and the cramped, uncomfortable berth, I did not get much sleep. Each time we stopped at a station, I went to the bathroom, and then had a smoke at the end of the carriage. Why do night trains waste so much time? Nobody gets on, but they sit at a station for ten, fifteen minutes. If they cut out the time spent waiting the trip would be hours faster. I wanted to be home as soon as possible, and the waiting was killing me.

The train was mostly empty. Few people use sleepers these days.

How long has it been?

Twenty years. Since I was eleven, and they sent me to live with relatives in Osaka.

That long?

It surprised even me. I had tried not to think about it, but I still remembered everything that had happened. Saki's pale face flashed across my mind, and I could no longer stay still. The hand holding the cigarette shook. My sister-in-law still had a death grip on my heart.

I suddenly felt like I was making a terrible mistake. I hadn't decided to go home because my father died. I just wanted to know how Saki was getting on, alone. I almost threw up. Memories of my sister-in-law always brought with them the stench of blood.

– 2 –

IT WAS EARLY morning when we reached Matsue. There were no buses for another hour. I went out on the broad street next to the station, looking for a hotel. I would be able to eat there, even this early. I was in the fifth grade when I moved away, so it was like I'd never been to Matsue before. I remembered nothing. But there were towns like this all across Japan. I found a business hotel before I'd walked five minutes. I ordered bacon and eggs, toast and coffee, and picked up a newspaper. I was nodding off almost immediately. All my nervous tension had drained away. Or perhaps it was the opposite, and being so nervous had exhausted me. I had barely slept a wink.

The morning sunlight was very bright. I closed my eyes.

"Um, sir...."

I opened my eyes to find the waiter looking at me uncomfortably.

"What?"

"Would you like a fresh cup of coffee?"

For a moment, I had no idea what he was asking.

"That one must be cold by now."

I turned my gaze to the table and discovered my food had arrived without my noticing. The coffee had gone cold; it was black and repulsive. I looked at the clock. I'd been out for twenty minutes.

"I'll get a new one," he said cheerfully, relieved that I was awake. A new cup arrived a moment later, filled with hot coffee. I watched the steam rise from it and felt like throwing up again. I clapped my hand over my mouth and tried to stand, but my knee caught on the table. I couldn't help myself. I threw up into my hand. Stomach acid gushed from between my fingers and dripped onto the table.

"Are you all right?" the waiter asked, concerned.

"Yes," I said, "Much better now."

He handed me a napkin, and I wiped my mouth, apologizing. Some young female guests shot me disgusted glances. I could not stay a moment longer. I picked up the check and went out.

Coffee....

I knew it was the coffee that had made me throw up. Memories of what had happened twenty years ago remained deep within me. Thinking of Saki had revived them. I drank coffee every day, but just recalling her made me feel nauseated. Was this really a good idea? Perhaps I should turn around, head for Izumo and take a plane back to Tokyo. I should never have come. Throwing up had made me cold, I thought, shivering.

– 3 –

RAIN STARTED PELTING down while I was on the bus.

Weather in these mountains had always been fickle. The bus trailed forlornly along the slopes of the rounded hills so unique to Izumo. I had not seen them for years but felt no attachment to them. The closer I got, the more I regretted coming. The rain only served to darken my mood. I imagined someone would be waiting for me at the stop, but I dreaded walking for an hour in this downpour. My family name went back three hundred years in these parts, and the mountain forest was theirs. They could easily have made a road wide enough for a car to pass, but our ancestors had chosen to respect the sacred forest and had left things as they had always been. Our servants lived at the bottom of the hill and were forced to clear the road every day in winter. This was easier said than done, however. After years in the city, this state of affairs no longer felt normal to me. I pitied the servants, having to climb that hill every day.

The driver called out the name of my stop. I peered through the rain-streaked windshield. Black clouds covered the town.

There were a few people waiting for the bus. One of them must have been waiting for me. I had not been back in twenty years; not many people knew me any more. I could tell at once which of them was here for me. I could see an umbrella bearing the crest of my family. It was held by a woman. I waved through the window, alerting her to my presence, but my arm froze mid-wave.

The woman had a black eye patch covering her left eye.

Saki....

Why was Saki waiting for me? My knees shook. I had not expected to see her so soon and had no idea what to say. I stood petrified until the driver grumpily ordered me out. I had no choice but to move forward. An elderly couple followed me out.

"Shirō?" Saki asked, looking me over from head to toe. Her face was very pale.

"Saki," I said, bowing my head and accepting the umbrella she offered. "It's been a long time."

I tried desperately to avoid staring at the eye patch. My chest hurt. I did that to her. It was my fault she'd lost her eye.

"I didn't think you'd be the one to meet me."

I'd been told she'd moved into a place of her own ten years ago after my eldest brother died in an accident. Tradition held that only the main branch of the family was allowed to live in the Sabashima residence. With the second son in charge, his elder brother's widow was given a new place to live. Effectively, they had cut her off. If she'd had a child, things might have been different. My mother had privately informed me that my surviving brother's wife hated Saki.

She had lived in my father's house for ten years, so it made sense for her to attend his funeral. But for her to come meet me....

"I was asked to meet the guests," she said, as if it were only natural.

Our family kept a second house in town. The mountains were not always easily accessible, and we had often used the town residence as a guest house. As a child I had lived there during the school year.

"The rain has left the mountain road impassable," Saki said, guiding me towards the town residence. "Such a shame. But it should be clear by morning."

This was not an uncommon event. I nodded, somewhat relieved. I was not in the mood to struggle up a muddy hill. And now that I was actually speaking to Saki, it felt like a weight was off my shoulders. She treated me exactly as she always had, much to my delight. I had once believed her to be a terrifying monster....but that had only been a figment of my ignorant, childish mind. I had been sure she despised me, but that had been my only remaining reason to fear her.

"I am sorry, you know," I said, the apology sounding so simple I could not believe my own ears. Saki's easy smile had drawn it out of me.

"The eye? Don't worry about it," she said, smiling.

She was only eight years older than I was, making her thirty nine. But that smile was the same as it had been when she was nineteen, the year she married my brother.

Nineteen....

The realization made me want to cry. She had only been nineteen when she lost her eye. For a girl her age it must have been devastating. She had been so beautiful. After my brother's death she could easily have remarried. He had died ten years ago, when she was not even thirty. But with only one eye, that path had been closed to her... and all because of me.

"Just the two of us tonight," Saki said, opening the gate to the town residence. "The other guests moved to the main residence yesterday. I hope you don't mind. I can only offer you leftovers for dinner, I'm afraid."

Just the two of us? I could feel my heart beating faster. Not from fear, not any more. I had loved Saki the moment I laid eyes on her. The glimpses of her pale skin through the folds of her kimono had made me a little boy again.

– 4 –

THE TOWN RESIDENCE was just as I remembered it. I had always liked it better than the massive, labyrinthine main residence. Not that it was by any means cozy—there were more than twenty rooms. It was only small by comparison. The same eight-mat room I'd used as a child was prepared for my stay. I'd never felt comfortable in rooms larger than twelve mats. The garden outside the room's windows looked just like it used to. I recognized the pine trees immediately. I had a strange feeling I was tumbling backwards through time. Beyond those white walls lay the world I had left twenty years before. My desk was no longer in the room, but the color of the walls, the stains on the ceiling—everything else was exactly the same. The building was a hundred years old. A mere twenty years was not enough to change it.

I changed clothes and took a nap. I had not been hungry for lunch. There had seemed little point in wandering around outside in the rain, and I was utterly exhausted. I pulled a futon and a pillow out of the closet and lay down. The thick bark roof soaked up any sound, turning even the pounding of the rain into a soft lullaby.

"HAPPY YOUR NEW sister's so pretty?" Hikozō said, flashing his yellow teeth as I came into the dark kitchen, where he and the other servants were drinking. I grinned back. The first time I saw my sister-in-law I thought she was as beautiful as a princess. I had no sisters of my own, which meant I was more proud of her than anything else in the world. And I was pleased by all the commotion her arrival had brought. The house was always so empty, just the family and a few servants, but on this day there were nearly two hundred guests, many of them relatives I had never met before. It was a bit odd that they were all my relatives and guests of my father. Saki had no guests, but my mother told me that was the rule, and I accepted it. I didn't really care about anyone but Saki. I didn't understand the whole marriage thing anyway. It was more like I suddenly had a sister. My brother was seventeen years older than I was, and we were not really close.

From that day on, I was always with Saki. She must have assumed being friendly with the youngest child would help her fit in, and she was always nice to me. Summer vacation had just started, so I had moved back to the main residence. My brother was out of the house all day, working in the mountains or in town. My father and mother were usually in the town residence, meeting with guests. Most of the time, Saki and I were alone in the massive house. My other two brothers lived in dorms at school in Matsue and did not return home. I'm sure Saki was lonely. She was nineteen, still young. When she was done working, she never refused to play with me. There is nothing fun about Old Maid with only two people, but she laughed a lot.

Saki liked coffee, and when it was just the two of us, she used to make me some, in secret. My mother had scolded her, saying I was too young for it. But the bitter taste of it tempered with plenty of sugar became our little secret.

Then one day, I saw Saki coming across the garden from the main building. I positioned myself to jump out and surprise her, but she never appeared. When my legs started going numb, I went looking for her. I heard the door to the lavatory open. I went closer, moving quietly. I had assumed someone was leaving, but in fact the person had just gone in. I held my breath, and hunched over in front of the toilet. This would really surprise her. I heard a pleasant splashing sound. Saki's pee. It was a pit toilet, and the sound echoed. She must have been relaxed, confident she was alone. I felt my heart beating faster. Why did it do that at the sound of her peeing.... I felt dizzy, and had to crouch down. I heard the rustle of toilet paper. I had ceased to exist but for my ears. Saki was wiping herself. The sound of her tying her kimono obi was equally exciting.

I fled before she came out. I felt a pain at the front of my shorts. I reached down and was surprised to find my penis was hard. I couldn't tell anyone about this. Saki passed by without noticing me hiding in the shadows.

When I was sure Saki was in the kitchen, I stepped into the toilet. We often had guests, so the toilets were large and luxurious. There was a mat on the floor. I opened the door to the stall, pulled down my pants and squatted like Saki had. That alone was enough to give me a strange, bittersweet feeling. I looked between my legs, peering into the dark tank below. It was frighteningly deep. It took a while before I could make out anything. I gulped. There was a bit of white paper caught on the beam of the floor. Was it the paper Saki had just used? If it was anyone but her, it would have been dry by now. I could hear my heart beating loudly. I lay down on the mat next to the toilet and reached down into the hole. Almost there. My fingers were just a few centimeters away. I stuck my head and shoulder into the hole, straining to reach. The waste lay a good two meters below, and the stench was not that bad. Even if it had been, I would still have done it.

At last my fingers touched the paper. I pulled it up gingerly, careful not to drop it. It was hers. The center of it was still damp. I sniffed it. The sweet smell was from the paper; we used perfumed toilet paper in our house. I wasn't sure what to do next. So

I stuffed the toilet paper in my pocket and left the toilet feeling like I had found a great treasure.

In the hall, I heard Saki calling my name. I froze. I thought she had seen me follow her into the toilet. But when she poked her head out of the kitchen, her smile was the same as always. She was just asking if I wanted coffee.

I took the coffee and went to my room. I lied and said I still had summer homework to do. I couldn't face Saki after what I had just done. But that wasn't the only reason—there was something I wanted to try. I stared down at the black coffee. I pulled the toilet paper out of my pocket. I hesitated for a moment and then squeezed the paper over the cup. Drip, drip, drip—golden drops fell into the coffee. Saki's pee. My heart was racing again. Was there something wrong with me? I couldn't help myself. I took a moment to savor the smell of the coffee, then began to drink, one sip at a time. It didn't smell like pee, but I felt like I had made Saki my own.

After that I was even more obsessed with her. I kept careful watch, and every time she went to the toilet I snuck in after her and looked for her toilet paper. But my good fortune did not repeat itself. It was always out of reach.

I began to wonder if I could reach it from the hatch on the tank. If I went around to the garden and lifted the lid on the tank, I could easily reach inside. Saki would use a wad of paper, so I might be able to catch it as it fell.

This idea got me even more excited. There was a flight of stairs next to the toilet that led down into the garden. If I snuck down there and quietly opened the hatch, Saki would never know. I waited for my chance.

I did not have to wait long.

Saki and I were alone in the house. I heard her footsteps heading for the toilet. The toilet door opened. I quickly went 'round to the garden and quietly opened the tank hatch. The hatch extended out from the house, so it was impossible to look up, but I could tell if toilet paper was being dropped. I waited impatiently.

Something fell from above. I looked down into the tank. Something black had fallen onto the pile of waste. What was it? Not poop, clearly. My shadow fell across it, and I could not see clearly. I pulled back a bit to let in some light.

Fear and nausea assaulted me. It was a crimson lump of blood. I almost fainted. It was clearly blood. But why? Was Saki hurt? No, she was fine. She had been smiling happily just a few minutes ago. I fought to stifle a scream.

I heard a rustle of toilet paper. I looked back in the tank. The paper dropped. It too was covered in blood. I fled.

Saki terrified me. What had she been doing in the toilet? What had she been secretly eating? That might have been something's head, covered in blood.

I ran to my room and hid in the closet. I was scared. If Saki found out what I'd seen, I was sure she'd eat me.

Saki came to my room. I was shaking like a leaf. Saki went away, looking puzzled. I didn't leave the closet till my parents got home. I meant to tell everyone, but Saki was smiling, just as she always did. That smile fooled everyone. If I had seen her true nature anywhere but the toilet I could have said something, but as it was I knew I would just get in trouble.

Watching my parents and brother gave me courage. I needed proof. Evidence I could show them.

The next day, the house was filled with guests. A group of important prefectural officials had come to visit the mountains, and my mother and Saki spent all their time looking after them. My father had hired performers from Osaka to entertain the visitors in the evening. Our servants were allowed to watch as well, so it was like our home had been turned into a theater. Family members sat in the front row. I had to pee really bad, but the doors on the left were closed off by the curtains. To get to the toilet I would have to go past the servants and into the hall through the back doors. I tried to wait until the *rakugo* comic recitation ended, but it proved impossible. I looked at Saki, and went pale.

I stood up and moved quickly towards the toilet. I almost pissed myself in the hall. I threw open the door and made it just in time. I breathed a big sigh of relief and then realized that someone was in the other stall. Slippers were outside the door. Without thinking, I opened the door and looked in.

Saki was squatting inside.

Our eyes must have met, but it was as if she wasn't looking at me. I screamed, but Saki still did not respond.

I tumbled out of the toilet and fled. I ran back to the theater and looked again. Saki was sitting in the front row, listening to the *rakugo*. I looked back down the dark hall. Saki was standing there. She walked right through the wall into the theater.

"She's a monster! Saki's a monster!" I shrieked. Everyone turned and looked at me.

Someone laughed, and soon everyone was laughing with them.

"I saw her! I did!" I sobbed. Hikozō came over and led me out of the room.

"The young mistress was with us the whole time," he said. "These guests are really important. Your father's going to be very angry with you."

He took me to my room, where I stayed, trembling.

It was not a dream. Saki had definitely been in the toilet. I was so scared I dove into my futon. I looked up at the ceiling. My heart almost stopped. Saki was clinging to the ceiling, staring down at me.

I pulled the futon over my head. I remained there for ages. I only looked out again when I heard my father's voice. Saki was not on the ceiling any more.

"I'm scared! Saki's going to eat me!"

"What did you see?" he asked. I told him about the lump of blood in the toilet.

"You'll understand that when you grow up. Forget about it. We'll tell you about it later," my father said, nodding seriously and patting me on the head. "This visit is good for our family. Try not to say anything odd in front of company," he admonished, and went back to his guests.

The next day, I was abruptly ordered to move to the town residence. I was sure Saki had insisted on this, now that I knew the truth. She wanted me exiled so she could eat my parents without interference. I wasn't going to let her. If no one believed me, I would have to defeat the monster myself.

I went into the shed and found a poker. If she came after me again, I would stab her with it.

I waited until Saki was alone.

She went to change the flowers in the guest rooms. I followed.

"Shirō?" she said, turning around. The hallway was very dark.

"I know! I know about you," I said.

"Your father told you?" she said, laughing.

I shivered. My father was in on it. Feeling very sad, I thrust the poker forward. There was a scream. Saki lay on the floor, clutching her left eye. Blood was coming out. I got very scared. I dropped the poker and ran outside. It was all too much for me.

HAD I BEEN dreaming, or just reliving the past? I came to myself, staring up at the dark ceiling.

It took a long time before I realized I was in the town residence. I must have been dreaming. I looked at the clock. It was well past five.

What an awful dream.

But it was not quite a dream. It had all happened. Returning to my old home had brought back vivid memories, horrible memories that echoed in my dreams. I was grown up now and could explain everything logically. Saki had just been menstruating. The lump that had fallen was cotton, soaked in the menstrual blood. It had only looked like an animal's head to my eleven-year-old eyes. Seeing Saki in the toilet was certainly odd, but was probably some kind of astral projection. She had probably been holding her pee, had wanted to pee so badly she had created a second self. I had read books about that, and it was common enough. I just happened to witness it. Her appearance on the ceiling was the same. She had been worried about what I would say. All of which was terrifying enough, but she was not a monster.

Poor Saki. Marrying into an old family like ours must have been a constant source of stress. That kind of pressure often leads to astral projections. She would not have known this was happening. It must have been utterly bewildering when I suddenly attacked her. She had not been the scary one; I had. Perhaps she had noticed how I was watching her and thought I was a creepy little kid.

If I were her, twenty years would not be long enough to forgive me. I had taken her eye. And my family was so old and powerful that my crime went unpunished.

I wept at Saki's generosity. How could I ever have hurt someone as nice as she was? How could I ever atone for my crime? I could not begin to imagine how hard it must have been for her.

– 5 –

I LOOKED ALL over, but there was no sign of Saki. The rain had stopped, so perhaps she had gone shopping. There was food ready in the parlor. I had not eaten all day. The meal was cold, but delicious. While I was eating, the phone rang. I thought it might be Saki, but it was my mother. When she heard my voice, she gasped, "What are you doing there?"

"I heard the road was impassable."

"Didn't Hikozō meet you?"

"No, Saki came to meet me."

This seemed to terrify her.

"You didn't know?" I said.

"Your father didn't tell you anything?"

"About what?"

She fell silent.

"What's going on?" I said, raising my voice. My mother's silence was unsettling.

"Before your father died... he said the family would prosper again, like it used to."

What did that mean?

"He said O-Saki-sama would return with you...."

A chill ran down my spine. I didn't know what she meant or why she'd used the honorific, but it terrified me.

"Don't stay there! Come home. Nobody uses that house any more. Only Hikozō ever goes there. But there's been no sign of him all day."

Impossible. The house hadn't changed at all. I looked around. There was a lot of dust on the floor.

"O-Saki-sama? You mean Saki?"

"Enough! Hiroshi was more than enough! I don't care about the house, I don't want money!" she sobbed. Hiroshi was the name of my dead brother, the one who had married Saki. He had taken over from my father, but after he had died, the family business had gone downhill. My father had been worried about it and had asked me to come home several times.

The phone went dead.

I dialed the main residence, but the call did not go through.

All my fear had returned.

I opened the sliding door to run, but it led to a closet. Saki was sleeping on the shelf. I jumped back. Saki did not move. She looked dead, but I listened carefully and could hear her breathing. She had slipped out of her body again. I knew she had cut the line. This was her empty husk.

I had known all along. I realized that now. I had always known, but it had been too terrifying. I had driven it out of my memory. But the answer lay beneath that eyepatch.

I had seen it when I stabbed her in the eye with that poker. The poker had gone into her and pulled out her eyeball. And I had seen. Seen the hairs spill out from her torn skin. I had to be sure.

With trembling fingers, I reached out and touched Saki's eyepatch. She didn't move. I lifted the eyepatch. My finger felt the hair underneath. Hair was growing out of her eye socket. Saki was still sound asleep. I looked down at the soft hair under her eyepatch. I felt a warm breath on my neck. I no longer had the courage to turn around.

A Short Night

短夜（Mijikayo）

Uchida Hyakken（1921）

内田百閒

English translation by Andrew Clare

I LEFT THE house intending to see with my own eyes the moment a fox transforms itself[1]. It was a dark night and the wind was blowing.

Having gone a little way, I cut through a narrow side street and climbed an embankment behind the town. I walked along the embankment, following it upstream. Below the embankment was a grassy plain with pools of water dotted about here and there. As I walked along, from time to time the puddles shone a dull white around the roots of the grass.

A bamboo grove ran along the far side and beyond that flowed a large river, although it couldn't be seen from that side of the embankment. In times of flood, even the water that flowed by the base of this embankment became a river, and so there were a number of bridges here and there. I came to the foot of one of those bridges and wondered whether or not to cross. If I were to cross at this point, it would take me into the grove.

Although foxes were in the grove, I went up the embankment again, thinking it would be better to get a little further ahead. For some reason, I suddenly felt uneasy, and when I casually turned and looked behind me, fifty or sixty large fireflies flew in a line directly above the bridge I had considered crossing earlier, quickly moving towards the grove on the opposite bank. Just as I was thinking how strange it was, the fireflies disappeared.

---

1. The supposed ability of a fox to transform itself into human form is well documented throughout Japanese history. One of the earliest recorded stories is found in the *Nihon Ryōiki* (日本霊異記) compiled by the priest Kyōkai (景戒) in the 9th Century. The story concerns a man from Minō in the 6th century whose wife turns out to be a fox that has undergone a transformation. *Nihon Ryōiki.* Various editions, notably, Tokyo: Iwanami Shoten, 1996. Translated into English as *Miraculous Stories from the Japanese Buddhist Tradition: Nihon Ryoiki of the Monk Kyokai* (*Harvard Yenching Monograph*). Harvard: Harvard University Press, 1973. Possession by a fox is usually uninvited, and involves the fox taking over the host's body or personality. Smyers, Karen Ann. *The Fox and the Jewel: Shared and Private Meanings in Contemporary Inari Worship.* Honolulu: University of Hawaii Press, 1999, page 90. Foxes were frequently given to manifest themselves as lovely young women or sometimes Buddhist priests.

I came to a place where the flood water had formed a large pond. At that point I climbed down from the embankment and went along the edge of the pond. There was a rock just where the water had dried up, and sitting down on the rock, I gazed across to the other side. Occasionally the wind rose and then died down again.

The sky was overcast with low-lying clouds, although the cloud cover appeared thin, and in places faint, white stars were visible. After a while, a large fox slowly emerged from the dark grove opposite. The fox came into view clearly from out of the pitch darkness. After looking hesitantly about, the fox came to the edge of the pond and repeatedly stirred the water with its forepaws as if searching for something. Small ripples spread out across the dull surface of the pond and I heard a faint lapping sound.

The fox lifted its forepaws and began, in a curious fashion, to drape its head with pondweed[2]. Just then, there came a sudden splashing sound from the middle of the pond, and, as I looked on in surprise, I could see quite clearly a large carp swimming vigorously about a foot or so beneath the water's dark surface. Then I saw, much closer to the bottom of the pond, an even bigger carp, likewise swimming energetically in the same direction; it was so clear, in fact, that I could almost count each of the scales on its body. Just as I wondered what was happening, both carp vanished from my sight.

Then I noticed a young woman who had thus far escaped my attention standing on the far side of the pond. Just as I had heard

---

2. As a common prerequisite for the transformation, the fox places objects such as reeds, a broad leaf, or a skull over its head. Nozaki Kiyoshi. *Kitsune - Japan's Fox of Mystery, Romance and Humor*. Tokyo: The Hokuseido Press, 1961, pages 25-26. The word *Amendoro* is likely to be a contraction of the word *Kaamendoro* which in Chichibu dialect means pondweed or algae. There is a Meiji period woodblock print dated 1875 by the artist Kawanabe Kyōsai (河鍋暁斎) depicting a group of foxes changing shape. Notably, one fox has draped duckweed over its head to effect its shape-shifting. Kawanabe Kyōsai Memorial Museum, Saitama prefecture.

tell, what struck me most was the kimono she wore, with its bold vertical stripes. Although she had a beautiful face, with her hair done up in a married woman's style, I could not see clearly what she looked like.

The woman appeared to be doing something as she crouched down by the edge of the pond. Although it was dark, only the area immediately around her was clearly visible. It looked like she was raking up leaves and blades of grass around her with both hands, earnestly rolling them into a bundle. Before I knew it, the bundle had turned into a baby. Carrying the child in her arms, she came around the far edge of the pond and began to make her way up the embankment. She had the appearance of a lovely country wife, and I was captivated by her. Picking up a stick that was lying nearby, I quietly followed the woman.

On and on, seemingly forever, the woman walked at a brisk pace along the top of the embankment. Taking care not to let her out of my sight even for a moment, I followed. At length, the grove on the opposite side petered out and I came to a point where the embankment adjacent to the dry riverbed I had just walked by converged with the embankment abutting the large river.

There was a small, solitary house where the two embankments met. The woman paused at the entrance and knocked lightly on the door. I stopped a little way before the house and quietly watched. Repeatedly rapping at the door, the woman called out "Mother, I'm home."

A clattering noise came from inside the house, followed by the sound of the door opening. I thought I heard two or three words spoken by an old woman, and then the young woman, who had been standing at the door holding the baby, disappeared inside the house and I heard the sound of the door starting to close. At that moment I sprang forward and stood in the way of the closing door. A small old woman of about fifty stood on the other side.

"That woman is a fox!" I said abruptly.

The old woman looked at me in surprise. She stared at me for a long time without saying anything. The young woman stood behind her, still cradling the baby. She too stared hard at me with an astonished look on her face.

"She's a fox. Turn her out," I repeated. "I saw the fox transform itself into this woman. I'm going to reveal its true identity," I said again.

"Don't be absurd," said the old woman, losing her temper. "This is my daughter-in-law. What do you want, coming here at this time of night?"

"I'm telling you, that is a fox from the grove. Don't be taken in by it."

"What are you talking about? You're the one who has obviously been possessed by the fox. Either that or you are a pervert."

"That's not true," I said levelly. "I saw the fox transform itself into this woman by the big pond near the grove. The baby that the woman is holding is a pile of leaves. I saw it all quite clearly. Having changed into that woman and picked up the baby, I felt sure it intended to trick someone, and so I followed it here to this house. If you think I'm lying why don't you smoke the baby with fresh pine needles? You can be sure it will reveal its true form right away if you do."

"Good heavens! You're talking nothing but a lot of nonsense. You talk of smoking my grandchild with fresh pine needles. And what will happen if it's not a bundle of leaves? It would be unforgivable if anything should happen while my son was away. I can't do it, no matter what you say. Enough of your jokes. Please leave right away."

"You've already been tricked."

"No, that's not true. It's you that should calm down and think again about what you are saying. Blocking someone else's doorway in the middle of the night—if you were in your right mind how could you say such things?"

"And what will you do if she really is a fox?"

"But that's not possible. Hurry on home now and don't waste my time."

"But, if she is really a woman, would she stand here so coolly while I repeatedly call her a fox? The reason she hasn't said anything is because I saw the instant she changed shape. It is precisely because you haven't realized the truth that she is so unconcerned. But if you allow her to stay in your house and fall asleep, there is no telling what fate may befall you during the night."

When I said this, the young woman took two or three paces forward and suddenly began sobbing loudly.

"Mother, what are we to do? What are we to do?" she cried.

"It's alright, it's alright," said the old woman. "We needn't take any notice of someone like him. If you carry on like this you'll wake the baby."

"Oh?" I said. "If the baby wakes up the bundle of leaves will fall apart."

"Mother!" The woman began crying loudly again. "This is awful. What are we to do?" she said, her whole body shaking.

"If it's so awful why not smoke the baby, you old fox?" I said.

"Alright then, I'll smoke it," said the young woman in a shrill voice.

"What are you saying?" said the old woman, shocked.

"Leave her be. I'm going to reveal it for what it really is."

"No, I won't let you do that. A baby isn't a toy."

"No, I'll smoke it. But, if it turns out to be a real child then I'll make you sorry I did it."

"You needn't worry. We will know as soon as we pass it through the smoke from the fresh pine needles. If it is a real baby, as you seem to believe, then wafting a little smoke gently over it will not cause it any harm. You wait and see. The baby will turn into a pile of grass and that woman will sprout a tail and run away. But I'll chase after it with this stick and smash its backbone to pieces."

As I said this, the young woman emerged from the back of the room carrying a handful of fresh pine needles. I heaped them up and set fire to them on the path in front of the door. Red flames crept between the needles, and as the flames died down and flared up again, pale gray, choking smoke rose into the air.

"Well now, hand over the baby," I said, taking the infant from the woman's arms. I had no idea what trick she might play were the young woman to do it herself. The baby squirmed in my arms. Supporting it with both hands, I plunged it into the midst of the pale, swirling smoke. As I did so, the baby coughed two or three times. Then its body moved jerkily. Thinking this strange, I pulled it out of the smoke and found the baby was already dead. The woman let out an ear-splitting scream and collapsed unconscious right in front of me.

"See what you have done!" screamed the older woman in a strangely tearful, snarling tone of voice. Pale and trembling, she made no attempt to help the fallen woman.

I was at a loss as to what to do. Perhaps I had been led to do this by the fox. I thought that perhaps I had been tricked while watching the carp. But that couldn't have been true, as I was certain I had seen the fox's every movement. All the while following the woman along the embankment, there had been no indication whatsoever that I had been tricked. And yet the baby was dead, and because of that, the woman I had thought was a fox lay unconscious before me. I felt I had committed an inexcusable blunder.

I tried various things to resuscitate the baby, but so small, it could not be saved. Splashing water on the woman's face, and raising her up in my arms, I tried everything I could to bring her around, but she remained unconscious. The old woman stood stupefied, her face ashen, and she did nothing at all to help. I sighed deeply as I carried the unconscious woman out under the eaves of the unfamiliar house.

Confusing thoughts crowded my mind, but being vague and confused, they were soon dispelled, only to be replaced by other thoughts. Before I knew it, I broke down in floods of tears. I tried to think about the baby that I had killed with my own hands, but, for some reason or another, I found it all the more difficult to stop other thoughts coming into my mind.

Just then I heard voices coming from the river below the embankment. The light from a lantern danced above the water as it drew nearer. After a little while, I heard the sound of oarlocks, and I realised that people were rowing a boat by the foot of the embankment. It would be extremely trying to meet these people in my present predicament, and I didn't know how they would react. But it was a fact that the baby had died while the master of the house was away, the old woman was shattered and the wife had not yet regained consciousness. Were someone to come now and offer assistance, such assistance would be gratefully received in my hour of need.

The boat arrived below the embankment and five or six men came noisily over. They clambered up the embankment, and, as if by design, assembled in front of us. Looking about at the scene before them, they appeared extremely shocked. One of the men said he wondered what had happened because the door to the house was open.

Among the travelling companions was an elderly priest who did his utmost to console the old woman. A young man wearing a cap prodded the young woman, who still lay in my arms, in the ribs and somehow or other caused her to regain consciousness. Realising she was in my arms she pushed me away, stood up and began crying again in a deafening voice.

I told them the whole story, without omitting any details. As a result of their comings and goings on the river, this group of young men from the neighbouring village had grown friendly with the people who lived in this house. The Buddhist priest was the chief priest of a temple on top of the distant mountain.

At length, the old woman regained her composure and in front of the priest she repeatedly lamented the calamity whereby through my thoughtlessness I had killed her one and only precious grandchild. She broke down in tears, saying that when her son returned the following day she would have no excuse for what had happened. The young woman was inconsolable and cried continually while holding her dead baby.

Then the chief priest spoke, "This tragedy is all this man's doing. He ignored your pleas for him to stop and caused the child to breathe in the smoke. I know you will hate him forever for his insistence on having his way. But there is no malice in this man. Believing that the young woman was possessed by the fox, and even explaining this to her, was a mistake born, so to speak, out of kindness. In other words, because this man was himself possessed by the fox, it is pointless to talk of reason. He meant no harm. And since no one possessed by the spirit of a fox can be responsible for their own actions, I would ask that you forgive him. I apologize on behalf of this man. And while the baby's death is certainly a wretched story, you would do well to accept this as the child's fate, and I will attempt to persuade your son to accept it as such."

Strangely, because he was speaking so rapidly, he managed to say this in a single breath. I felt truly grateful and, glancing at his face, I was surprised to see an enormous pair of spectacles balanced on the end of his nose.

"As a result of my indiscretion, I have done something inexcusable," I said, apologizing to everybody.

"In any case, because he has killed a person, it must be reported to the various authorities. However, for the time being I will take care of this matter. For now, you must accompany me to my temple. I will take you into my charge," said the chief priest.

The group that had come ashore from the boat together agreed unanimously that that was the best thing to do. The old woman and the wife eventually agreed, and I was released into the priest's care. The priest read a simple sutra over the dead baby and then took me out of the house. The group of young men remained behind, in all likelihood to hold an all-night wake.

Following behind the chief priest, I walked for what seemed an eternity along a dark and unfamiliar path. From time to time I could hear the croaking of frogs, their voices sounding somehow as if they were heralding the imminent arrival of daybreak. But, although we seemed to be walking forever, the sky showed no sign of growing light.

Passing through dense thickets, we went along the top of a dry culvert before eventually coming out at the foot of a mountain. The chief priest didn't utter a word as we trudged along. Then, as we began to climb the mountain, he simply said, "You must not look back." His words were terrifying, and I felt paralysed with fear.

The mountain path was formidable. Lumps of earth, dislodged by the chief priest's feet as he climbed ahead of me, rolled down the slope, and each time they hit my toes my hair felt like it was standing on end. In the pitch darkness, I couldn't tell where the mountain ended and the sky began. Breathing became difficult as I rose into the unfathomable heights.

When at last we reached the summit, there, looming in the darkness, was a large temple. As the chief priest went in through the dark front entrance, a small, pale apprentice monk emerged from the back carrying a candlestick.

Guided by the chief priest, we went through countless spacious rooms before entering the inner hall of the temple. The dim light from two all-night lamps shone cold and bright. The chief priest sat me down in front of the image of the *Nyorai* Buddha and asked me to chant. Then, moving behind me, he shaved my head. As he did so, I continued to intone the *Namu Amida Butsu*[3].

Told to pray to the Amida Buddha for the child I had killed, I struck the gong. Then the chief priest disappeared. Sitting alone in the middle of the inner hall of the temple, I repeatedly struck the gong. From time to time a breeze came out of nowhere and moved ever so slightly the heavy banner that hung from a pillar. The peals of the gong, like flowing silver, resounded clearly all around. My mind, too, seemed gradually to have become calm. Calling to mind the face of the child I had so easily killed, I continued to pray earnestly for the repose of its young soul. I seemed to be ringing the gong forever, and while I was doing so the short night suddenly came to an end.

As the dazzling, yellow morning sun shone down, striking me directly on my face, I suddenly sensed that something was not right and looked about me. The pillar, the banner, the image of the Buddha, and the gong were all gone.

I was sitting in a rough, clay-flecked depression on top of a bare mountain, the branch of a dead tree in my hand. In front of my knees, near where the gong had been, was a single fragment of roofing tile. Other than that there was nothing there. My scalp began to smart where my hair had been shorn. Shocked, I stood up, but unable to orientate myself I did not know which way to go.

---

3. This is the Japanese pronunciation of the original Sanskrit 'six-character form' of the *nenbutsu* (念仏), or oral invocation of the Buddha Amitabha and means 'Hail to Amida Buddha.' The invocation is chanted in Pure Land (浄土教) Buddhism in order to achieve rebirth into the Pure Land after death.

The *Kudan*'s Mother

くだんのはは「Kudan no haha」

Komatsu Sakyō「1968」

小松左京

English translation by Mark Gibeau

ONE HOT JUNE afternoon in 1945 my house in Ashiya was burnt to the ground in an air raid.

I was in my third year of middle school at the time and had been mobilised to work in the Kobe shipyards building midget submarines. Like all the kids my age, I was hungry to the point of malnourishment— just a filthy kid, all skin and bones, with sharp, bitter eyes.

WHEN THE MASSIVE Kobe-Osaka air raid hit, we sprinted from our factory on the western edge of the city to shelter at the foot of a large hill in Hirano. As it turned out, however, the evacuation hadn't been necessary, and we complained about missing our lunch. I heard Ashiya had been hit, but at the time I was too angry at having to make the long walk home to pay much attention. Whenever there was an air raid, all the trains on the Hanshin, Hankyū, and National rail lines came to a halt, sometimes not moving again till the following day. It was thirteen kilometres under the burning sun to Ashiya, and now I would have to walk the whole way, wracked with hunger and faint with exhaustion. No matter how many times I underwent that ordeal I could never get used to it. The very thought of the long trek home made me want to weep with despair.

So, on that day too I walked home from the factory with a couple of friends. As I dragged my legs, numb with exhaustion, across the rail ties, I could see columns of brown smoke rising here and there throughout the countryside. One house by the tracks still burned, spitting sparks and flames from its charred frame. When Ashiya Station came into sight I suddenly stopped. I was at a complete loss. The landscape had been utterly transformed. It was as though I had arrived at some unknown land. My corner of the city had been burned clean away, leaving only a small mountain of red earth, still too hot to approach. Only the occasional concrete wall or stone lantern still stood. That and a single tree, burned naked by the fire. It took me ten minutes just to find the place where our house once stood, and even then I was only able to locate it after recognising the small stone bridge that crossed a ditch near our house.

OPPOSITE WHERE OUR house used to be stood a moustachioed man wearing the khaki green national uniform,[1] his mouth agape. My father. He didn't even turn to look at me as I approached. I asked where we would spend the night, but he merely grunted in reply. My father built the house and it was a large part of his very small fortune. Before the war it was a big deal to have a house in Ashiya. As a typical white-collar employee, my father was a man of small ambition, but this feat at least he had managed to accomplish. Now he stared at the ruins, stunned that his meagre wealth and all his dreams had been reduced to this tiny handful of charred earth.

In the end it was O-saki who saved us from having to choose between spending the night out in the open or making the long walk in the dark to the dormitories run by my father's company. We had been standing there for about an hour, too exhausted even to move, when I saw a woman walk by, a large work apron over her national uniform, goggling at the destruction. She seemed not to notice us at first but then hurried over.

"Oh, sir! Young master! How terrible!" O-saki said, on the verge of tears.

O-saki would have been about fifty years old, and she had worked as our maid for many years. She was a gentle person,

1. In 1940 the Japanese government issued a proclamation outlining the new "national uniform" to be worn by all men in place of their daily work clothes. Resembling a military uniform, it was intended to conserve resources and foster a sense of unity. A female version, known as the *monpe,* was also devised.

fond of children and adept at housework. Being the eldest, I wasn't that close to her, but my brothers and sisters were much younger than I and were very attached to O-saki. My youngest sister preferred O-saki even over our sickly mother and clung to her day and night, to the point where O-saki couldn't go home until my sister fell asleep. She was never careless or rough with the dishes or other household items, and she would do anything asked of her without complaint. She was never idle. I realize it's difficult to believe, but in the old days there really were housekeepers like that.

One of the reasons O-saki was so conscientious was probably because of her faith. I remember seeing my younger sister ape her odd hand gestures and thinking that O-saki must be a member of Tenrikyō.[2] She was with us for a little more than three years, quitting when my mother, brothers and sisters all evacuated to the countryside. We pleaded with her to stay, saying that with all the women gone there would be nobody to look after my father and me and that if she left the house would be deserted in the daytime. But, apologising, she refused our entreaties, saying that she was obliged to her new employer.

"But don't worry, ma'am. I'll still be in the neighbourhood and will stop by whenever I have the chance. And, unless my new household is in danger, I'll come right away if anything terrible happens."

"Where is it?" my mother demanded.

"It's an estate just down the road, by the shore."

"Oh, well, if it's one of *those* estates the money must be pretty good, right?" Mother said. Despite everything O-saki had done for us, Mother started complaining as soon as the smallest thing didn't go her way. This tendency to act like a spoiled child was one of the things I hated about her.

---

2. The *teodori* (hand dance) is a key ritual of Tenrikyō, a religion established in Japan in the mid-nineteenth century.

"I didn't accept the position for the money, ma'am, though it is very generous. The work is lighter, and despite the pay they haven't been able to find anyone who lasts beyond a week. And the head of my church asked me especially. Our sacred teachings tell us to aid those in distress, ma'am, even if it means doing something that others might find distasteful."

O-saki left to work at the estate, but she still stopped by to check in on my father and me from time to time. She made short work of our accumulated mess and brought us various foods that had become very difficult to get—all gifts from the estate, it seemed. On the day of the air raid she rushed right over as soon as she heard that the area near the station had been hit. Standing there and looking at O-saki's face my resolve wavered, and I suddenly felt tears starting to well up.

"Oh, what horrible luck, sir! I had to stay to protect the estate, but I was so worried about the two of you. I was in such a panic!"

"It's all right, O-saki. This is war after all, isn't it?" my father said with a hollow smile.

"But you don't have anyplace to spend the night, do you?"

I looked at my father. He was beyond confusion and simply stood and stared at the burnt ruins in the deepening twilight, his face expressionless.

"If you wouldn't find it unpleasant, won't you please come and stay with me, sir? I've been living down at the estate ever since the Maid Association's dormitories were burnt down," O-saki said with a smile. "I'll ask the mistress. There are certainly plenty of rooms, and you and the young master can spend the night in my quarters if you don't mind."

THE TRULY GRAND houses in Ashiya were not near the Hankyū or National Rail lines but rather further down toward the shore, by the riverside and the Hanshin Rail station. The area around the hills belonged mainly to the nouveau riche, but the houses of the old, established merchants of Osaka were clustered down by the shore, at Kōrōen in Nishinomiya and in the area surrounding Shugukawa. Most of these houses were built on tall stone retaining walls and were surrounded by high fences topped with spikes to discourage intruders. From the outside all you could make out were second-story roofs beyond thick, manicured gardens of trees and shrubs. To me, the glittering gold and platinum tips of the lightning rods seemed to symbolise the whole area and the class of people who resided there. O-saki's house sat on a quiet corner on the edge of the district. The estate was separated from the sea only by a small grove of pine trees, and I could hear each wave crash on the shore and smell the salt on the breeze that passed through the trees. Dressed in ragged clothes and legs trembling with exhaustion, my father and I dragged ourselves up the stone stairway to the gate.

O-saki led us into the entrance hallway and, bidding us to stay there, went inside. My father and I sat on the stone floor in silence, listening to O-saki's footsteps fade into the distance as she disappeared into the estate. I suddenly sensed a presence and, turning around, saw a figure dressed in a kimono standing behind me. The person stood in the shadows of the corridor beyond the entrance hall and seemed to be peering out at us. I couldn't make out a face in the darkness, only the white tips of the feet, clad in light summer socks. The figure just stood there, gazing wordlessly at us. Just then O-saki returned, calling out "Oh, there you are!" The figure in the shadows at last revealed herself. She was tall and elegant, neatly dressed in a modest summer kimono and looked about forty years old. She had a slender, aristocratic face, and her skin was so white it seemed almost transparent. Perhaps she suffered from weak eyes, for she wore rimless, octagonal spectacles—their lenses tinted a faint purple. Though she seemed not to be wearing powder, her face appeared pale and wan, and her hair was meticulously arranged. She looked down slightly as O-saki described our situation, her thin face as devoid of emotion as a Noh mask. Eventually, however, her brows drew together in a crease and she spoke in a quiet voice.

"I see. That is a bit of a problem."

It was immediately obvious that she wasn't simply saying this to be difficult. Rather, we understood that our presence really might cause a problem. I went to pull at my father's sleeve.

"Yet, if they are your acquaintances...."

The relief was visible on my father's face. At these words he pulled off his hat as though suddenly recalling himself, held out his business card and formally introduced himself.

"In times like these we must all do what we can for one another," she replied quietly. "O-saki's room—the maid's quarters—is quite small. O-saki, why don't you lay their bedding out in the detached room at the back of the house? It might be best if they took their meals there as well."

WE WERE LED to the room of about six tatami mats in size that had been set aside for us. O-saki walked across the corridor that connected the room to the main house, bearing black lacquered trays of food. We ate so much I couldn't help feeling a little ashamed.

"Please, sir, eat as much as you like," O-saki said, smiling as she stood in the shadows beyond the flickering light of the candles. "The mistress has ordered it. In such difficult times as these it may seem terribly wasteful, but there is no shortage of rice in this house."

Though it was mixed with two parts barley, the rice seemed nothing short of a dream to us. We were usually fed on wormy beans and corn and sometimes even acorn flour and pressed soybean skins. And there was meat! It was thinly sliced and tough but meat all the same, with an egg and vegetable broth. Each dish seemed a miracle in itself.

O-saki hung the mosquito netting for us and we crawled into the summer bedding, which, though slightly damp and smelling faintly of mould, was nonetheless soft and cool against my skin. The room was plunged into darkness once the candles were extinguished, and, though I was utterly exhausted, I couldn't manage to fall asleep.

"Everything's gone, isn't it?" I asked my father. "My textbooks, our shirts, all our clothes...."

"Yes," Father replied.

"What will we do now?"

Father heaved a deep sigh and rolled over, turning his back to me. I understood his dilemma. The war had taught kids my age a lot about the various shades of meaning contained in the phrase "daily life." I fell silent, thinking I had said something improper. We were too busy just trying to get through each day. We didn't think about the future, not even about what would happen with the war.

I wanted to comfort him, to apologise to his turned back. I wanted to tell him that I understood, that I knew it must be so much harder, so much sadder for him to see the house destroyed than it was for me. But even as I thought about that, the realisation that I would have to drag myself to work at the factory once again the following day hit me. We would have to leave this place and find somewhere else to stay. I felt my insides burn with despair.

Would we end up going to one of the dormitories run by my father's company in Toyonaka or Minō or wherever it was? Or would we take refuge in the elementary school's assembly hall along with all the other people made homeless by the air raids? Without so much as a single pot of our own? Maybe we would dig out one of the air raid shelters among the ruins and live there, like some of my friends did. These thoughts ran through my mind as I stared blankly into the darkness. Then I heard something. A faint voice. I strained my ears and realised it was simply the whine of a mosquito. The high-pitched buzzing of the insect suddenly made me itch all over, and I was soon wide awake again. Lying still in the darkness I could make out the sounds of the wind rustling through the pines and waves hitting the beach. Then I heard the voice again, but clearly this time.

"Father, someone is crying," I whispered. But he was already snoring. The thin, weak cries—like those of an infant—continued to echo and die away in the deep silence of the estate, sometimes sounding very close, other times distant.

The next morning, before I left for the factory and Father for his office, we agreed to meet up again at the estate at the end of the day. At the factory I told everyone how my house had been destroyed, but nobody seemed to care very much.

When I returned home that evening Father was already there and was deep in conversation with O-saki.

"The timing is terrible," he said, looking at me. "Today they suddenly decided to put me in charge of the company's evacuation site out in the country—the person who was running it was killed in the air raid.... So I'm being sent to the site for a month and a half."

Father looked at me as though to ask what I would do. I looked from him to O-saki and back. O-saki, who had been kneeling on the raised wooden floor just inside the house, suddenly smiled and slid herself forward on her knees.

"I've already asked the mistress. How about it, young master? Will you let O-saki look after you for a little while?"

"The mistress says you can stay—if it's just you," Father said.

I fell silent. Only now, when I faced the prospect of losing my father, did I realise how much I relied on him. My face flushed as a wave of loneliness washed over me. Perhaps noticing this, he peered down at me.

"Or you could take some time off school and go stay with your mother. What do you think? It would be a rough trip by train but...."

"I'll stay," I said curtly.

"Behave yourself then," Father said, getting to his feet. "O-saki tells me there's an invalid here as well."

"You—you're leaving tonight?" I asked, taken aback.

"Yes, tonight. I'll do something about getting us a place to live when I get back."

With that my father entrusted me to O-saki's care and departed. I didn't accompany him all the way to the Hanshin Railway station, walking with him to the gate to the estate instead. I watched him disappear into the distance down the white path. His retreating figure seemed strangely sad as he walked down the road, skinny and shoulders hunched, the small bag containing his air raid hood swinging from his belt.

The company was being unreasonable, I thought. Sure, we're in the middle of a war, but even so you'd think they would avoid sending someone on a business trip the day after his house has been burnt to the ground. But this was war. Eventually the enemy would land, and, unless a divine wind intervened, we would be fighting them with bamboo spears and everyone would die. To a middle school student of today all this must sound hopelessly naïve, yet as these thoughts occurred to me my eyes actually filled with tears as though I were but a small child. I had absolutely no idea my father had really left me with O-saki so he that could stay with his mistress, one of the secretaries from his office.

I DIDN'T MOVE in with O-saki but stayed in the detached room by myself. The biggest change for me was my diet. For the first time in ages I had rice for breakfast and dinner. O-saki even offered to make me a lunch to bring to the factory, but I had to refuse. Just being able to eat rice for breakfast and dinner was enough to make me feel guilty when I thought of my friends. I knew their lives at the factory were hard and cruel and getting worse by the day.

The air raids had increased in ferocity, and it wasn't unusual to see squadrons of B-29s pass overhead three times a day, in the morning, afternoon, and night. Then, once every three days or so, a massive formation of bombers would pass overhead to lay waste to Kobe, Osaka or one of the outlying cities. When there were no bombings, we had to endure strafing by the low-flying planes coming in from the aircraft carriers. Throughout the day the news reports and military marches we listened to on the factory radio were interrupted by an irritating buzzer announcing special bulletins from Central Military Information. In a mechanical voice the newsreader reported that enemy planes were attacking, sirens started to wail in the distance and the evacuation bell began its clamour. Ringing seemed to fill the air, and throughout the city we could hear the sporadic fits of coughing that were the anti-aircraft guns coming to life. Then the familiar buzzing thump, like something slapping into sand, filled our ears and we were surrounded by the tearing cracks and roars of explosions. Choking on smoke, we were forced to sprint through the sea of fire to the refuge of the foothills.

It was hot every single day. Not only did we have to deal with the sweltering heat, but the air reeked of acrid smoke, and even at night the heat from the burnt ruins radiated up from the ground, roasting us from below. The soldiers and teachers, made irritable by the heat, beat us worse than ever. I felt like my stomach was filled with boiling water and that, at any moment, diarrhoea might stab down from the pit of my stomach like a pair of red-hot tongs. Amid the din, the explosions, the angry yells, and the oppressive heat, we felt as though we were shrivelling, parched black under the blazing sun, like a frog's desiccated corpse.

Inside the estate it was different. It was as though the trees and shrubs shut out the confusion and heat of the outside world. My room was always still and cool. The long-neglected garden was overgrown with thick summer grasses, but there were still carp in the pond. The fish, some mottled and some red, were more than thirty centimetres in length and swished their tails lazily back and forth at the bottom of the muddy pool of spring water. Cicadas gathered amid the gracefully shaped branches of the magnificent black pines and in the rich foliage of the blue-green paulownia trees. Though the buzzing of the cicadas was loud, it somehow seemed to highlight the gentle stillness of the estate.

It's just like being deep in the mountains, I thought as I sat day-dreaming on the edge of the veranda. Whenever I got a day off from the factory because the trains had stopped and such, I would spend that time in the gardens. Going into the garden through a wicker gate, I walked over to the spring and, sitting on one of the stones by its edge, would stare into the water for hours on end.

"Do you know what that carp is?" a voice suddenly asked one of those afternoons.

The lady—that's what I called her whenever I thought of her—stood behind me, her kimono impeccably arranged as always. I glanced at the whitish fish she was pointing to, but I didn't recognise it.

"It's a German Carp. It only has a few scales here and there. It's a kind of deformity," the lady said. "But sometimes deformed things are the most valuable."

Those days I rarely had the energy to be curious. Once, my friends and I were walking home from the factory when we came across a man sitting atop the rubble of a burnt building, glaring fiercely at everything around him. His shirt was pulled aside to expose his stomach and one hand was clutching the naked blade of a Japanese sword. We walked by without a single glance. It wasn't until five years after the end of the war that I found myself thinking about that strange scene, wondering if he had actually gone through with it. The only things capable of rousing my curiosity periodically were the lady and her estate. Was it true that the lady and a sick child were the only people living in this giant house with all its rooms? Were there really no men about at all? How come the lady never wore the national uniform, dressing instead in kimono? Even if she never went out, how come the Civilian Defence Corps and the Neighbourhood Association—normally eager to stir up trouble—let her be? The flails and buckets of sand for putting out fires were nowhere to be found. At a time when so many people had been made homeless by fire, how come nobody complained about all this space being wasted on just two people? She seemed to have money, but where was all the food coming from?

On this last point, at least, I was able to unravel the mystery a little bit. One night when there had been a blackout, I was looking out the window of my room and saw a man with a kerchief about his face and a bundle on his back sneak in through the back gate. As he walked through pools of moonlight I caught a glimpse of a face heavily scarred around the eyes. The next morning we had meat for the first time in days. Ultimately, however, I lacked the energy to pursue these questions. They simply occurred to me from time to time but never translated into any sort of action. More than anything, I found myself intrigued by the occasional sound of crying that came from the second floor of the main house.

"The invalid, it's a girl, right?" I asked O-saki. "It sounds like she's really suffering."

"Did you hear her?" O-saki whispered, her face sombre. Then, with an almost frightening directness she said, "Please, young master, avoid coming into the main house as much as possible."

"How old is she, the sick girl?"

"I don't know," O-saki replied. As though deep in thought, she first bowed her head and then shook it. "Like you, I've never seen her."

Another thing that puzzled me was that there wasn't a single radio in the estate. Nor did she subscribe to the single-page broadsheets that passed for newspapers in those days of paper rationing. With all the blackouts we were experiencing I supposed that unless they had a battery-powered radio it wouldn't have done much good, but even so I wanted to hear the latest news about the war. People were spreading all sorts of rumours at the factory. Most were about some kind of new, secret weapon or a new kind of bomb or rocket that would wipe out all the enemy in one go, but there were other strange rumours about riots in America or that the war was going to end any day.

On the night of the enormous Nishinomiya air raid I jumped up from my bed and ran outside to see the eastern sky filled with the light of orange-black flames and great balls of light that crackled through the dark like magnesium. I had long since started to sleep with my puttees wrapped about my legs, but this was the first time I thought we might really be facing the total destruction of the region. I started packing my things so I could evacuate at a moment's notice.

"I wonder if they'll come here," asked O-saki, wearing her national uniform.

"They're close. They're hitting the area around Higashiguchi now," I replied. "The next wave might go for Ashiya."

"It's getting closer and closer," O-saki said quietly. "Wasn't that Kōrōen just now?"

Suddenly I noticed something white standing beside me. Turning, I saw that it was the lady wearing a brown *haori* half-jacket over her light summer kimono. Holding the jacket close around her shoulders she gazed up at the sky over Nishinomiya.

"Shouldn't we evacuate? It'll be safer by the foot of the hills," I said.

"No, we will be fine," she said in a soft voice. "They will make one more pass and that'll be the end of it. We are in no danger here."

Something about the way she spoke upset me. It made me think that maybe she wasn't quite right in the head. But her face remained as placid as a Noh mask. The distant flames glittered red on her rimless glasses.

"Something much worse than this air raid is going to happen," she muttered. "Something horrible...."

"Where?" I asked quickly.

"To the west."

"Kobe?"

"No, further west."

With that the lady suddenly covered her face and went back into the house. As the sky grew light I returned to my room. On my way to my room, however, I stopped and peered up at the main house. The door to one room had been left open, and in the darkness of the room I could make out a white figure. The lady was sitting stiffly in the middle of the ten-mat room. About three kilometres to the west flames and smoke blocked out the sky. The fire brought with it a hot wind that filled the air with ash. Deep within that wind I thought I could make out the agony-filled cries of those trapped in the fires. As I left the garden, however, I realised I was mistaken. It was only the sound of sobbing, once again penetrating the tightly fastened window at the far end of the second floor.

FROM THE FOLLOWING day I was kept home from work by diarrhoea. Since the detached room had no toilet of its own, I had to cross the corridor leading to the main house time and time again. There was a household toilet nearby, but I walked to the end of the long hallway by the garden and used the guest toilet by the side of the stairs instead. This was both a product of my own selfishness and an act of rebellion against the estate's magnificence. One of my uncles on my mother's side ran a prosperous farm in Saitama prefecture and I had visited him once when I was quite small. I remember being filled with a vague sense of pride at how the many servants and farmhands made such a fuss over me, at the grounds so vast they contained as many as ten storehouses, at the thick wooden rafters over two hundred years old. The fact that this house made my uncle's estate look tiny by comparison made me feel strangely oppressed, and that annoyed me. Of course, curiosity played a role as well. I simply could not accept that this estate, so vast that the far ends of the long corridors were hardly visible, could be inhabited by so few people. In other words, going to the toilet had become something of an adventure. As I walked, I noticed the dark lustre of the floors, and it occurred to me how hard it must be for O-saki to keep the hallways polished. Partway down the corridor I stopped and listened closely at the doors of the rooms on either side, but they were shut firmly and there was nothing to indicate that anyone was inside. A thin layer of dust coated the frames of the grimy paper doors. Rounding the corner I jumped back in surprise as something loomed up before me. Looking more closely, however, I saw that it was simply an ancient wooden statue of Buddha standing silently in the corner. A bronze *gigaku* mask, its mouth agape in voiceless laughter, hung on the wall. Across from the toilet there was an old wooden plaque with the words "*Monstrum Sui Generis*" written in faded white characters, though to this day I don't know what it means.

The main toilet was opposite the room with the men's urinal and was about four and a half tatami mats altogether. Three of the sand-stucco walls had latticework windows, and the new tatami mats were bright and cool to the touch. The ceiling was made of straight-grained cedar, arched as though in the manner of a ship. In the centre of the room was the toilet, coated in black lacquer. The lid was also coated with the same black lacquer but with a finely detailed *seigaiha* wave pattern painted in gold leaf. A crystal weight in the shape of a Chinese lion sat atop a small pile of toilet paper in a wicker basket. A red lacquered washstand in front of the toilet, about thirty centimetres tall with cabriole legs, held the green porcelain washbasin. This basin sometimes held water lilies, sometimes water lotuses. In the northeast corner of the room stood an eight-legged stand made of black persimmon, about sixty centimetres in height. A silver incense burner stood atop it, emitting a thin haze of smoke and filling the room with its delicate fragrance. It seemed that keeping the guest toilet clean was one of the more important tasks in O-saki's daily routine. I once saw O-saki carrying a dustbin full of green cedar leaves. Whenever I opened the lid of the toilet, the rich scent of fresh cedar leaves wafted up from the unseen depths. It gave me something of a wry thrill to sit on this toilet amid such spaciousness and luxury and battle with the diarrhoea brought on by my steady diet of beans. Yet the biggest surprise came when I ran into O-saki as she was coming down the second floor stairs by the toilet. I don't know why, but the sight of me standing there caused her to freeze in shock.

Nearly dropping the basin she was carrying, she cried out, "Oh! Young master! It's you!" She had gone completely white, and her breath was coming out in gasps.

"What are you up to, all the way over here...."

"What? I'm not allowed?" I asked defiantly.

"Well, no, it's not that...." O-saki said, struggling with the basin as she adjusted her grip on it. It was emitting a strangely putrid smell. I made as though to peer into it, and, noticing this, O-saki hurriedly shifted it to her side, hiding the contents from me.

"You mustn't look!" she whispered and started to hurry off. Seeing something dragging behind her, I called out. "You've dropped a bandage, you know."

O-saki turned around, and at that moment the contents of the bowl were completely exposed. It was full of bandages, stinking and soaked with blood and pus! O-saki, now completely flustered, fled toward the kitchen.

After that I became obsessed with a strange notion. What was the girl suffering from? Could it be *that*? The very thought made my skin crawl. The pale, translucent skin of the lady, like that of a newly hatched silkworm—they say that's a symptom too. The idea grew more and more unbearable, and that afternoon I went to the kitchen to see O-saki. Peering into the big, dark kitchen I saw her heating water in a large kettle and boiling the bandages. Next to her was the basin, about sixty centimetres in diameter, that had held the bandages earlier. Now it was filled to the brim with a steaming, mud-like liquid that emitted a sickening odour. The nasty, vomit-like substance appeared to be food. I called out to O-saki, catching her by surprise yet again, and this time she responded with a slightly angry glare.

"The kitchen is no place for young boys!" she said.

"O-saki, what's wrong with the girl?" I asked, undaunted. "What if it's leprosy?"

"Young master!" O-saki scolded, her face suddenly serious. Wiping her hands, she came over to where I stood. We sat down on the raised threshold of the kitchen door.

"Now, young master, you know that it's not polite to poke your nose into other people's private family matters."

"But what if it is leprosy?" I asked. "The lady is hiding a sick person, and you're the only person she lets get close. That must be it. What if you catch it?"

"I am not going to catch leprosy. And even if I did it wouldn't matter." O-saki said piously. "God is with me. You've heard the stories about Kōmyō Kōgō,[3] haven't you?"

"But that's just a legend! If it's leprosy, she needs to be quarantined," I insisted.

"Now listen. This is all I can say about it. The girl does not have leprosy."

"So, what is it?"

"I don't know.... But it's her mother I really feel sorry for."

"What, living in this huge mansion? In all this luxury? What's there to feel sorry for!" I shouted, driven by a combination of my jealousy and propaganda about "Supporting the Divine War." It was an explosion of that disgusting, cowardly, and malignant indignation that gripped virtually everyone during the war.

"She.... She's a traitor! She buys off the black market, she doesn't wear the uniform, she doesn't even work! I'm going to tell the military police!"

"Young master!" O-saki said reprovingly, her voice trembling.

"Fine, I won't tell anyone. I won't tell the police," I said in a despicable, threatening voice. The military police were, in any case, far too terrifying for people like us even to consider approaching. But I took advantage of O-saki's ignorance. "But then you have to tell me what's in that basin."

---

3. Empress Kōmyō (701–760) was an influential empress and devout Buddhist during the Nara period (710–794). In addition to using her influence to spread Buddhism, she is said to have established facilities to aid the poor and the sick. One of the legends surrounding her says that while caring for the sick she was asked by a leper to suck the pus from his boil with her own mouth. When she did as she was asked the leper was revealed to be Ashuku Nyorai, or Akshobya—one of the Five Wisdom Buddhas.

O-saki blanched, her lips pressed tight. I continued to bully and cajole O-saki. How could I have been so horrible! Though I had been bullied and abused so much myself, or perhaps *because* I had been bullied and abused, once I got a little power of my own, even if it was only illusory, I was quick to exploit it to bully others. O-saki grew agitated and after a little while finally admitted it was food—a mixture of various things.

"I truly don't know anything," O-saki said. "I'm only allowed to go as far as the corner in the second floor hallway. I leave a basin full of food three times a day, and each time an hour later the food is gone and the basin is filled with the bandages instead."

O-saki's expression seemed to be twisted in pain as she spoke. I felt a sharp stab in my chest at having threatened her, forcing her to betray her mistress. Yet this stab of conscience only made me grow colder.

"O-saki, you know what is wrong with her, don't you?" I said, leading her on.

"I have a vague idea. But this is one thing I can't tell you, young master. To tell you that would be a terrible betrayal of the trust the mistress has placed in me."

O-saki sounded so resolute that it was now my turn to feel embarrassed. The selfishness of a spoiled child doesn't stand much of a chance against the firm opposition of an adult.

"Listen carefully, young master." At some point O-saki had gotten up to kneel formally on the wooden planking of the floor, her back straightened as she stared straight down at me. I felt myself shrink before her gaze. "Whatever happens, under no circumstances are you even to think about going up to the second floor to snoop around. If you were to do something so foolish, why there's no telling what misfortune might befall you."

PERHAPS O-SAKI'S ADMONITION had sunk in because for a while I felt no desire to pursue the "secret" any further. Only now it was the "secret" that was pursuing me. A couple of days later, I heard the sound of a piano coming from one of the back rooms. Drawn by the sound of the instrument—the first I had heard in a long time—I made my way around to the back. The lady was playing. An upright piano sat in the ten-mat room near the end of the corridor, and the lady was singing in a thin, pure voice. Though my memory is a bit vague, the words went something like this:

Rapidly approaching, the twilight of an age
Unseen lands are everywhere covered
With black clouds and falling rain.
Flashes of lightning, the roar of thunder
You the revellers, with fear tremble
You the haughty, prostrate yourselves in humility.

The lady spotted me and smiled.

"Yoshio?" She called to me, "Come over here by me." I felt a little guilty about my earlier encounter with O-saki, but now that I was alone with the lady the old curiosity start to burn once more. As I stepped into the room the lady poured me a cup of iced tea from her thermos.

"Every day is such a trial," she said, pushing aside the clothes she had been folding. "Each day is such tedium. Of course it's inexcusable, yet...." I found myself on tenterhooks as she spoke, wondering if O-saki had told her what I had said. Avoiding her gaze, I looked down at the pile of clothes and saw a red satin patterned kimono of the kind a girl of thirteen or fourteen might wear.

"I feel so sorry for young people like you. It must be terrible."

"There's nothing to feel sorry about." I said, flaring up. "It's our duty. The upperclassmen have gone to flight school, and some have even sacrificed themselves in *kamikaze* attacks. We are ready to offer up our lives at any moment too!"

At this the lady gave a faint, mysterious smile. But the sadness and the foreboding in that smile sent a shiver down my back.

"That won't happen, Yoshio," she said. "That will never happen. Soon all of this—everything—will be finished."

"How can you know that?" I asked, suddenly serious. "The enemy has occupied Okinawa. The fleets are coming from the Ogasawaras and the Philippines. They are going to land. And when they do this whole area will become a battlefield." I paused for breath, coldly calculating the impact of my words on the lady. "And when it comes to that, even this house will be burned to the ground."

Suddenly the lady raised her delicate voice in an abrupt laugh.

"This house won't burn," she said, lightly covering her mouth with her hand. "That's already been decided. You think it's odd that I never evacuate during the air raids, don't you? But even if everything around us is reduced to a scorched field, this house alone will remain untouched. We have a spirit protecting us, you see."

"But even the Minatogawa shrine in Kobe burned down," I replied.

"Oh, a shrine can burn. But this one plot of land will not be bombed, because my house is on it."

A terrible notion flashed through my mind, and I suddenly felt hot all over. At the same time, I felt my heart shrivel up inside me, as though pierced by a lance of ice. It made perfect sense, everything seemed to fit together. Why didn't they bomb the estate? How was the lady able to spend her days all alone in this vast house, without having to do any kind of work? Who was she concealing on the second floor? I stiffened, and the words rushed out of me.

"You—you're a spy, aren't you?"

This time the lady did not laugh. She rose to her feet, displaying the elegant profile of her face, beautiful and shrouded in faint, forlorn shadows. She leant against a pillar, and, gazing up into the blistering azure sky, whispered, "If only it were as simple as that...."

The stillness of a summer sky like molten glass was interrupted yet again by the wailing of air raid sirens. The reverberations seemed almost to shake the enormous, pillar-like clouds. I thought I heard someone keening from somewhere within the estate, as though in imitation of the siren. I must have been mistaken, however, and concluded that it was probably just a dog or a cow.

"This house has a spirit protecting it. It is the cursed fate of our line. Do you know what a cursed fate is, Yoshio?" Slumped against the pillar, the lady continued in a hollow voice.

"You see, my family is of a very ancient line in the provinces—a very old and a very large family. Deep in the mountains of Kyushu there is a vast estate—as big as a castle. It had numerous farms and mountains and many hands working the lands. Yet that vast wealth contained within it the malice of many, many people, of many peasants. The accumulated malice of generation upon generation—that's our curse."

I found myself drawn into her story, listening intently. The lady continued in a quiet, rhythmical voice, as though she were chanting a sutra.

"My ancestors were once Christians, you see. But in the end they turned other Christians in to the authorities one after another so as to steal their wealth. They conspired with the authorities and even turned in non-Christians, lying to get them thrown in jail just to get their hands on the farms and estates of the families that were arrested. It's their accumulated malice that has left generations of women in our line barren. And if one of us should manage to have a child it never lives for more than three days."

But you, I started to say before pressing my lips together.

"My husband, not surprisingly, is also of a venerable family from the Tōhoku region. For generations it was also known as one of the wealthiest families, but it is said that, through the ages the peasants and tenants were horribly mistreated by every head of the household. If a village failed to pay its annual taxes its women and children would be chased out into the wild mountains to collect firewood. They say that sometimes they would even hang the village headman upside down and set starving dogs upon him. However, since the master of the house was also a distant relative of the lord of the domain and since he was in league with the local officials, the peasants could do nothing about it. Because of this, as soon as each eldest son was elevated to head of the household he would inevitably go mad and die in mysterious circumstances.

"There's a guardian spirit attached to his—and my husband's—house, a spirit that only the mad head of the household can see. Though it is a guardian spirit, it takes the form of a vicious beast and is terrifying to behold. When the spirit appears, the person who sees it is driven mad and starts to behave erratically and wildly, recklessly killing peasants and behaving abominably. When I visited my husband's family in the provinces where they lived I saw his father. He was locked up in a room in his own house. His bloodshot eyes were bright scarlet and he crawled about the room on all fours, drooling and screaming that the beasts were coming, that the ox was coming.

"Yet for all that it is still a guardian spirit. Once, when one of my husband's ancestors had gone too far and done something too horrible to be endured, he was attacked by a group of outraged peasants. They were about to kill him. But then the spirit took the form of a giant, black beast and scattered the peasants, saving the man's life. Another time a massive fire swept the neighbourhood, burning everything in sight, but the spirit protected my husband's house. It was the only building left standing. During the fire the spirit spoke to my husband. "I'm one of the peasants tortured to death by your family," he said. The spirit said that he tormented my husband's line out of hatred, but in return he would protect the house and wealth they had gained through the pain and misery of the peasants."

I held my breath as I listened to her tale. A sudden ringing pierced the vast blue sky as the alarm bell began to sound, indicating that people should take cover. From somewhere beyond the clouds I heard a deep rumbling, a sound like the earth shuddering.

"My husband left home very early so he was able to avoid going mad. He's still alive somewhere in China or one of the other colonies. Instead of going mad it seems that he has killed many, many people. The spirit came to this house because I married such a man. And so the spirit protects my house. The spirit.... is the child. The spirit is the accumulation of all the curses wished upon this household. That cursed fate protects us all. It's strange when you think about, I suppose. For generations our family has been shielded by the hatred of untold millions."

Just then the first bombs sent a ripple through the distant core of the earth. Suddenly moving away from the pillar, the lady walked over to the piano and started to play again, though very quietly. It was from Mahler's "Songs on the Death of Children," a song that for some reason I knew quite well. I was entranced by the sight of the lady, her feet clad in pure white pressing against the pedals as she played, and forgot all about the violent explosions of the falling bombs. It took me a little while to realise that the lady was playing for someone else. Across the garden the second floor window that was normally tightly shut had been cracked open. Behind it I saw a black shadow standing and listening intently to the piano.

AROUND THAT TIME the war began to take on a strange quality. It was as though the war itself had become a kind of whirlwind of misfortune, raising clouds of flames and ash. All day and all night, violent winds swept ceaselessly across the face of the earth. Just beyond the raging of the wind I could almost make out the faint sound of screaming, and, though I seemed to sense its meaning, I couldn't express it in words. One voice in the wind pronounced, "Off toward Ise a barren plum tree bore fruit this year, so the war will end soon. It was the same during the Russo-Japanese War." Others said that a vast nettle tree at such and such a shrine split completely in two despite there being no wind. Another told of a famous fortune-teller who predicted that the war would end without victory or defeat. Yet another claimed that somewhere deep in the mountains two newborn infants had suddenly started to speak, saying that Japan would lose the war. There were many such voices.

We didn't believe any of those stories.

Yet at the same time something reverberated within us from deep within the screams, a scream like the wailing of the wind. Who was it that told us a new Imperial General Headquarters had been built in the mountainous Shinshū region and that the Emperor had been evacuated there, or was going to be soon? I do know it was the banker's son who told us that the banks, expecting defeat, had already started hiding their assets. We listened to the tales with bated breath all the way to the end and then beat up their bearers for being unpatriotic.

One of the machine operators loved any talk of secrets no matter how outlandish, and in the hushed tones he was fond of adopting when revealing confidential information he would breathe stories about a new and terrible secret weapon that Japan was preparing. It supposedly possessed such tremendous destructive power that, do what they would, all of the enemy's tanks, infantry and even their aircraft would be annihilated in one blow. Headquarters was concealing it as a weapon of last resort. It was so powerful, he said, that it would inflict terrible damage even upon friendly forces, so they were debating whether or not to use it even as they waited for the perfect moment to employ it.

At the same time, debate over the impending battle for the mainland raged. We constantly argued over whether the first troops would land in Kyushu or at the Kujūkuri Beach near Tokyo. After one of these debates a forty-year-old conscripted Korean labourer who had been listening in called me aside, his expression serious.

"What are you going to do if the Americans land?

"We'll grab bamboo spears and sacrifice ourselves, of course." I responded instantly. Then I put the same question to the horse-faced man. "What will the Koreans do?"

He thought for a moment before replying with a nod, "We Koreans will do the same."

Occasionally, a single B-29 would fly low over us, scattering leaflets as though to mock us. None of us picked up the leaflets, but we heard stories about how kids at other schools got dragged away by the military police for reading them. We heard that they were about something called the Potsdam Declaration, but the name didn't mean anything to us.

"Young master, I wonder what will really happen with this war," O-saki would sometimes ask with a sigh. She wasn't talking just to me but to the picture of her son as well. He had been killed in the war, and his picture—that of a young man with a boyish face, dressed in the uniform of a naval petty officer—hung in O-saki's quarters.

One day the lady stopped me in the corridor.

"Yoshio, your family—where have they evacuated to?"

"My father's hometown," I answered. "In Hiroshima."

"Hiroshima?" she asked, her brows furrowed. "In the city of Hiroshima?"

"No, on the outskirts, in the mountains."

"Oh, well, that's good then," the lady said, visibly relieved. The 'horrible' thing the lady hinted at on the night of the air raid took place the following day. On the sixth of August the atomic bomb was dropped.

On the night of the sixth I was on my way to the toilet and saw that the lady was in one of the rooms that was always locked. Candles burned on the Buddhist altar, and she clasped a rosary in her hands.

"My husband has died," she said in her usual, quiet voice, "in Manchuria."

The next day, the seventh of August, the Soviet Union joined the war against Japan. I also remember it as the day when I found a soiled bandage in the corridor. O-saki must have dropped it, and in addition to the blood and pus there were a number of hairs—thick and brown like those of an animal—stuck to it.

The night of the thirteenth arrived. That evening the lady called O-saki and me into her parlour, which was quite unusual for her. Her eyes were red and swollen in the flickering light of the candles, as though from crying.

"O-saki, Yoshio," she said, her voice slightly thick with emotion, "the war is over. Japan has lost."

I felt a jolt of anger and glared at the lady.

"O-saki, thank you for everything you have done. You are welcome to stay in the house, but the child will not need your assistance any more. Yoshio, you may stay here too, but your father will be coming for you soon."

The lady turned her face into the shadows and whispered, "The child will not live long, not now that Japan has lost...."

"How do you know we've lost," I shouted. "It's a lie! The government hasn't said anything, has it? The military is telling us to prepare ourselves for the sacrifice of a hundred million souls, isn't it! Japan won't lose. People who talk about defeat are unpatriotic! Traitors!"

"The child told me. From tomorrow, there will be no more bombings because we have lost," the lady said quietly, still looking into the shadows, "though the Emperor won't announce it until the day after tomorrow."

I fled from the room. *The old bitch! Japan lose? Never! Unthinkable!* I shouted in my mind. Filled with rage I was practically running down the corridor when I suddenly froze in my tracks. The sound of weeping came down from the dark hallway on the second floor. The cries were much sharper than usual and went on and on. It was as though the owner of the voice was writhing in agony, unable to endure the sorrow and torment of separation.

AS YOU KNOW, things turned out precisely as the lady had predicted. We didn't feel the slightest shock when we heard His Imperial Majesty's voice. The only thing that surprised us was the voice itself, which we were hearing for the first time. It was high-pitched and nasal, and we had a difficult time figuring out what he was saying. It took quite a while for it all to sink in, and even after we heard the broadcast we all returned to our work. But eventually, like water poured onto sand, the voice telling us that Japan had lost soaked into each and every one of us, and the factory grew quieter and quieter. At three o'clock all sound came to a stop and everyone looked out at the sky with slightly foolish expressions on their faces. People gathered together and sat in small groups. Some yawned or scratched their heads, looking lost as a result of the sudden inactivity.

I returned to the estate in something of a daze. But as I sat in the detached room I was suddenly filled with an inexplicable sense of rage and resentment. I ripped my military drill book into pieces and threw my hat on the ground. I wanted to break and destroy everything in sight. I wanted to grab someone, a target onto whom I could vent all the indescribable misery welling up in me.

I jumped up and ran to the kitchen. I called for O-saki. No response. Thinking I would get back at the old lady who had made the damned prediction in the first place, I ran down the long corridors, my feet pounding loudly as I went. As I went down the corridor I pulled the tightly shut doors open one after another, yanking each of them back with a crash. But the lady was nowhere to be found. The deserted estate fell back into serene silence. No, it wasn't completely deserted. There was still 'the child.' Once again the thin, desperate cries made their way down from the second floor. I suddenly decided that I would have a look at the child the lady called her guardian spirit. Already I was demonstrating the first signs of the sacrilegious impulse that would plague me in later years. *It's because of her prediction,* I thought, *that Japan lost.*

I sprinted up the stairs to the second floor. *I'll see the girl for myself, the sick girl she has been trying so hard to keep secret.* The hesitant curiosity that had possessed me since I arrived at the estate had been awakened by this sacrilegious impulse and tinged with a desire for revenge. It exploded within me. I ran down the U-shaped corridor to the last room on the second floor and threw open the door from which the cries emerged.

What I saw behind that door, wearing the long-sleeved, delicately patterned crimson kimono of a young girl, sitting atop a damask cushion, eyes bloodshot and swollen from weeping was... an ox! Though it had the body of a thirteen or fourteen year-old girl, the face was that of an ox. Two horns sprouted from its forehead, its nose protruded and its face was covered with brown, bristly fur. It had the lugubrious eyes of a ruminant, brimming with a gentle pathos. The sound of a young girl weeping faintly as though she might vanish entirely came from its mouth. Bandages soaked with blood and pus were wrapped thickly around the base of one of the horns, around its upper arms and, with the exception of the fingers, around the hands that covered its face. The smell of the bandages and the animal scent washed over me. My eyes went wide and I stood rooted to the spot in front of the beast not daring even to breathe.

"So you have seen her," an icy voice sounded from behind me. It was the lady, sliding the door closed with a snap. Her face was hard and frozen, like a Noh mask. But in the shadows of her expression I thought I saw a flash of anguish.

"You have finally seen her. The child... the child is a *kudan*."

SO THAT WAS a *kudan*. According to the lady, the word "*kudan*" was written using the Chinese characters for "person" and "ox." *Kudan*, the lady told me, were born from time to time, but their existence was usually concealed by their parents. What's more, *kudan* have the ability to predict the future. The lady, thought to be barren, had given birth to just one child—this child. She had horns at birth, and as time passed they grew longer and longer. As her horns grew, her face also transformed into that of an ox. There is plenty of medical data on people born with horns, cases in which the skin becomes tough and malformed or the bones themselves become twisted. In the old days, she said, such people would probably have been feared as demons. But a *kudan*, she said, was altogether different. A *kudan* was a monster from its very core, and it possessed supernatural powers. Perhaps they are like the Minotaurs of the Greek myths, from the Isle of Crete. The birth of a *kudan* is a harbinger of some great, epochal calamity. And when that calamity strikes, the *kudan* dies. But while the *kudan* lives, it can predict everything related to the terrible event.

The lady was very insistent that I keep all of this—that I had seen the *kudan* and everything else she told me—strictly secret. If I didn't, she said, misfortune would befall my house as well. So, all this time I have never said a word about it. I kept it secret even from O-saki. Yet now, twenty-two years later, I have no choice but to make my story public. In doing so I hope to gather whatever scraps of information I can about *kudan* from my readers. Does anyone know anything about *kudan*? Does anyone know what was in that thick, muddy soup? Is the saying that "Whoever sees a *kudan* will give birth to a *kudan*" really true? I'm making this story public because I'm at my wit's end. My first child—our daughter—was born with horns! Is this, as I fear, the harbinger of yet another terrible catastrophe to come?

The Clock Tower of Yon

猫の泉（Neko no izumi）

Hikage Jōkichi（1961）

日影丈吉

English translation by Rossa O'Muireartaigh

– 1 –

I CANNOT REMEMBER what month it was when I travelled to the town of Yon. I am too lazy to take notes on my travels, so I have forgotten many things. I do remember that I had a Rolleicord camera around my neck and that I walked around carrying my jacket. But it was not summer. In fact, connecting these images with other memories, I know that it was winter.

I had a plan to hold a modest exhibition after returning to Japan, and so I had been taking a lot of photographs. I had left Paris and its sleety skies and was touring *le Midi* region. After photographing Marseille Port I got on a train to Nice.

Nice, Cannes, and Monte Carlo are all famous wintering grounds everyone seems to want to go to. But I wasn't so keen on these places myself. Such places do not pay much heed to the solitary and penniless traveler. There was nothing much to be gained there. It would have been nice to have the passion to photograph the *beau monde* of these cities, but I had no inclination to photograph the bare backs of fashionable women.

I was mostly a landscape photographer, or, failing that, an animal photographer. I am not good with people, and this has prevented me from photographing them professionally. If I were ever to find someone I wanted to photograph I have no doubt that my legs would tremble so much I wouldn't be able to even point the lens properly.

Basically I was scared of people. Why had I wanted to become a photographer? It was not because I thought I would be successful at it or even be able to do it. It was, to put it succinctly, because I felt comfortable looking at existence through my small camera. Perhaps that was why. Or perhaps I was searching for something through the mechanical eye of my camera—the non-human things that infiltrate the apertures of society and fill them in without us noticing them; or to put it another way, those things whose nature we do not notice as we infiltrate and fill the fissures of their existence.

This might all sound rather pompous, but really I was quite apathetic about my motives. It is just to say that if someone at the time were to have pointed at my camera and said, "You won't see anything looking through that camera. There is nothing more than that which exists before you, or rather in your field of vision," I would not have disagreed, but I would have still kept a stubborn smile on my face.

I must have had something approximating self-confidence, although, alas, I am not so sure now. At the time I believed that my camera could erase metaphysical problems from my field of vision.

Very few of my photographs seemed to capture what I wanted. My pictures were filled with bland hills of heather, and villages of brick and plaster houses clustered into a single mass. To others they would probably have looked like run-of-the-mill photographs with none of the photographer's conceptualizations manifest.

Unfortunately, even I, looking back, do not have any way of proving that at the time I was seeing with my camera, which is invisible to others. When I take out the two or three works that still remain and look at them, I have no idea what was so interesting that I was trying to capture. All I see now are mediocre, amateur snaps. Even so, I do not feel that what I so firmly believed then was complete nonsense. The methodology I believed in at that time was, at its simplest, one of gazing upon two or three fragments in isolation, a methodology that cannot be expressed in photographs.

Either way, I did have a particular concept or, to be more accurate, methodology in mind. I truly believed that I could make something of this methodology, and it was in pursuit of this goal that I scheduled my travel in those days.

Because of that I shunned snapping my shutter in those locations thronged with people in scenes that could be termed *rendezvous*. I had not planned to go to the Riviera but to head to Arles, a town with Roman ruins, and the marshes of the Rhône estuary, which better suited my purposes.

However, as it turned out I was going to have to skip Arles and content myself with only a part of the Rhône estuary. This was all because just before I was leaving Paris an acquaintance had pressed me into agreeing to meet a certain man in Nice. The man was Japanese, the same as myself, and my acquaintance. He was a highly regarded, much commended university professor, and I was asked to take a message to him.

The message was an invitation for him to come to Paris some month soon. A letter, of course, would have sufficed, but my acquaintance insisted that a letter was out of the question. He was quite adamant that since I was travelling in the region I should meet up with this professor and persuade him face to face to come up to Paris. So strongly did he urge me that I felt obliged to do so.

Timid person that I am, I always regret taking on tasks like this. And once agreeing to do such favors, I end up regarding them as unavoidable obligations to the extent that I could not relax until they have been carried out.

I went to Nice on the date arranged by my Paris acquaintance and sought out the Hotel La Jetée where the professor was supposed to be staying. I was told a telegram had been sent to the hotel saying when I would be coming and stating that my intentions were to engage in casual chat. So I did not feel apprehensive about visiting. But the professor, it turned out, was no longer staying at the hotel. The *gérant* of the hotel told me he had left two days before.

The scholar had actually stayed there, and my Paris acquaintance had actually sent a telegram. But this renowned scholar, unlike me, was perhaps on a tight schedule and probably felt that my schedule and that of my Paris acquaintance were of little consequence.

It was not my first encounter with this kind of nonsense. I wasn't surprised or angry. In fact, on second thought I was delighted not to have the bother of meeting the professor. I left the plush hotel straight away and strolled along the shore. I was planning to look for a café in the back streets, drink some cheap Italian wine, and consider my options.

After a while I sat down on a bench and gazed at the sea. Seen from this shore it was too tame to tempt my camera, but I stayed ensconced in the *le Midi* sunshine with its power to allure one to linger till sunset. As I sat there planning my next moves (to eat cabbage rolls and leave the city after sunset), I suddenly realized there was someone beside me trying to talk to me. A man with a high nose and the dark skin of a Moor had sat down next to me.

"Are you Portuguese?"

"No. I'm Japanese".

"Ah, Japan...."

Peering out through the glasses poised on his nose, the man's eyes narrowed as they searched my face. His own face resembled the poet Jean Moréas[1] as he appears in *The Book of Masks* by Gourmont[2].

"Are you Greek?"

"No. I'm from Menton. I came here to buy fishing tackle. I'm just waiting for the train to go home. Are you staying here?"

"I'm just thinking about whether to go back to Paris or go to Arles."

"Are you going to Arles for sightseeing?"

"Yes. There're some Roman ruins there."

1. Jean Moréas: A Greek francophone poet and writer (1856–1910).

2. Remy de Gourmont: French poet and writer (1858–1915).

"Roman ruins? Well then, wouldn't you be better off going to Italy, the land of Rome itself?"

I knew that I could not explain my feelings to this man and that I had no obligation to do so. But his mocking smile was provoking so I said as though to justify myself, "I want to photograph the Alyscamps."

"The Alyscamps?"

The man pondered this for a moment and then pointing at my Rolleicord, this time with a slight air of respect, said, "Ah, yes. The Roman burial ground. Of course. I take it you're a student of ancient history." He continued. "Speaking of burial grounds, there's a town deep in these mountains that has one. It's called Yon."

"Yon? I've never heard of it."

"It's quite a bit beyond Vence, deep in the mountains. Not many people go there. In fact, I've never been there myself. I heard about it from someone. It's a tiny town in the valley. It was a fortress during the time of the Kingdom of Arles. Now it's a well preserved medieval town."

"It sounds like a strange place," I said, my interest aroused.

The man, who resembled so much the Athens-born poet, Ioannis Papadiamantopoulos[3], touched his glasses and nodded.

"The people living there are strange as well. They till the land up in the mountains and herd mountain sheep. They don't mix with outsiders. They're self-sufficient, stuck up there in the valley."

"Do they have their own particular customs?"

"Well, that I don't know. As far as I know the only man who has been there is the one who told me about it. And he was a strange man."

"You say 'he *was*.' Is he dead now?"

---

3. Ioannis Papadiamantopoulos is the real name of the writer Jean Moréas.

"About three years ago he went missing. He lived outside Menton and worked as a trader.... In fact, I had no idea such a town existed in France until I heard about it from that man."

"Whereabouts is it?"

"I think it's somewhere between Alpes-Maritimes, Basses-Alpes and Var."

"How do you get there?"

"Well. I can safely say that transport wouldn't be too convenient. No one comes out of that town, or rather village. I haven't really heard of anyone ever going there. You wouldn't be thinking of going there yourself, would you?"

The man looked at me with concern as I sat in silence.

"I'd like to go there if I could get there. Did you hear any other strange things about the town?"

"Well, let me see."

He took off his glasses and, still looking at me anxiously, stroked his chin.

"Oh, yes. There are Tibetan cats there. They are strays. No, hang on. Are there Tibetan cats there? Am I confusing things?"

The man stared at me looking concerned.

"My memory is a bit vague. I'm not lying or trying to make fun of a foreigner, but it was quite a long time ago, and the man I heard it from was very odd. I only remembered about it just now. The more I tell you about it the more I start to disbelieve it myself."

Seeming timid now, the man looked around restlessly.

"The man might have been fooling me. When you think about it, I've never heard of Yon apart from this man's story. If you want to see burial grounds, you're definitely better off going to Arles."

Looking embarrassed, the man stood up saying that it was time for his train. He put his glasses back on and rushed off. I stayed on the bench a while longer in a state of utter amazement.

Living together with Tibetan cats in a medieval town with ancient ruins? What could the plain people of this town be like? How do they spend their days? That alone would made it the perfect destination for taking photographs. But then again, Yon probably doesn't exist. That trader who disappeared from Menton about three years ago was probably a bit strange in the head. The man was probably just spouting nonsense. Those were the thoughts going through my mind.

I stood up and went for something to eat. I found a small restaurant and asked a large man in a cook's uniform who seemed to be the owner if he had ever heard of Yon. An old man facing the counter holding a Milanese pepper mill in one hand asked me to repeat the name again and again. It seemed he hadn't heard it properly due to my strong accent. Eventually, as he turned the pepper mill using both hands to operate it, he said, "I was born in Lespelle, but I've never heard of a town called Yon in these parts."

After my dinner I got on a bus to Vence. My idea was that if no one in Vence knew where Yon was, I would just take photos of the old towns in the surrounding mountains and then head back to Paris. Arriving in Vence, I found a small room to stay in.

The young *fille de chambre* had never heard of Yon. The old lady at the reception desk had heard the name but couldn't remember anything about it. Still, just because these people had never heard of Yon didn't mean that it didn't exist. While it still had the remnants of an old town it was now only a small village and so it was quite natural that people generally wouldn't remember it, even if it was not very far away.

I lay on the bed in my austere lodgings—I was very much the thrifty traveler in those days—and with a feeling of great excitement began to imagine Yon, a medieval town of stone, brick and mortar with frugal folk and feral felines. It was full of the kind of material I had been searching for. Just the thought of it made my heart race with excitement. Arles was nothing compared to this. It was all I needed to create my first masterpieces.

Photos of the group life of stray cats and dogs are clichéd when done badly, but I had taken a fair number of them, as such material very much expressed my artistic intentions. Still, I had yet to find a gathering that suited my purposes.

During this trip I had been able to take photos of a pack of dogs I had encountered unexpectedly on the sand banks of the Rhône delta. There were around twenty of them. I don't think I really succeeded in photographing them properly as there was quite a large bunch of them and I was too close. Any closer and I could have been bitten to death. So just the thought of this old town with its wild cats was enough to trigger a want in me to go photograph it.

By the time I left my hotel the next morning, I was obsessed with Yon. But where was it to be found? I took a coarsely folded motoring map from my bag and perused it intently looking for a town of that name, but I could not find it. In two or three places in the town I asked some men who looked as though they might know where it was but to no avail. No one seemed to know.

However, an old man lazing in the sun next to an open-air bookshop said, "If you're looking for a region between the departments of Var and Basses-Alpes, then it would be upstream of the Loup and Lane rivers. I don't know about any town called Yon, but I think you'll find the lay of the land to be as you say in that area, my Chinese friend."

I made up my mind then to go to Grasse. If I could not find Yon from there I would go back to Paris. Travelling through the region, I felt as if I were being pulled along by something outside myself and felt anxious that I might lose the power of this extraneous force. My mind was a blank, and I could not take in anything of the views along the way.

It was then that I remembered I had neglected to post a letter I had written to my acquaintance in Paris. I rushed off the bus, but with the obsessive trance as I was in I cannot remember if it was the town of Le Bar or Châteauneuf or some other town or village. As I ran into the post office in front of the bus stop, I realized something I should have thought of before—that the very function of a post office is to connect people from different locations and to know the names of places. Why hadn't I thought of going into a post office before?

The postal clerk was a middle-aged man. I do not remember his face, not because the small post office was so dark but because I was so overjoyed to finally meet someone who had heard of Yon. All other details of the scene escape me now. The clerk peered over the counter and said, "This post office has never handled any post for Yon. But, yes, there is definitely a town of that name. I haven't been there myself, but I have an idea how to get there."

The clerk with his tenebrous visage told me the route, remarking that he only vaguely knew the way. He anticipated that the transport would be lacking, but I was determined to surmount such difficulties. I spent no time in Grasse but headed straight to Saint-Vallier. From there I continued on to the regions upstream of the Loup River. It was a difficult journey, indeed a journey of an archaic quality involving the use at one point of an ancient-looking horse cart.

– 2 –

AS EXPECTED, THE journey was arduous. It reached a point where I could no longer use any form of transport, so I climbed the rest of the long path on my own. Even at that point, coming as far as I had, I was still haunted by doubts about whether the town of Yon existed at all. All was silent amid the mountains, and it seemed as though no one would be living all the way up there.

But indeed there was a town. A fortress from the days of the Kingdom of Arles had been built on the flat mountaintop and had collapsed some centuries previous. In its place were meager fields of tillage. Away from the fields stood lines of old olive trees, and underneath them lay Roman period sarcophagi. There were six of them lying to the left and the right. The line of trees spread along the slope like the curved shape of a saddle. From the top of the slope a path led down to a town that could be seen in the valley below. Trees lined the path as though forming a gateway to the town.

There could well have been a gate there when it was a fortress. The splendor of the valley town made me think so. Going down that slope it was as though I was entering a dream.

The road ended at a small but distinctive plaza. On the left-hand side of the plaza stood a building with a tall clock tower that seemed to be the town hall. It extended back to the base of the mountain behind it. In front was a small church with a small bell tower, and on the right was a plain but large and sturdy two-story building. These three buildings formed the perimeter of the plaza. Behind the church, rows of uniform homes spread out, filling the valley. It was a small but quite splendid town.

I looked around and entered the plaza. There was no one around. The town was deserted.

The door to the entrance of the building on the left was firmly shut. Above the door was what seemed to be a town crest. It had a motif showing a shield inside of which was what appeared to be a wolf with teeth shaped like a saw. Written on the crest was "Yon Town Hall." Feeling as though I was moving in a dream, I walked up the stone steps of the entrance and pushed on the door.

The door creaked open—the first sound, apart from my own footsteps, I had heard in Yon.

"*Personne?* (Anyone....)" I called out.

My voice echoed in the high-ceilinged hall. One side of a double door opened, and a small man wearing a hood emerged. When he saw my face he froze and stared at me, wide-eyed. He was a seemingly ageless man with eyes like a bird.

"Well, who might you be?" he asked.

"I am Japanese, and I have come from Paris. I came here after touring Nice."

I showed him my passport. He stamped his feet, out of astonishment it would seem, and cried out, "*Étranger! Vraiment étranger!* (A foreigner! Real foreigner!)"

Still holding my passport, with the nimbleness of a mouse he scampered back behind the door from which he had emerged. His murine agility astonished me. The same door opened again, and a fat, reddish face peaked out. The face disappeared again for an instant before the whole person emerged. He was a short, fat man. Outlandish curls hung down to his shoulders from what seemed to be a wig. The man with the hood popped out from behind him and said,

"*Monsieur le Maire* (Mayor), this is the Japanese man."

The man in the hood, who seemed to be the town clerk, leafed through my passport, which he still held in his hands. He suddenly stretched out both hands and said,

"What do you think, Mr. Mayor? It's a real foreigner."

"Be quiet, you," said the mayor, pompously chastising the town clerk, keeping his beady eyes fixed on me all the while.

"What is your purpose in coming here?"

"To take photographs." I raised the camera that hung around my neck. "I heard that there are Tibetan cats here, so I came to photograph them. I'm a photographer, and I photograph animals."

The mayor didn't seem to take in everything I said. He searched my face in wonder. The town clerk remained restless. He tugged the mayor's collar and whispered something to him and then the two of them hastily surrounded me, ushered me into a room and then disappeared. They scurried and scampered about the place—like a fat mouse and a thin mouse.

I hesitantly placed a glass of wine the town clerk had poured for me to my lips. It was a full-bodied wine like a Burgundy. When I had drunk half of it, the church bells began to ring and the sounds of people outside could be heard. I put the glass down and went out into the front hall. The door had been left open, and I could see three men standing in the middle of the plaza: the mayor, the town clerk and another man with a bluish face wearing clothing like a Jesuit monk's robes.

I went outside and found that there were people standing all around the plaza, all of them staring at me. Old people, young people, children. There were about thirty in all, including babies in their mother's arms. All of them were small-built and looked the epitome of dogged mountain people.

When the three men noticed me, they walked towards me with great ceremony, the mayor in the lead. Standing at the bottom of the steps, the mayor looked up at me and spreading his arms announced with the solemnity of an official declaration, "*Monsieur Japonais*, I welcome you as the thirtieth visitor to our town."

I had not expected this kind of treatment. I was very surprised and looked around me.

The mayor smiled, the town clerk blinked his eyes with an absent expression, and the monk looked at me with sad eyes. The people standing around the square watched me with the lugubrious look of mice peeking out from a hole.

I was then taken to the other building, the large three-story edifice facing the town hall. Inside it looked like an inn, but with no signs of anyone dwelling there. People were working busily in the downstairs hall, which contained an old fireplace. It seemed as though they had been hastily assembled for the task. An upstairs room had also been prepared in a rush for me. But it was clean, and I surmised that I was in a civic guesthouse of some kind that was usually vacant.

After a while the three men came to see me again.

"We have a request, *monsieur*," the mayor said in a portentous manner.

"The fact is there is a custom in our town that every tenth traveler who comes here tells the town's fortune for us, and you are our thirtieth visitor."

"But I can't prophesy," I said, surprised.

"This is not about prophesying. It's just that only every tenth traveler understands the meaning of its words, so we want you to listen to them."

"Whose words?"

"It's not a human. It's that!"

The mayor wheeled around and pointed through the window of the inn at the clock tower that loomed above.

"The town hall was built three hundred years ago. It is the most recent addition to this town, along with this inn. Since then, there has been a custom of listening to the town's fortune at that big clock tower. It started when the tenth visitor to the town heard the grinding noise the clock makes before it strikes the hour and understood the meaning of the prophecy."

"So, are you saying that in the space of three hundred years this town has only had thirty visitors?" I asked, astonished yet again.

"There is nothing surprising about that. This town has been most secluded for many years. When we were still powerful, no outsiders got past the gates of the town. Even now, no one comes into the mountains this far."

"Did a trader come here from Menton about three years ago?"

The mayor turned to the town clerk and glared at him. It seemed that the mayor knew but it was not his place to say. The town clerk quickly nodded and answered for the mayor.

"Yes, yes, he came. According to the town records, he was the twenty-ninth visitor. Of course I remember him even without the records."

"So, what exactly should I do?" I asked, perplexed.

"Five minutes before the hour go up there and listen to the grinding sound the big clock makes," the mayor replied.

"But I don't know if I can do that."

"According to legend you had the ability as soon as you set out to come here. Please try."

The priest, who had been quiet until then, suddenly spoke up. "According to the records, the prophecy heard by the tenth visitor was wonderful. But the prophecy heard by the twentieth visitor was unlucky. The town's fortune always turns out as the prophecy says. This time perhaps we'll hear a good prophecy."

Hearing that, I realized that what they were asking me to do was not necessarily a pleasant task. I was hesitant, but I could not leave.

"All right. I'll try, but I don't know if it will work or not," I said. "In return, may I have your permission to see the town and take photographs?"

The three of them gathered by the window to ponder my entreaty. Eventually the mayor said, "Apart from when the clock strikes, you are free to walk around the town. But you must not speak to the townspeople. They don't have the knowledge to converse with a stranger."

The mayor shrugged his shoulders, said they would be back to get me before the clock struck, and then left, followed by the other two.

It would be a long time until sunset. I rested awhile in my musty room. Soon the town clerk came, alone this time. He led me up to the clock tower. The entrance to the base of the tower was tucked away near the door to the entrance hall. Climbing the steep steps was a strain.

We went into a passageway behind the big clock. The town clerk had me sit in a chair and signaled me to listen carefully. Then, just before the clock struck the hour, a formidable sound rose up like a throaty wheeze. The first gasps seemed to be just tuning up. They were followed by a continuous growling sound and finally, with a loud din that made me want to plug my ears, the hour was struck.

The town clerk cast me a sidelong glance, but I just shook my head.

He then said, with a tone of resignation, "Well, once is probably not enough."

After we descended, the town clerk reported to the mayor, who had been waiting below. I promised them I would go up again in an hour's time and with that went out into the plaza. There was no one around. Everyone seemed to have gone home.

I wondered why they were so surprisingly unconcerned for the fate of their town. Perhaps I was partaking in nothing more than an old ritual passed down through the ages and even these mountain people were not taking the legends seriously. I began to feel that the whole thing was ridiculous.

I cut across the plaza to return to the inn, but something in the center of the plaza to my side, like a large stone water basin, caught my attention. When I looked at it carefully, I saw it to be the remains of a fountain. Once it had probably gushed with water, but the course of the groundwater must have shifted at some point leaving just this bone-dry stone basin with its exposed base.

Just then one of the many statues around the rim of the basin suddenly moved. I jumped. These were not sandstone statues as I had thought. Amber eyes flicked open and stared at me. They were cats! Three or four large grey cats, of a type the French call *chat-bleu,* lazing around the fountain.

I was elated. I lifted up the camera hanging from my neck (I always had my camera when outside) and went to snap them. But it was no good. In an instant the cats turned around and raced away towards the town hall, disappearing from sight.

I was disappointed, but I was sure there would be other opportunities. The cats were bound to return to this dried-out fountain, their napping spot. The next time I would be more subtle. I lingered in the plaza for a bit and then decided to try the church.

The church was slightly different from the regular Gothic-Roman style one frequently sees in the south of France. It had none of the usual brightness but instead stood gloomy and cheerless. Entering the church, I was surprised to find it so unkempt. I wondered if the town had any believers at all. The crucifix at the center of the altar at least was not covered in dust, but it was a crude and oversized construction unsuited to such a small church. Its incongruity was creepy.

I felt repelled by the place and decided to leave at once. At that moment I saw the priest stand up from beside the altar. It looked as though he had been on his knees praying. His face was as pale as a ghost.

"Did the big clock say anything," he asked with concern.

"No, nothing I could understand. It just made a mechanical kind of noise."

"It's awful. The people here don't believe in God. They want to listen to the prophecy of the clock. I can't get them to return to the faith."

"Do they have no religion? And what happened to this church?"

"There are only non-believers now. This church is a relic of the past."

"But surely not everyone in a town of this size is a non-believer?"

"A town of this size? Are you saying that because of the long, narrow street you see behind the square? "

"Yes. However small it is, it's amazing to find such a fine town here in the middle of the mountains."

"It was a splendid town long ago. There were hundreds of people living here. Now it's only a shell of its former self. The people have either died or gone away. Only a handful of the houses here are habitable. The rest are just abandoned ruins."

"That's unbelievable."

"Calling this a 'town' is a just an old habit. Even referring to it as a 'village' is an exaggeration. It's just a small hamlet. You saw the people gathered at the plaza, didn't you? That is almost everyone in this town. It can hardly be called a town with just forty people living in it."

"But there's such a lovely town hall and everything."

"There are only two people there, the mayor and the town clerk. They are not needed to govern a hamlet of forty people. All they do is look after the clock— keep it oiled, tighten the screws."

I stared at the priest, stunned.

"If there are so few here, do I still have to follow this town tradition and interpret this bizarre prophecy?"

"Unless you leave this town right now you'll certainly have to. You'll be like me, a priest administering to an empty church."

A hideous smile rose to the priest's lips.

– 3 –

THE CATS AROUND the fountain had increased to five or six, but again I failed to photograph them. I had made up my mind to leave this eerie town the next day, but I was determined to take photographs that would capture the lives of these cats before going.

For a second time I was brought to listen to the bell chime, but again I failed to hear a prophecy, which seemed perfectly normal to me. The mayor, however, peeved at my lack of supernatural powers, glowered, "Well, you really don't hear much, do you?"

"All I hear is GRUU-LU-LU"

"I don't know what that is. It's just noise."

One hour later, I climbed up the clock tower a third time. The sun was hidden behind a ridge, leaving the hamlet completely covered by its shadow. From this vantage point, the town did seem to consist of uninhabited houses. Although it was still daytime, the town slumbered in complete but curious silence.

I sat on the chair behind the clock feeling forlorn, thinking that were I to continue doing this it was unlikely that these two self-appointed officials, with their loyalty to their forefathers' conventions, would let me leave the next day. The town clerk monitored me as before, standing beside me to offer encouragement.

Feeling cornered, I listened even more intently than before. It gave its grinding growl once more.

Then, with its next mechanical expiration, I heard the clock say, "*Vas-t'en! Jeune homme!* (Go away! Young man!) *Déluge! L'horloge!* (Floods! The clock!)"

I heard it distinctly. I turned to the town clerk to report, but I stopped myself and instead just shook my head.

Of course, if I had told him what I had just heard I would have fulfilled my duties. They would have been free to interpret what the clock said as they pleased, and I would have been free to go. But I hesitated to say something I did not believe myself. I reckoned instead that the clock's clamoring must have been somehow distorted by my sense of being trapped.

"Go away, young man!" I was in fact eager to depart this valley. "Floods!" This did not make sense in the middle of these mountains. There was no river flowing here. The fountain was dry. The people of the town had to pump up water from behind the mountains. "The clock!" It was right in front of me.

In other words, my mind was in tune with the chiming of the clock, and my own thoughts were randomly resonating back to me. Feeling deflated, I descended the clock tower's narrow stairs.

The mayor looked at me like I was an imbecile and said, "The sun is about to go down. Let's try again tomorrow."

I went back to my lodgings. The woman charged with looking after me fed me a tasteless supper she had cooked for me. After a while I went to bed, but I could not sleep.

Vas-t'en! Jeune homme! (Go away! Young man!) *Déluge! L'horloge!* (Floods! The clock!): The sound of the clock kept ringing in my ears like a chant. What did it mean? My sleepless mind failed to make any sense of it all.

I nodded off for a moment with exhaustion but soon woke up again. There was not a sound to be heard in this old building where I slept or from the plaza outside. When the woman on duty left I was completely alone in the large old inn. The thought of this made me perk up.

I got out of bed and looked out the window. A large moon had climbed to its zenith with a brightness that lit up every part of the plaza. I could see some movement at the edge of the dried-up fountain. It was the cats. There were more of them now, perhaps about ten. They were pattering around the edge of the fountain with a blue shine undulating across their fur.

In the moonlight, I could clearly see the numbers on the big clock. It was near midnight. I quickly dressed, slung my Rolleicord camera over my neck and went downstairs and out into the plaza. In the silence of this small valley town of just forty peasants with its air of medieval solemnity I could sense that it was mostly ruins.

There were more cats than I had thought, twenty, maybe thirty of them. I stood still and trembled at the sight of so many. They were clustered around the stone edge of the fountain. Some were strolling among the crowd. The light of the moon, shining deep blue, revealed the tough but calm composure of these feral cats.

This time they did not run away when I aimed my camera. As I approached the fountain, they repositioned themselves so that they appeared to be seated in a circle around me. Maybe it was my imagination, but I felt that they were staring at me as though they wanted to ask me something.

Even with such a bright moon it was impossible to take photos. This clowder before me did seem a tad creepy. Though they were wild, they were quiet, and I did not feel they meant me any harm. Either way it seemed better to be there than to be alone in that old inn.

Perhaps I could not bear the loneliness. Since coming to this town, those three strange men were the only human voices I had heard speak to me. The other villagers were as quiet as mutes. In contrast, I felt an affinity with these cats, who probably numbered as many as the townspeople.

Compared to the people living in this valley, the cats had strong physiques with healthy-looking fur. It was proof that whatever they were eating was nutritious. I had no need to fear they would eat me alive. And they presented wonderful subjects for my camera.

There were many empty houses in this town, so the cats were no doubt easily able to secure a place to live. I intended to discover their abode and to photograph their environs when the sun came up. With this in mind, I planned to stay beside them for the evening and monitor them.

There were tomcats among the group. Two or three of them crawled along the edge of the stone fountain and with faltering steps dropped down onto the bottom. One of them had begun this, and the rest had followed. After a while I could hear a gurgling noise.

I looked into the bottom of the fountain and saw that some water had accumulated there. In the moonlight it shone the color of a crushed sapphire. I presumed that some water emerged there each evening.

I sat on the edge of the fountain and watched the cats as they sat or sprawled around me. Being with them, I could share my loneliness. Then from above the town hall clock croaked into action and struck twelve o'clock.

After the last stroke of the clock, I then returned to staring at the cats. But the strange feeling I had about them returned. They were all looking at me. The one that had been lying down had sat up. It seemed as though they were expecting something from me.

"What? Do you also want to know the prophecy of the clock?" I mumbled inadvertently with a wry smile. Then I paled with the realization, amazing though it was, that that was indeed what the cats wanted.

"All right, I suppose I won't feel guilty just telling you. But this is only what I think it said. The clock said, 'Go away, young man! Floods! The clock!'"

I may well have been making it up, but I did feel a sense of apprehension that I had, in fact, been the recipient of some kind of revelation. It seemed as though the words had forced themselves out of my mouth. While it was never my intention to acquire supernatural powers, anyone can become strange in a strange situation.

After I made my pronouncement, one of the cats peered up into the sky where the moon shone and yowled. Then she turned around and started making her way to the town hall. The other cats followed. In single file they marched up to the porch of the town hall.

I stood up, quite astounded by the sight. I assumed they were going off to their homes, so I decided to go with them to spend the night in their company and wait for morning.

The cats disappeared inside a gap in the door to the entrance to the town hall, and I followed in after them. The lead cat was already climbing the stairs to the clock tower.

Eventually the column of cats, with me following behind, reached the top of the clock tower. I sat down on the chair in the corridor behind the clock. The cats stretched themselves out all along the corridor to the top of the stairs. Two or three tomcats jumped onto my lap, and I cuddled and stroked them. I was not afraid of these Tibetan cats now. The corridor was illuminated by the moonlight shining in through the window. All was silent.

It was my first chance to relax since coming to the town. Perhaps it was because of my easy-going nature, but I was not irritated by the intrusive click-clack noise from the clock.

At one point I was awakened by the chiming of the clock. I stretched and looked out the window and saw part of the plaza and the fountain basin now brimming with water shining blue in the moonlight. Apart from that there was nothing else out of the ordinary. Then I fell back into a sleep that lasted until dawn.

While I was still in that slumber I sensed a sound like some kind of earthly shudder, and I felt the clock tower shake slightly. But I was so exhausted after walking the mountain path and going up and down the stairs all day that I assumed I was having a bad dream and kept my eyes shut.

When I did open my eyes it was morning. And—to my regret—there was not one single cat left in my company. I hurriedly bounded down the stairs.

Halfway down, the stairway was drenched and I had to take care not to slip and fall. I assumed that even with the clear moon, given the capricious nature of mountain weather, rain must have blown into the tower. But that was not what had happened.

The walls of the front hall on the lower floor were completely wet. Water dripped from the ceiling and had seeped into the crevices of the stone floor. Without stopping to ponder what might have happened, I darted out of the town hall.

Looking at the plaza it seemed as though there had been a torrential rainfall. The houses were soaked up to their ceilings, and there was water between the flagstones. I sensed that something horrendous had happened.

When the sun came up, the town was shrouded in mist. I almost screamed with fear. There was no sign of anyone about. Was there anyone left in the town?

I rushed around the town wanting to cry. I ran down the road beside the church, the road leading to the distant cliff and other lanes, but, because of the small scale of the town, I was soon back at the plaza.... Yon was empty. No signs of life remained.

Coincidence or not, the big clock's prophecy had been right. During the night, whatever the cause, a flash flood had struck, and the forty people of the town had been swept away in an instant. Or had they escaped behind the mountain just before the flood?

Either way, if they were still alive I didn't want them to see me. I couldn't face them. If my sense of rationality hadn't prevented me from telling them of the prophecy, even if it had been a coincidence, I could have saved them and their few belongings.

I made my way to my room in the old inn and picked up my bag, now full of muddy water. I quickly climbed the slope, glanced back at the burial ground below the line of torchwood trees and left Yon.

I have told only two or three people this story. When they heard it they asked, "Is that a true story? Did that really happen?"

Perhaps the reader shares the same doubts, but I must reply thus: I do no intend to lie, though I sometimes wonder myself if these things really did happen to me. Human memory is not consistent, and these events have no abode save my memory. Truth resides in the question of what your true self is. So there will be differences with the reality conceived by others no matter how objective and faithful a record we may keep.

The Mummy

木乃伊 (Miira)

Nakajima Atsushi (1942)

中島敦

English translation by Ruselle Meade

WHEN THE PERSIAN King Cambyses II, the son of Cyrus the Great and Cassandane, invaded Egypt, among his troops was an officer by the name of Pariscus whose ancestors, it is believed, hailed from the region of Bactria to the far east. Lengthy residence in the city did nothing to rid him of his provincial air, and he forever had the disposition of a particularly dreary peasant. His predilection for falling into reveries meant that, despite considerable professional advancement, he was often the subject of ridicule.

After the Persian army had crossed Arabia and were making their approach upon Egypt, Pariscus's abnormal behaviour began to attract the attention of his officers and subordinates. He was bewildered, transfixed by the unfamiliar surroundings. The thoughts in which he was immersed agitated him. He seemed to be troubled by an inability to recall something. When some prisoners of war from the Egyptian army were brought into the camp he overheard one of them speaking. He listened attentively for a moment with a strange look on his face. After a while he realised that he could understand what they were saying and mentioned this to the person beside him. Although he could not himself speak their language it seemed that, for some reason, he could understand it. Pariscus summoned a subordinate to find out if these men were indeed Egyptians. (The majority of the Egyptian army were actually Greeks and other mercenaries.) He replied in the affirmative. Pariscus became perplexed again and plunged into unsettled thought. He had never once, at least not until now, set foot in Egypt. Never had he had the merest association with any Egyptian. Even in the midst of the raging battle, Pariscus was alone in his thoughts.

The Persians pursued the defeated Egyptian army, and when they entered the ancient, white-walled city of Memphis Pariscus's depressive agitation became even more marked. Some thought he was on the brink of an epileptic fit. His colleagues who had mocked him earlier grew concerned. He stood in front of the obelisk outside the city of Memphis and mumbled as he read the hieroglyphics that had been carved onto its surface. Then, in a similar tone he translated for his companions the name of the king who had erected the monument as well as his exploits. The other commanders grew uneasy and glanced at each other. Pariscus himself was also extremely perplexed. No one (Pariscus included) had been aware of his knowledge of Egyptian history or language.

Shortly thereafter Pariscus's master, King Cambyses, grew violent and his mental state deteriorated. He forced Psammenitus, the Egyptian king, to drink the blood of a cow, and then killed him. Not content with this he sought to exact revenge on Amasis, Psammenitus's predecessor, intending to violate the corpse of the former king who had died half a year earlier. He took personal command of one of his troops and headed to the city of Sais where Amasis's mausoleum was located. Once in Sais he ordered his troops to find the king's burial place, to dig up his corpse, and to present it to him.

The Egyptians, having anticipated the likelihood of such reprisals, had cunningly hidden the mausoleum, so the Persian army had to expend much effort searching numerous gravesites both within and outside the city, examining them one by one.

Pariscus was amongst the troops looking for the king's corpse. While his fellow soldiers were obsessed with the thought of plundering untold treasures—the jewelry and the furnishings typically buried alongside Egyptian nobility—he alone was indifferent. His countenance remained dour as he proceeded from grave to grave. On occasion, one might have been able discern on his face an expression akin to a faint ray of sunlight penetrating an overcast sky, but no sooner would it disappear and he would lapse into his former solemn mood. It was as if there was inside him an irreconcilable tension caused by a constant struggle to make sense of something.

One afternoon, a few days after they had started their search, Pariscus found himself alone in an underground tomb. It appeared that he had become separated from his troops. He was completely disoriented. He had awoken to the realisation that he was indeed alone, in this old, dark tomb.

As his eyes became accustomed to the dimness, he could make out various sculptures and utensils that had been scattered about, and was impressed by the murals and embossed carvings around him. The lid of the coffin had been cast aside, and two or three heads of clay dolls had also fallen to the ground. It was clear that this was the aftermath of a pillaging by other Persian troops. The cold smell of old dust invaded his nose. In the recesses of the darkness he perceived a large statue of a hawk-headed god. It regarded him with a cold, piercing stare. On a mural close to him was a gloomy procession of gods with heads of outlandish beasts: jackals, crocodiles, blue herons, and the like. Amongst the procession was a large faceless, trunk-less eye from which sprouted long, thin arms and legs.

Pariscus lumbered on in a daze toward the back of the tomb but stumbled after five or six steps. He looked down to see that he had tripped over a mummy. Still in a daze he took the mummy up in his arms and rested it on the base of the statue of the god. The mummy looked like any of the many others he had seen over the past few days. As he was about to proceed he glanced at the mummy's face. A sensation—whether it was a hot or cold he did not know—pierced him to the spine. He was unable to avert his gaze from the mummy's face. It was as if there was a magnetism drawing him in. He could not move. He could not but look into his face.

He stood there transfixed for an eternity.

In that time there was an extremely unsettling transformation within him. The elements constituting his body started simmering and bubbling beneath his skin (just like the contents of the test tubes in which future chemists would conduct their experiments). After a while, the fomentation subsided leaving him completely transformed.

Pariscus was now in a state of complete peace. The root of his discomfort, a feeling not unlike the frustration of failing to recall the dreams of the preceding night's slumber, was now clear. It had now dawned on him why he had been so agitated since his arrival in Egypt. "Is this why?" He had, without realizing it, uttered these words out loud. "I am this mummy. This is certain."

When he said these words, the mummy's mood appeared to soften and the corners of its lips curved almost imperceptibly into a smile. Was light appearing from somewhere? The mummy's face alone was illuminated making it rise conspicuously from the gloominess surrounding it.

In an instant, like a brandishing of light tearing through darkness, memories of long-past lives shot back—memories of the time when his spirit resided within the body of this mummy. Sun rays scorching desert sands, the rustle of a breeze though a shade tree, fetid mud left behind by receding floodwaters, white-robed figures crossing bustling streets, the aroma of bath oils, the coldness of the stone on the knee during prayers in the fading light. These vivid memories sprang from the abyss to subsume him.

Had he been a priest in the Ptah temple? Perhaps, because although everything he had ever seen, touched or experienced had now been brought back to him, his own appearance from that time would not emerge into view.

Then, suddenly, he saw the despairing eyes of a bull he had once brought as a sacrifice before the gods. They resembled the eyes of someone he knew, someone who had been close to him. Yes. It was her. At once, her eyes, her face lightly dusted with powdered malachite, her slender body, her familiar gestures and her scent all became real to him. Oh, how he longed for her. Like a flamingo in a lake at dusk she cut a forlorn figure. Of this there was no doubt, she had been his wife.

Strangely, he could not remember names, not the name of a single person or place. Memories of shapes, colours, smells, and movements from some unknown time in the past would appear and fade away in the midst of a perverted silence.

He could no longer see the mummy. Had his spirit escaped from his body and entered that of the mummy?

Again, an image appeared. He was lying prostrate, incapacitated by a sweltering fever while his worried wife gazed upon him from his side. Behind them were others—old people and children, perhaps. He longed for a drink. When he moved his hand his wife gave him some water and he slipped back into slumber. When he awoke the fever had left him. With still sleepy eyes he could see that beside him his wife was crying. The old people behind them were crying too. Then quickly, the shadows of rain clouds darkened the surface of the lake, and a great dark shadow enveloped them. His eyes drifted downward into a slumber.

The memories of his past stopped abruptly. Then, there was nothing, just the darkness of hundreds of years of consciousness. When he snapped back to reality (that is to say, when he was back in the present) he was back to being a Persian soldier (after decades of life as a Persian soldier) with his own mummified body in front of him.

Although these bizarre visions had shaken him, he felt a sense of transparency. His spirit had been stretched taut like the ice on an arctic lake. Yet, he was still transfixed by the buried memories of his former life. Like the fluorescence of those blind fish in the oceans, the revelations revealed only the impenetrability of the surrounding darkness.

Then from the depth of this darkness his own mysterious figure from his previous life emerged.

The apparition of his former self stood facing the mummy in a dimly lit room. His previous self trembled with the realisation that the mummy in front of him was from a yet earlier life. They were in a similarly dim and cold room. And, there was the same musty smell. All of a sudden, his previous self realised that he too had had an even earlier existence....

He shivered. What was happening? What did this all mean? Was this revelation of his previous life not the same that his previous self had seen? And the same that the self before that had seen? Was he, like the infinite chain of images produced by multiple mirrors, always the same?

Goose bumps broke out all over his body. He tried to escape, but his legs would not function. He could not look away from the face of the mummy. He stood like a figure frozen in perpetuity facing the discoloured, dried-out corpse.

When the other Persian soldiers discovered Pariscus the following day he was lying on the ground holding the mummy stiffly in his embrace. He was nursed back to health but had grown insane. He was now a lunatic making incoherent pronouncements, but no longer was he speaking Persian. He could now speak only Egyptian.

Only Child

一人娘

Akiyama Ayuko (2002)

秋山亜由子

English translation by Stephen Carter
Graphics by Dorothy Gambrell

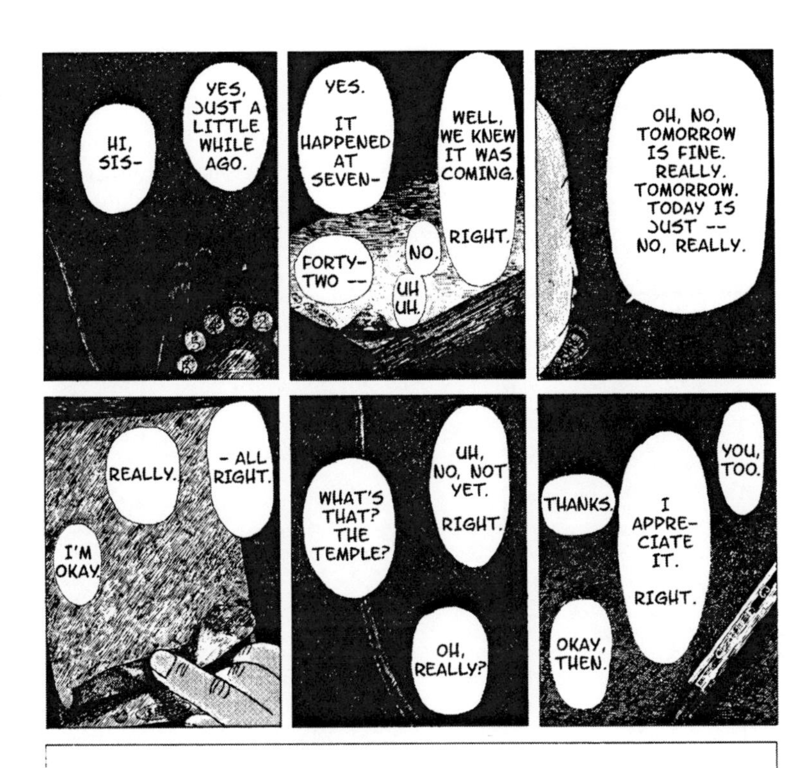
HI, SIS-
YES, JUST A LITTLE WHILE AGO.
YES. IT HAPPENED AT SEVEN-
FORTY-TWO --
WELL, WE KNEW IT WAS COMING.
RIGHT.
NO.
UH UH.
OH, NO, TOMORROW IS FINE. REALLY. TOMORROW. TODAY IS JUST -- NO, REALLY.
REALLY.
- ALL RIGHT.
I'M OKAY.
WHAT'S THAT? THE TEMPLE?
UH, NO, NOT YET. RIGHT.
OH, REALLY?
THANKS.
I APPRECIATE IT. RIGHT.
YOU, TOO.
OKAY, THEN.

チン
DING
Only Child

OH -- THE INCENSE.
ミシ
CREAK
CREAK
ミシ
CREAK
CREAK
CREAK
ミシ
CREAK

シュバッ
FLOOSH
WHICH WAS IT AGAIN?
...OR TO SHAKE IT OUT?
NOW, WAS IT BAD TO BLOW IT OUT...
WELL, LET'S NOT WORRY ABOUT IT.

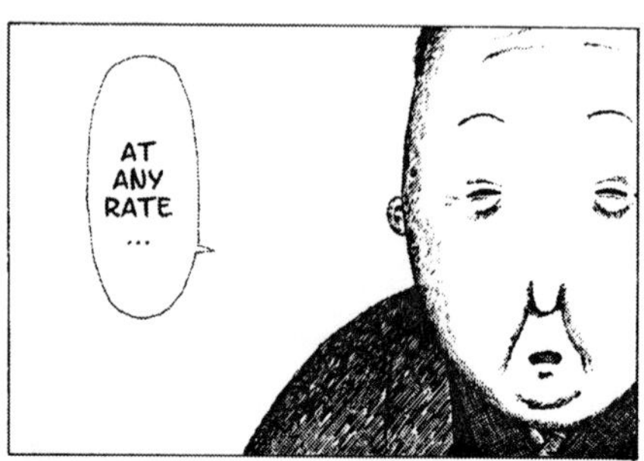
AT ANY RATE ...

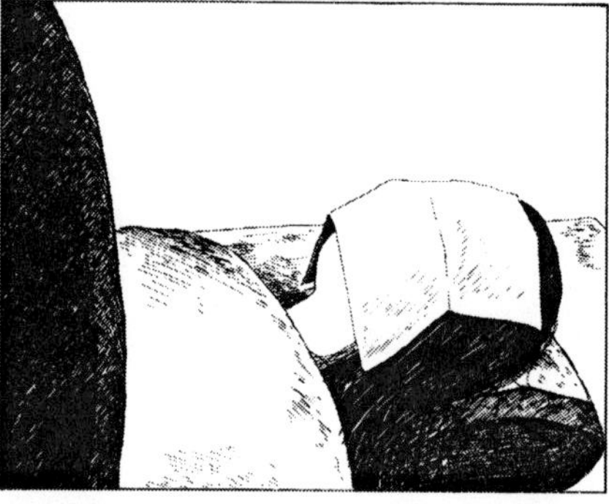

AT ANY RATE, KEEPING THE INCENSE BURNING IS THE IMPORTANT THING.

CAN'T GO TO PIECES.
むぎゅう
RUB RUB RUB

つーん

IT DOESN'T MATTER NOW, ANYWAY.
JUST HAVE TO ACCEPT IT.

"TICK TOCK, TICK TOCK"

TICK TOCK...

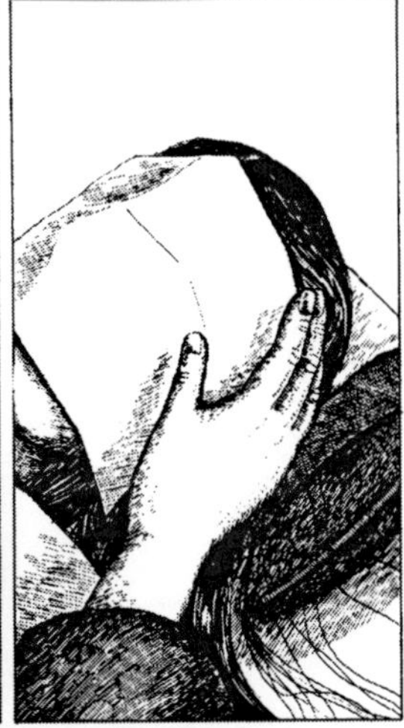

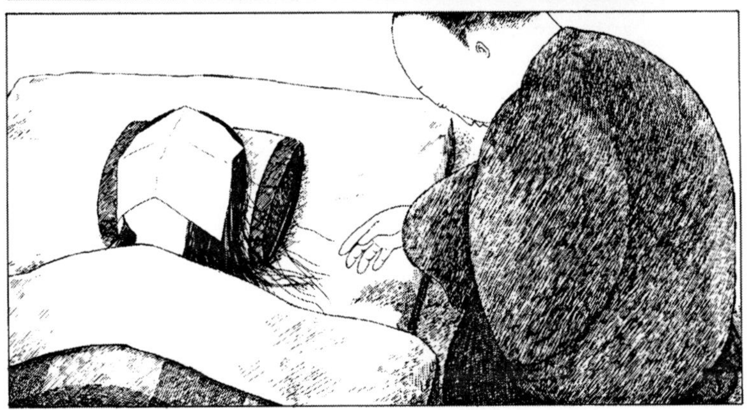

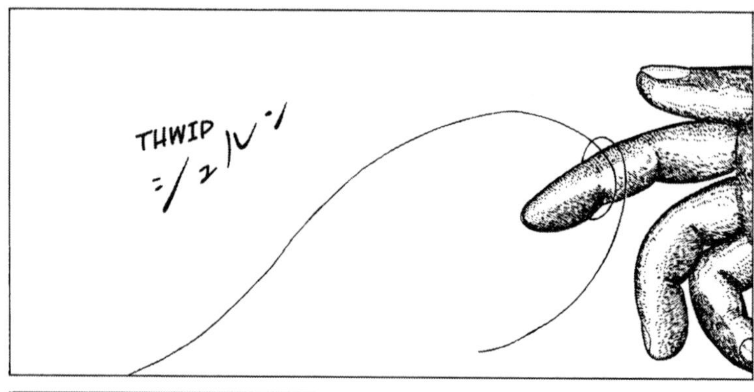
THWIP
シュルン

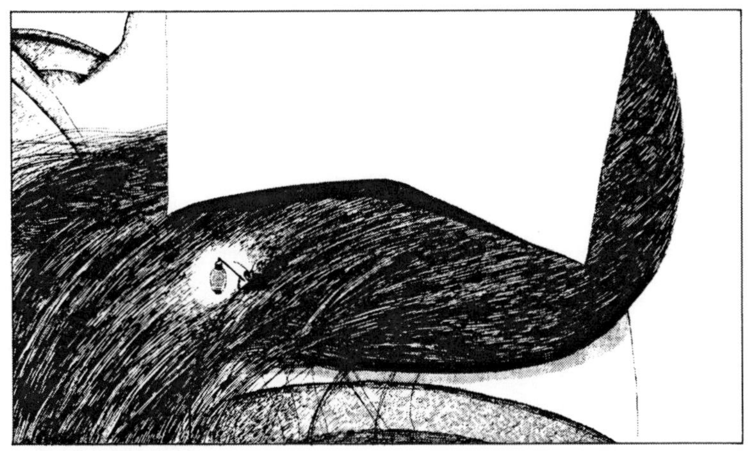

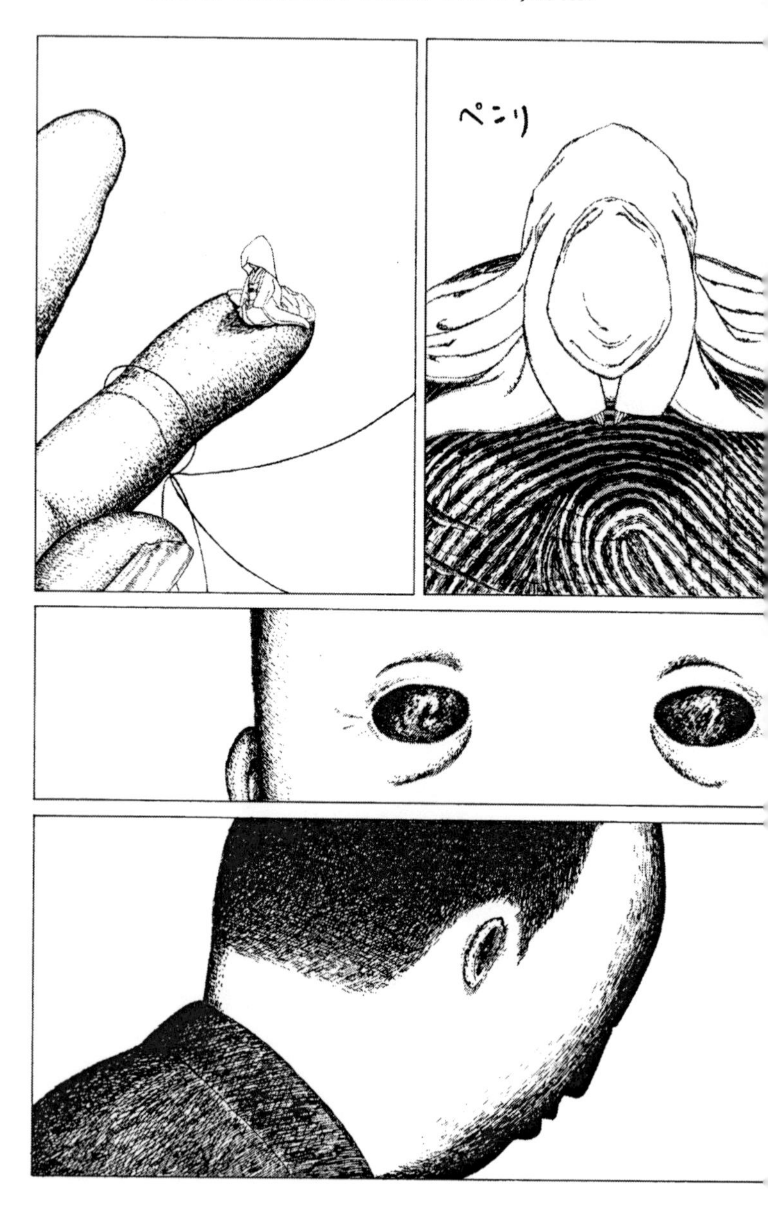
ぺこり

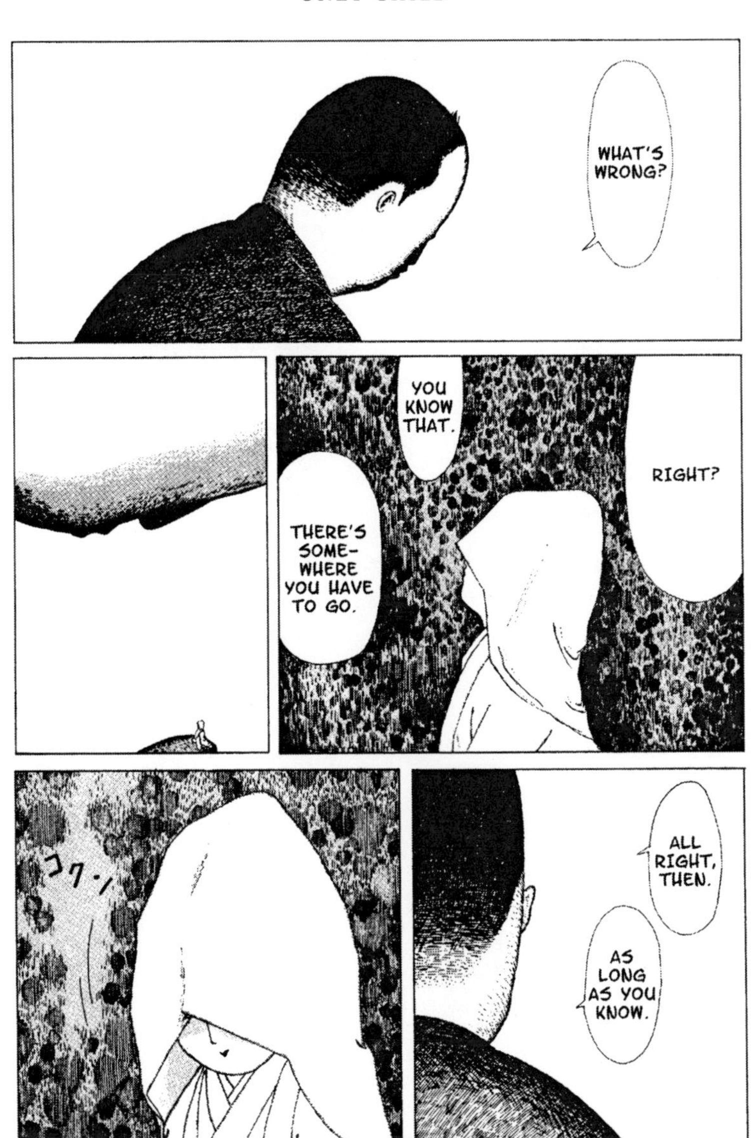
WHAT'S WRONG?
RIGHT?
YOU KNOW THAT.
THERE'S SOMEWHERE YOU HAVE TO GO.
ALL RIGHT, THEN.
AS LONG AS YOU KNOW.
コク

Contributors

Stephen A. Carter
("Only Child")

US-BORN STEPHEN CARTER is a long-time resident of Nagoya, Japan, where he lives with his wife and a large friendly spider, finds it fascinating how the new Japan is replacing the old, and doesn't drink nearly as much beer as he'd like.

Andrew Clare
("A Short Night")

ANDREW CLARE, A partner in an English law firm, lives with his wife, Deborah, and their three children, Lawrence, Esther and Patrick, in a small town north of Manchester, England. A graduate of Sheffield University (B.A., Japanese Studies) and Kobe University (Master of Political Science), he is passionate about Japanese literature. His translations include Matsumoto Seichō's *Pro Bono* (Vertical, Inc., October 2010), and he is currently translating a collection of stories by Noma prize-winning author Yoshiyuki Junnosuke.

Andrew Cunningham
("Reunion")

ANDREW CUNNINGHAM SKEDADDLED sideways into translation when he discovered he was a terrible storyteller, but was pretty good at the parts of writing that translation required. He owns more Japanese books than there are dollars in his bank account, and his dizzyingly varied translation career ranges from manga (*Parasyte, Otogi*) to young adult novels (*Boogiepop, Goth*) to anthologies (*Faust*) to video games (*Style Savvy*). He currently resides inside a volcanic crater.

Dorothy Gambrell
("Only Child")

DOROTHY GAMBRELL, who localized "Only Child," has neither a career nor hobbies. She has spent the last ten years self-publishing cartoons at catandgirl.com

Mark Gibeau
("The *Kudan*'s Mother")

I AM A LECTURER IN JAPANESE LANGUAGE, literature and culture at The Australian National University in... Australia. My interest in Japanese literature was first sparked by the Abe Kōbō story "The Magic Chalk" in Van Gessel's wonderful anthology of short stories, *The Shōwa Anthology*—an interest that (much to my own surprise) ultimately led me to graduate school and a Ph.D. dissertation on Abe Kōbō. In addition to teaching, trying to improve my literary translation and slowly converting my dissertation into a book, I am interested in Okinawan literature and the work of Medoruma Shun in particular.

Higashi Masao
("Introduction: The Rise of Japanese Weird Fiction")

HIGASHI MASAO is a noted anthologist, literary critic, and the editor of Japan's first magazine specializing in *kaidan* (strange tales) fiction, named *Yoo* (幽).

In 1982 he founded Japan's only magazine for research into strange and uncanny literature, *Fantastic Literature Magazine* (幻想文学, Gensō bungaku), published by Atelier Octa, serving as editor for twenty-one years until the magazine folded in 2003.

It was an invaluable publication not only for its content, but also because it discovered and nurtured a host of new authors, researchers and critics in the field.

Recently he has concentrated on compiling anthologies, producing criticism of fantastic and horror literature, and researching the *kaidan* genre, active in a wide range of projects. As a critic he has suggested new styles and interpretations in the field, including the growing "Horror Japanesque" movement and the "palm-of-the-hand *kaidan*" consisting of uncanny stories told in no more than eight hundred characters. He is well-known as a researcher of the uniquely Japanese *hyaku monogatari* tradition, with numerous books and anthologies published.

He serves on the selections committees for various literary prizes in the kaidan genre, and since 2004 has written the Genyō (幻妖) book blog on uncanny and fantastic literature cooperatively with online bookseller bk1, at http://blog.bk1.jp/genyo/

Pamela Ikegami
("Selections from Legends of Tōno")

PAMELA IKEGAMI, a native of Portsmouth, NH, teaches Japanese language and culture at the University of New Hampshire. She has a BA in Japanese and Asian Studies from the University of Colorado Boulder and an MA in Japanese from the University of Hawai'i at Manoa. She has also worked as a freelance translator since 1990. She loves to read scary Japanese stories, but can't bear to watch Japanese horror films.

Ruselle Meade
("The Mummy")

RUSELLE MEADE IS a UK-based freelance translator working from Japanese and French into English. Ruselle originally trained as an engineer but a three-year stint in Japan convinced her to combine this expertise with her passion for languages, and she started working as a patent translator. She has since broadened her range to include literary and academic translation. Ruselle is currently working on a doctorate on Meiji-era technical translation at the University of Manchester.

Miri Nakamura
("Introduction: The Rise of Japanese Weird Fiction")

MIRI NAKAMURA IS Assistant Professor of Japanese Literature and Language at Wesleyan University. She specializes in Japanese fantastic fiction, and she is currently working on a book on the rise of the uncanny in modern Japan. She has translated several academic works, which can be found in *Robot Ghosts and Wired Dreams* (University of Minnesota Press, 2007) and *Pacific Rim Modernisms* (University of Toronto Press, 2009).

Rossa O'Muireartaigh
("The Clock Tower of Yon")

ROSSA O'MUIREARTAIGH IS a freelance Japanese to English translator. He has previously studied Asian philosophy at Nagoya University in Japan. He has also lectured in Japanese studies at Dublin City University, Ireland and in Japanese translation at Newcastle University in England. He has written various academic papers on translation, drama, and religious studies. Married with one adorable daughter, he is currently enjoying a change of scenery residing in Malta.

Kathleen Taji
(“The Third Night, from Ten Nights’ Dreams”)

A THIRD-GENERATION JAPANESE American, Kathleen Taji has been involved in several literary translation projects with Kurodahan Press beginning with the four-volume *Lairs of the Hidden Gods* anthology where her translated works include “Import of Tremors” by Yamada Masaki, “Terror Rate” by Konaka Chiaki, “The Road” by Aramata Hiroshi, “C-City” by Kobayashi Yasumi, “Quest of the Nameless City” by Tachihara Tōya, and “City of the Dreaming God” by Yufuku Senowo. She also translated the novel *Queen of K’n-Yan* by Asamatsu Ken, and is presently working on the translation of the SF novel *Crystal Silence* by Fujisaki Shingo. She lives in the suburbs of Los Angeles with her two African parrots and her desert tortoise, Miz Pamie.

Ginny Tapley Takemori
(“Sea Dæmons”)

GINNY TAPLEY TAKEMORI started out translating Spanish and Catalan, and went on to work as a literary agent specializing in foreign rights (with Ute Körner in Barcelona) and as an editor with Kodansha International in Tokyo, before returning to translation, this time from Japanese. She holds a BA (Hons) in Japanese from SOAS (London University) and is currently studying for an MA with the University of Sheffield. Now based in Tsukuba, Japan, she has long enjoyed roaming other worlds, and hopes to similarly touch the hearts and minds of readers with her own translations of fiction and nonfiction.

Robert Weinberg
("The Subtle Ambiance of Japanese Horror")

ROBERT WEINBERG is the author of sixteen novels, two short story collections, and sixteen non-fiction books. He has also edited over 150 anthologies. He is best known for his trilogy, the *Masquerade of the Red Death*, and his non-fiction book, *Horror of the Twentieth Century*. Bob is a two-time winner of the Bram Stoker Award; a two-time winner of the World Fantasy Award; and a winner of the Lifetime Achievement Award from the Horror Writers Association. www.robertweinberg.net

Brian Watson
("Midnight Encounters")

A PROFESSIONAL TRANSLATOR for nearly twenty years, Brian Watson began his career while teaching at a senior high school in Saitama Prefecture as a favor for another teacher. Although his client base has been expansive, covering everything from cosmetics to computer games, his love for Japanese prompted him to begin translating fiction in 2008. He can be reached at brian.watson@gmail.com

"The Heavy Basket"

Print by Yoshitoshi Tsukioka, courtesy of the John Stevenson Collection

A folktale tells of an old man and an old woman who were neighbors. Every evening the old man fed a sparrow that visited him, but one day the sparrow did not come. He asked his neighbor whether she had seen it. She replied that the sparrow had eaten some rice paste she had made, so she had cut its tongue out.

The old man searched the forest for the sparrow, finally finding it and being invited to enjoy a feast. The bird showed him two hampers, one large and one small, and told him to choose one as a present. With typical humility, the old man chose the small one, later finding it full of gold, silk, and jewels.

His neighbor was envious and hurried off into the forest looking for the sparrow, pretending to be overjoyed to see him again. The sparrow also offered her the choice of two baskets, and of course she chose the large heavy one. A host of ghosts and goblins were inside, and quickly devoured her.

Yoshitoshi Tsukioka (芳年月岡), aka Yoshitoshi Taiso (芳年大蘇) (1839-1892), is generally recognized as the last master of ukiyo-e woodblock printing, as well as one of its great innovators. His career spanned the Meiji Restoration, covering from the feudal era to modernizing Japan, and while Yoshitoshi was interested in new ideas from the West he was concerned with the erosion of traditional Japanese culture, including traditional woodblock printing.

His life is perhaps best summed up by John Stevenson, in his book *Yoshitoshi's One Hundred Aspects of the Moon* (Hotei Publishing, 2001):

> Yoshitoshi's courage, vision and force of character gave ukiyo-e another generation of life, and illuminated it with one last burst of glory.

The cover is from his *New Forms of Thirty-Six Ghosts* (1889–1892), a series of 36 prints now recognized as one of his greatest achievements, together with the one hundred prints in his masterpiece, the *One Hundred Aspects of the Moon* (1885–1892) series.

KURODAHAN PRESS

CPSIA information can be obtained at www.ICGtesting.com
Printed in the USA
LVOW122234240812
295733LV00001B/19/P